CARRILLO'S DEFIANT DAUGHTERS

Loren Nicholson

Loren Luis Nicholson

PublishAmerica
Baltimore

At the specific preference of the author, PublishAmerica allowed this work to remain exactly as the author intended, verbatim, without editorial input.

ISBN: 1-4241-6569-5
PUBLISHED BY PUBLISHAMERICA, LLLP
www.publishamerica.com
Baltimore

Printed in the United States of America

Acknowledgment

With sincere appreciation to Bernice, my wife, who played a role in every aspect of moving this book to completion. She read it, critiqued it, executed the cover graphics, but left the final decisions to me. So, I take full responsibility for the end result, but many good ideas came from her.

1. Josefa in San Diego

Josefa's body stiffened. She wrenched from the arms of Governor Jose Echeandia and sprang up from the log bench where they sat. It was dark. They were alone on the pueblo plaza.

"You belong to me, Josefa. You must marry me! " he said. He reached and pulled her into his arms again. His black beard scratched across her cheek.

"I would be proud if one of my daughters married the governor," her papa once said, and he had given the governor permission not only to visit Josefa at the casa, but to walk with her unescorted on the pueblo plaza, even at night.

Feeling desperate, Josefa pushed the governor with all her strength. She broke loose and ran across the plaza, past the trader's stores, past the casas, all the way to Casa Carrillo. She slipped through the great hand-azed doors into the casa courtyard. The family was in bed. She crept along the portico into the adobe-walled room where her sisters slept. Without undressing, she climbed under the blankets covering her straw mattress, still trembling. I hate Jose Echeandia, she thought. Why does papa insist upon arranging these visits for her with this older man!

Of course, she knew the answer.

******

With the light of first dawn showing through the beaded curtains of the doorway of their room off the portico, Josefa awakened out of a nightmare, and for a time, listened to Rosa and Francisca breathing. She heard her papa leave his bedroom. Today, she knew he planned to ride to the hills and with Indian vaquero help, move his growing herd of cattle to new grass. She touched her rosary and gave thanks. After last night, she didn't want to face her papa yet. As soon as she heard the courtyard gate close, she knew he had left the casa. She drew a sigh of relief.

"Rosa," she whispered to her 15-year-old sister in the rawhide-constructed bed next to her. "Let's go to the river."

5

Rosa rolled over, yawned and immediately sat up. She touched Francisca, their youngest sister. "Are you coming?"

Francisca sat up. "To the river?" she asked. Since their mama had died some years earlier, they needed to talk often. They always went to their hiding place along the river bank when they had important things to discuss.

They pulled on colorful chemise dresses that hung straight from their shoulders. Their dark long hair hung loosely, uncombed and wild. They tiptoed barefoot along the portico past the herb garden and out the heavy double doors in the courtyard. Their younger brothers would be all right because Oupay, their Indian servant, would soon arrive and fix breakfast . With abandon, they scampered through an orchard of leafless mixed fruit trees. In open space, breathless now, Josefa stretched to her full lean height, taller than nearly all of the girls in Pueblo San Diego. For the moment, she forgot Governor Echeandia and her papa's expectations, but then she also realized she had forgotten to play the secret game their mother had taught them in dealing with men.

"You must learn to defy them, My Dears...but always with love," the ghost of their dead mother whispered. Josefa's sisters shook their heads as Josefa told them about her experience. They nodded with understanding when their mother again advised them.

Josefa watched Rosa sip in the cool morning air, then balance easily while walking the length of a fallen tree. Francisca followed, then ran ahead. High on the river bank, Francisca stopped short, looking out to the bay. She was seeing something beyond the rush of muddy river waters. She pointed.

Josefa and Rosa ran to meet her. Josefa gasped, holding her breath. During the night, a trading ship had anchored in the bay.

"What ship is it?" Rosa asked. She was kidding, of course. All of them knew nearly every ship that dropped anchor in the bay. Josefa smiled knowingly at Rosa. It was the Maria Ester, out of Valparaiso. Josefa didn't know the vessel's young captain, but she had seen him other times at the beach in the hidehouses with her papa.

The presence of the ship sent a rush through Josefa, but Rosa interrupted. "It's story time," she said. Their mama had taught them to make-up stories about their futures. After her death, they still sought her whispered advice. Their stories became precious secrets, but through them, the girls set goals and predicted joyous futures. "You begin, Francisca."

"You know my best story," Francisca said. "He was mine from the day I was born. Like mama said, he is my birthright. When I am sixteen, he will ride

6

his horse with silver spurs to the doors of Casa Carrillo and lift me up in front of him. The whole pueblo will follow us to the mission. We will be married. We will have miles of rancho land with herds of cattle and horses and five children. Our children will be musicians and writers and poets. When a trading ship arrives in harbor, my Mariano will take me out to its deck store to buy yardage and fans and scarves. We will enjoy fiestas, balles and fandangoes at our own hacienda."

Rosa took over. "I want the commandante of a presidio." It took a long moment for her to visualize the face of faraway Romualdo Pacheco. He will spoil me, give me what I want. He will want to please me."

"How many children?" Francisca asked.

"You said you want five. Then I want six. I want both boys and girls. I will teach them great things, and they will become great because of it. I will read to them everyday and they will read to me."

Josefa's head spun with all that her younger sisters dared expect in life. All three grew quiet. It was a fairy tale time. Francisca and Rosa smiled through their golden dream. Then both girls turned expectantly to their older sister.

Josefa tried. "I know I am tall," she said thoughtfully, "but he will be much taller than me. His cheeks will be fair, and his eyes...they may be as blue as the sky. The world will belong to him, and he will share it with me."

She stopped to gather her thoughts. Her heart was racing. The soldier-teacher from the presidio once told them about a Roman statue of a man named David. He was perfect in mind and body. "My husband, too, will be perfect," she added. Her sisters laughed.

It was Francisca who suddenly paused with mouth wide open. She jumped abruptly to a standing position on the river bank and looked soberly, unbelievingly up the slope. Then Rosa stood. Last of all, Josefa came to her bare feet in one motion, brown skin flushed and long dark hair spewing across her face.

There was no warning. None of the girls had heard the sound of hoofbeats in the soft wet earth. There was only the appearance of these two giant men peering down from their mounts. They were laughing. They wore seamen's caps and loose dark jackets with large pockets, both foreigners with light hair and fair skin. The youngest of the two leaned forward on his horse toward Josefa. His blue eyes met hers. In Spanish, he said, "We are looking for Don Joaquin Carrillo."

"Watch for him. You'll know him." she remembered her beautiful mama whispering.

7

Josefa remembered this man from a year ago when she had heard he had sailed the triangle from Valparaiso to the Sandwich Islands to Northern California ports and finally, to San Diego. She was once again seeing the captain of the Brig Maria Ester. It was his mop of light hair that compelled Josefa in that moment. No person in the pueblo was so fair.

"My papa is with the cattle now," she said. "You'll find him in the fields if you follow the mission trail. That way," she said, pointing.

"A long way?" asked the older man riding with the captain.

"No," she said, and started running across the field toward home. Francisca followed, but both girls paused when Rosa did not hurry. She was always the brave one.

"You must follow the river along the valley until you see cattle in an open place on the other bank," she told the men. Then, she, too ran.

On higher ground, Josefa paused and saw the men continuing their ride along the river trail. She could scarcely contain her joy when the young man stopped, turned his horse and looked back at her. A wisp of a breeze played about her cheeks. She closed her eyes. She was sure she felt his kiss.

******

The entire Casa de Carrillo was set into exciting motion when the girls announced the news about the trading ship anchored in the bay. Their three younger brothers scampered about the courtyard laughing and wrestling with one another. Even Oupay, their Indian servant, and her babies seemed inspired. The arrival of a vessel always changed the tenor of the pueblo. It was trading time. These ships carried goods they needed, offering manufactured wares in exchange for the pueblo's cowhides and tallow. Of course, the ship's captain and its supercargo sought out their papa first because he traded on behalf of both the mission and himself from large hide houses on the beach. The ship's crew would surely set up a store on the deck or on the beach. Everyone loved the thrill of a ride on one of the surf boats to and from the trading ship to see the array of goods available for purchase. The entire village would gather above the beach to watch the lighters move back and forth between brig and beach.

With their mama dead, Josefa always took leadership in preparations for company. She assumed these two men, the ship's owner and its captain, would be dinner guests because they sought out their papa ahead of others in the pueblo. Josefa assigned tasks to everyone. Everything must be made ready. It took all day to prepare the house, gather and cook vegetables, slaughter a lamb and roast the carcass on the skewer over an open fire in the courtyard. They had not had guests for a long time, and this was a celebration. Josefa wanted to make it perfect.

In anticipation of the captain appearing at the casa, Josefa kept feeling compulsions she scarcely realized were inside her. Something pushed her past her concern that this ship's captain might not be at all interested in her. For all of the work, the afternoon passed slowly. It had never happened before, but there was always the possibility that these men would not accept the invitation she knew her papa would offer.

She found herself thinking about every small thing that could happen throughout the evening. Her sisters could not believe Josefa's determined plotting. Then, toward evening, ready for company, giggling and teasing, they joined her in their room to help her plan. With Rosa's help, Josefa drew her thick black hair back across her ears into a tight but perfectly circular bun high on the back of her head. From one of the rosebushes in the courtyard, Francisca cut three miniature pink buds, carefully tucking them together over Josefa's ear. Her sisters understood her feelings, Josefa knew.

Francisca talked excitedly about the dress she thought Josefa should wear. All agreed that there was one above all others.

In the dimness of their candle-lighted adobe-walled room, Josefa whispered, "Mama would never allow it."

Francisca smiled impishly. "Let's not tell her."

Josefa felt the presence of their mama's ghost.

Josefa pursed her lips thoughtfully, so possessed with what she was doing that she could not think straight. "Francisca," she said, "Help me."

Both Rosa and Francisca smiled. Francisca did not hesitate. She left the room. Josefa watched her run quietly down the tiled portico. Soon, she reappeared with the most beautiful deep blue fiesta dress in the pueblo. It had belonged to their mama who had made it and used it only for special occasions.

Josefa worried, but how else could she impress the giant sea captain with blue eyes. She hugged the dress close to her.

"Now," Rosa said, "Francisca and I must go help Oupay before the boys start looking for us."

From the bead-covered closure of their room, Josefa watched her sisters and little brothers turning the lamb on the spit of the open fire. In the adobe beehive shaped oven, Oupay baked bread and sweet doughs.

Taking courage, Josefa tugged her way into the tightly-bodiced, ankle-length dress. The satin skirt fell gracefully into large pleated ruffles all of the way to her ankles, and because Josefa and her mother were the same size, the dress fit perfectly. From among several mantillas the sisters shared, she selected one in dark rose. It hung in lacy folds from her shoulders. She covered her neck with several strands of beads and one arm with brightly beaded bracelets.

She peeked out the doorway as often as she dared, wondering when the men might arrive. For a long moment, it again struck her that they might have declined their papa's invitation.

"Belief in yourself," the ghost of her mama whispered.

Then, through an opening in the beaded curtain of the doorway, she saw her papa come through the courtyard. But where were the guests? The world folded in around her. For a moment, she could not breathe. It had taken all of the courage she could summon to plan this daring move, and in one painful instant, she felt stripped and alone. She dropped to her bed, wondering how she could ever explain, even to herself, such foolishness. In the silence, she studied the outlines of the Madonna in the niche on the opposite wall. She felt cold. There was no end of passing time.

When she sat up again, the ghost of her mama stood in the doorway, arms folded. Josefa stood, head bowed. The silence was unbearable. Then her mama said, *"You must understand how much you are hurting your papa."*

In the dim light, Josefa moved closer to her mama. "I do, Mama. I do," she whispered. "But you must know, I am nothing! Papa would trade me for a piece of land. He cares more for his cattle than me. He would have me live my life married to an old man. I must defy him." She struggled against her tears.

Then her mama's voice softened. *"Then do what you must do."*

At that moment, Francisca appeared out of the shadows and their mama disappeared. "Josefa, why don't you come out?" her younger sister asked. "They are here! Papa introduced all of us except you. Hurry."

Josefa tossed aside her mantilla.

"What are you doing?" Francisca asked.

"I have made a mistake, dressing this way," she said.

"No, no," Francisca said, taking her hand.

"I cannot go out there looking like this."

Francisca held Josefa's waist and looked up at her. "You are beautiful," she said. "Make Papa proud."

Josefa looked over her sister's shoulder into the courtyard where the two men stood with their papa. She sighed, shaking inside. At last, she walked to the doorway and pushed aside the beaded curtain

"Wait," Francisca said. She handed her sister the silk mantilla from the bed, and took a fan from the wall, opened it and handed it to her. "Remember what mama said."

"Si," Josefa replied.

"If you must de...defy..."

"If you must defy a man...even your papa, do it with amor."

Yes, she could do it her mama's way. After all, she loved her papa dearly. That was the real secret. "Defy with love," she said softly.

Holding the fan at a tilt and arching her back, still trembling, Josefa moved quickly through the shadows of flickering candlelight along the portico to the path in the courtyard, then past the rose garden and the herbs. Her three little brothers...Joaquin, Julio and Jose...saw her first and came to her laughing and staring.

"Is there a fiesta?" Jose Ramon asked.

"Please," she whispered. "Behave." She touched Jose Ramon's head with love. He succumbed to her quietly and took her hand.

The men, including her papa, appeared dumbstruck. The young sea captain took a step toward her, then paused. She reached out to her papa, hoping he would forgive her. She had defied him in all of his efforts to bring her together with the governor. Now, she continued her struggle. She kissed him on the cheek.

Josefa did not try to interpret his thoughts. He seemed to take a deep breath. Then, with much flourish, he turned to his guests. "Senors," he said, "meet my eldest daughter, Josefa." To her, he said, "Our guests are Senor Oscar Virmond, the owner of many trading vessels, and Senor Enrique Fitch, captain of the Maria Ester."

Enrique, unlike a Californio, gripped her papa's hand until it probably hurt. From the corner of her eye, Josefa saw Rosa whisper to Francisca. and a faint smile crossed their faces. Her papa led his guests into the sala, and Rosa crossed quickly to Josefa.

"You look beautiful," she whispered breathlessly.

She held a tray in hand with a small jug of mission brandy and three cups. Traditionally, when their papa had guests, their mama had poured the first brandy or wine, but without a word, the ritual now fell to Josefa, the eldest daughter.

Josefa glanced at Rosa and Francisca. Then she broke into a smile, feeling a wonderful surge of warmth. Passing the beautiful ghost of her mama and then her clearly happy sisters, she carefully carried the tray into the sala. Somewhere high on Presidio Hill, soldiers played guitars and the music matched the throbbing in her breast.

She concentrated on every move, feeling the eyes of the men upon her as she carefully placed the tray upon the small straight-legged table alongside the cushioned bench where her papa was seated, then slowly, thoughtfully, she poured brandy into each small cup. She knew the fragrance of her perfume permeated the room; she felt the tight bodice of her mother's dress, and she thought she heard the young captain take an uncertain breath. How much she wanted to please him.

"Josefa is my eldest child," her papa told the men, "now eighteen years old."

"We need not tell you, Don Joaquin, that all of your daughters are beautiful," the older man said.

Josefa gave no sign of hearing. The elder man talked through loose heavy jowls, and he had a waist so large that his pants hung below his belly. He was not a good looking man, but his words were good, and Josefa hoped that the young sea captain agreed with him. Enrique remained silent, smiling pleasantly. She did not need to search for his blue eyes. They followed her every movement.

As she left the sala, her mama appeared again. She said nothing, but her presence helped Josefa overcome her nervousness. It was time to bring out the silver candelabra from Mexico City. It held six long candles. Rosa and Francisca set the table, using their pottery dishes with the blue flower design. All of them had joined their mama in selecting this design from a ship's store long ago.

Their papa had traded many hides for household items to please their mama. Josefa felt so elated that she could scarcely contain herself. The dining room, used only in rainy or very cold weather, was located alongside the sala with a wide doorless arch between rooms.

As they brought out the dishes, their mama appeared to all of the girls. *"Set the table for four,"* she told them. *"Josefa must join the men."*

Josefa looked at her mama's ghost in disbelief. It was only upon the rarest occasion that the women joined their papa and his guests at the same table. They usually served the men, and then sat down to eat at a separate table in the courtyard. Their mama would have them defy pueblo tradition!

"Are you sure, Mama?" Josefa questioned.

"A daughter does not question her mama!"

That settled that. As Josefa worked, she watched the men. From where the young seamaster was seated, she could see that he was too big and tall for his straightback chair. He looked over the head of her papa directly toward her. When she glanced at him, she found herself looking directly into his eyes. His smiles embarrassed her. At the same time, her mind blurred, and she felt a pulsing through her body that made her hands tremble so she could scarcely light the candles.

For a time, it seemed to her that all of the conversation of the men took place between her papa and Oscar Virmond, but she could not hear what was said. Her papa peered out across the portico to the courtyard where Oupay worked, then walked across the sala toward the opening to the dining room where Josefa smoothed the white lace tablecloth and appeared not to notice. He stared at her as though he intended to speak, then turned back to his visitors and sat down. Enrique continued looking her way. Something in his face told Josefa that he had spoken about her to her papa.

Each of the men took his place at the dining table. Josefa carried the thick pottery platter, made heavier with choice slices of roasted leg of lamb. Rosa carried a bowl filled with roasted vegetables smothered in the juices of the meat. The food was placed in front of her papa for serving, including a plate of tortillas and bowls of salsa.

Then Josefa cautiously took her place on the opposite side of the table from the guests, and somehow, it worked out that she sat directly opposite Enrique. Her papa looked sharply at her, obviously disturbed by this breech of custom. *"Defy, but with love,"* her mama's silent presence reminded her.

In the quiet adobe-walled dining room, the soft light from the candles in the candelabras flickered across the beams of the open ceiling. The flickering light was not kind to Don Virmond's face. What she saw reminded her of the masks worn during the traditional Dias de los Muertos, Days of the Dead fiesta. it was frightening. At the same time, the glow upon Enrique Fitch's high-boned cheeks and muscular jaw told her she was safe. He reminded her of the stature of the Angel Gabriel in the mission church. She grew increasingly self-conscious. From Presidio Hill, the guitars of the soldiers increased in tempo.

Josefa stared at her plate. She picked at her food without looking up. During all of this time, she felt the eyes of Enrique Fitch waiting for her. She could almost feel him. He held her in invisible arms. When he talked to the others, she closed her eyes, fearing he would sail away and never return. At last, she raised her head and saw the longing look in his eyes, felt it in her own.

"The mission," her papa was saying, "has hundreds of stretched and tanned hides and plenty of tallow for trade. The priests need many things. I hope you can ride with me to see them."

"Good," Virmond answered. "I want to meet the padres and trade with them."

Enrique Fitch broke into the conversation. "I must see the governor before I leave the pueblo," he said. "Part of our cargo must be delivered to the military."

Josefa froze. Somehow she could not imagine Enrique in the same room with Gov. Jose Echeandia.

Virmond said, "If I can talk Don Joaquin into taking me to the mission, I will leave you free to see the governor, Fitch."

When they finished eating, Josefa realized that neither she nor Enrique had spoken a direct word to one another. She covered her dress and helped her sisters clear the table while the men talked. She washed the dishes in the large iron cauldron kept on the yard table.

"Tell me about him," Rosa whispered while they put dishes away in the pantry.

Josefa shrugged. "We have yet to speak to each other."

"Let's stay up until they come out into the courtyard," Rosa whispered.

Josefa felt weary. "Maybe." she said. "There is much cleaning to do in the courtyard. Let's take our time."

They lingered over their work interminably. They carried the iron cauldron full of dish water outside the gate and poured it in a flower bed. They wiped the courtyard table until it was spotless. When it was time to put their younger brothers to bed, Francisca took the boys to their room. Josefa and Rosa continued miscellaneous chores in the pantry until they heard the men's voices in the courtyard. Now, the men sat down around the pit fire, and Josefa took a deep breath and went to them, standing beside Enrique.

"Papa," she said, "would you like fruit?"

"Fruit?" her papa asked, looking suspiciously at her. "This is not the season for fruit."

"Si," she said weakly. "I thought…dried fruit."

Her papa looked at both men questioningly. Both shook their heads.

Enrique Fitch stood and turned to her without a word. Then, he looked expectantly at her papa.

Her papa raised both hands in front of him and appeared to shrug. Josefa saw Enrique smile.

He said, "I have asked your father if you and I might ride horses on the beach tomorrow morning."

Josefa felt breathless. Then she blurted, "When will you see the governor?"

"Afternoon is soon enough."

Josefa turned to her papa. Enrique came to her side. "I am concerned that you have no older woman to escort you," her papa said. To Enrique, "That is the custom, you know."

"I've walked unescorted with others," she said. "Even at night."

Her papa knew that she referred to the governor. His face turned dark. He remained silent. Finally, he said," We shall see in the morning."

2. Enrique - San Diego

Henry Fitch had long grown accustomed to his Spanish name, Enrique. He was also very familiar with the customs involved in courting a woman. He had witnessed young men and women strolling together in the evening on the plazas of every pueblo from Valparaiso to Monterey, and he was amused by the inevitable presence of an older woman somewhere nearby.

While he and Josefa rode side by side down the brushy slope that led to the beach, Oupay followed some fifty meters behind. To fit his size, Fitch rode the largest horse in the Carrillo corral. Josefa rode side saddle, her long skirts draping the left side of her mount so that the pommel supporting her right leg was hidden. Watching the control Josefa exercised over her animal and the beautiful trotting gait she maintained told Fitch that it was not just the men in this part of the world who were superb riders. Even on horseback, Fitch thought Josefa the most feminine creature he had ever known. In her loose skirt and blouse, black braids of hair bouncing down the center of her back, she was a study in movement.

She appeared overjoyed, and Fitch felt like a man who had it all, now feasting in restrained passion for a woman who became more dear to him with every passing moment. They reached the beach by riding alongside a string of small buildings constructed of heavy timbers once serving as ballast in the holds of trading vessels. Traders making regular stops in California ports kept such buildings for storing hides and tallow until they were ready to sail to South American ports. Here, they met traders and importers carrying manufactured goods shipped around the horn from Atlantic and European ports.

"This is my papa's hidehouse," Josefa told him., pointing to one building above the beach.

Oupay found a place on the steps of the building out of the wind and brought out a basket filled with crocheting. When Fitch wondered what to do next, Josefa beckoned him. They rode out across the beach to the wet sand at waters edge. Here, Josefa suddenly threw herself full astride her mount and galloped. Fitch followed at full gallop, enjoying the motion of the horse just as he enjoyed the sensation of his ship rising and falling with the movement of the sea, and it made him feel good to see Josefa so filled with life.

Well down the beach away from Oupay, Josefa halted and waited for him to pull alongside her. She looked to the bay where the Maria Ester turned at her anchor.

"I like your brig," she said.

For such a wide-beamed vessel, loaded with cargo and setting low in the water, the Maria Ester did make a neat silhouette, Fitch thought.

"She is my home," he said. "I don't know what I'd do without her."

"You do not have a home?" Josefa asked.

"Not in the way you do," he answered.

With a helpless shrug, she said, "I was born in this pueblo. I do not know any other."

They climbed down from their horses and trailed them at water's edge. Along the way, Josefa stopped and turned to him. "How does it feel to sail so many places."

In the moment they stood facing each other, he wanted to touch her, but he was determined not to risk spoiling either the moment or the possibility of a lifetime of moments.

"I think I have felt all the feelings one can feel..."

"I would be lonely," she said.

"I have been lonely." he said. "For the home that doesn't exist, I suppose. For a family, too, but I have no family."

They climbed an embankment above the beach to another hidehouse. Enrique tied their horses and found steps to sit.

Josefa's questions stirred dreaded memories of his childhood...of returning one day from the New England country school house he attended to find his mother bleeding profusely, lying unconscious on the floor; of running a mile down the wagon road to get help from a neighbor, of returning to find that his mother had bled to death during a miscarriage. Since his father was a sailor faraway at sea, it was many months before he knew what happened.

Now, in this moment, Fitch again experienced the childhood terror and loneliness of standing next to his mother's bed crying until he was utterly empty inside.

Josefa leaned close to him. "What is the matter," she asked.

"I'm sorry," he said, straightening, "very sorry."

"You must tell me," she said. "It is important."

"After she died…" he started.

"Who?"

"My mother…"

Josefa's eyes filled with tears, thinking of her own dead mama. "I lived and worked on a neighbor's farm and continued school," he said.

They were silent for a time. Fitch changed the subject. "Is there a school in San Diego?" he asked.

"Si, I still go to school."

"Where is the school?"

Josefa laughed. "It is a log in the square."

"And who is the teacher?"

"At first, it was the priest from the presidio chapel. Now, it is a soldier. A very smart soldier."

"When the time comes," Fitch said, without thinking, "we must build a school house for the children of the pueblo."

She searched his face, appearing suddenly shy. He decided he must not explain, although their future together seemed so natural to him. Instead, he said, "When I was sixteen, my father introduced me to a sea captain who hired me. I sailed along the Atlantic coast and into the Caribbean Sea over and over. One time, I hired on for a trip around the horn to Valparaiso. From there, I joined the crew of a schooner sailing to the Sandwich Islands. Those were my days of learning about the sea and about trading ships."

"And now you are the captain of a ship," she said, smiling.

Just the way she said it made Fitch feel good about himself. It reminded him again that something important was missing in his life. She encouraged him to tell her more.

"I met Oscar Virmond at Acapulco, and he needed a shipmaster for short hauls along the coast of Mexico. The lengths of the trips gradually became longer. Now, for nearly three years I have sailed the triangle from Valparaiso and Lima to the Sandwich Islands, then followed the currents to California and south again."

"Why is Oscar Virmond sailing with you?" she asked.

"He owns the Maria Ester."

"I don't remember seeing him."

"That's true," he said, "but he wants to become acquainted with California. He is adding new vessels to his trading fleet, and he needs to know how to use them profitably."

Josefa stared into the sand below them. Fitch continued to talk. "Virmond has helped me in a thousand ways, but some day I want to have my own business."

When he stopped speaking, Josefa surprised him. She slipped the slim fingers of her hand into his big fist, and before he realized it, he put an arm around her waist and pulled her close to him. Neither looked at the other.

"Did I tell you," he said, touching his cheek to hers, "that I have applied for Mexican citizenship?"

"No,"

"I did it for business reasons. When I return to Acapulco, I expect to receive my papers."

Josefa heard what he said without comment. She did not realize its significance. He turned and studied the shape of her dark eyes...such unusually large, sad sleepy eyes. Now, he watched them brighten, and he was sure she wanted him to kiss her.

"I must have your father's trust," he muttered. He started to stand, but she touched his shoulder. This time, he cradled her in his arms, leaning her back to the hidehouse porch, tenderly kissing her cheeks, her neck, her lips.

"It is time for me to see the governor," he whispered.

He saw Josefa turn pale, and he could not decide whether she was unwilling or unable to speak during their ride back to the pueblo. As they parted, she said, "I know you will stand strong, Enrique."

******

Jose Echeandia was not only governor of Alta California, but also commandante general of the California military. He kept a small adobe casa in the pueblo, but also maintained a headquarters office and apartment at the presidio, and that is where Fitch found him.

Fitch still felt the mixed warmth and confusion of his time with Josefa as he rode through the presidio gate. The soldier on guard directed him to the governor's headquarters, a large apartment located beside the chapel. An aide invited him into the main room of the small apartment. Fitch glanced around the white-washed adobe. The place was clean with sparse furnishings that included a large elaborately carved linen chest next to one wall, a painted cupboard with carved doors in back and a plain table. A niche in the other wall contained a casting of the Madonna.

A man in his late forties with a short reddish beard appeared in the doorway from the next room. He was lean and unusually fair, clearly of Spanish heritage. His hair seemed brown in comparison with his beard, and his eyes ranged from hazel to green in the irregular light of the room.

"Our honorable governor," the aide said to Fitch, straightening himself. "Don Jose Echeandia."

The governor's office in the next room was primarily a sitting room with a pine writing table off to one side. He directed Fitch to a simple highback chair with raw leather seat.

The older man looked tired. Without knowing why, Fitch found himself lowering his voice, slowing his movements to match the lackluster appearance of the governor.

"Our cargo includes military equipment, Governor," he said, "and our orders are to deliver it to you." He handed the governor a bill of lading prepared by the Mexican central government military supply office in Mexico City.

The governor said nothing for a time, staring absently at the bill of lading. It struck Fitch that something was on his mind that had nothing to do with the business at hand. Whatever else he had heard about the governor, he still had been led to believe that he was usually an affable man. "Why have you delayed in coming to see me?" the governor said in a Castilian manner and pronunciation. Fitch held his reserve, considering what might prompt the governor's question. He felt forced to tell a bit of a lie. "Did I receive wrong information? Haven't you been too ill to see me?

When the governor did not answer the question, Fitch said, "We plan to sail south from here."

"No," Echeandia said firmly. "We will keep most of the equipment here, but I want you to take some small arms north immediately."

He checked the items on the bill of lading that should be transported to the Santa Barbara presidio, returning it to Fitch.

Fitch was disturbed by the idea that the governor was ordering him to sail north. Such a small amount of freight was not worth the trip unless he was going that way anyway. Instead of responding, he changed the subject. "I apologize, Sir, for not getting a message to you about the cargo sooner"

Fitch thought the governor's face softened slightly, but then the bearded little man leaned forward in his chair, brow suddenly distorted. "Is it true, Señor Fitch, that you are staying at the home of Joaquin Carrillo?"

"No, we stay aboard our brig."

The governor only seemed to show more irritation. There were no secrets in this small pueblo. Fitch now knew why he asked the question. The governor knew about his morning with Josefa. Seeing Gov. Echeandia now made it clear why a young and vibrant woman like Josefa would resent the prospect of marrying this tired old soldier. Fitch stood, saying, "Governor, we sail south from here. We must leave all of the military equipment with you as directed by Mexico. However, when we return, I can deliver it for you. I am sorry for the inconvenience."

"Never mind," Echeandia said. He was red with anger. "I will have the next ship coming this way make the delivery. Bring it to the beach. My men will haul it to the presidio."

******

The pueblo was silent. Only a few stray chickens and a mud-caked bitch dog shared the square. It was siesta time. Even the children remained behind the adobe walls that enclosed the yards of the casas.

There were three cantinas in Pueblo San Diego, and in each, Fitch found members of his crew. He ordered them back to the brig with instructions to start moving cargo from the hold to the deck. Tomorrow, they would shuttle loaded lighters between the brig and the beach.

But now, Enrique yearned to see and talk to Josefa one more time. He felt more confused than ever. It seemed to him that the rest of his life hung in the balance. Upon arrival at the Carrillo casa, he found both Carrillo and Virmond back from Mission San Diego and seated at the table in the courtyard drinking brandy which Virmond had brought from the ship. They were clearly enjoying each other's company and certainly happy about arrangements they had made at the mission for moving trade goods. Joaquin invited Enrique to join them in drinking, but he was intent upon seeing Josefa. Glancing about the courtyard, he said, "I want to thank you, Don Joaquin, for permitting me to ride with Josefa this morning. I hope I may see her again today."

"She...her sisters...wash clothes at the river," he said. His speech was slurred, and he smiled at Fitch through blinking unfocused eyes.

"Do I have your permission?"

Joaquin waved a hand. "Of course, Amigo."

The sisters were not difficult to find since clothes draped the lower limbs of the trees as well as the bushes all around them. When Josefa saw him, she twinkled all over, and he knew that she felt as he did. She scrambled up the embankment to where he stood. Rosa and Francisca looked at both of them knowingly and turned back to their work.

Fitch quickly took Josefa to a small clearing where he knew they were out of sight. "I won't waste time about saying what must be said," he said.

Josefa stood solemnly, clearly enjoying his touch.

"Since we were together this morning, I've had time…"

Her smile turned to a look of alarm as she obviously remembered where he had been since they separated. "How was your visit with the governor?" she asked cautiously.

"I learned some things," he said.

"Did you learn that the governor is looking for a wife?"

"I did, and I learned who the governor wants to marry."

Josefa came close to him, and he took her soft body into his arms.

"Please…" she implored, and tears came to her eyes, "If you love me, carry me far away."

Fitch looked down at her. "We scarcely know each other, Dear Josefa, yet I have never felt so sure. I want you for my wife. I want to talk to your father before I leave San Diego."

He felt the whole length of her body against her body. "Si…Si," she whispered. "Please don't talk now. Just hold me." For the next several minutes, they moved together heartbound in a world apart from all others. His kisses smeared her tears. Only Josefa's sisters constant chatter on the river bank below finally brought them breathlessly back to reality.

He held her quietly, searching above him through a lace of gentle willows for some kind of blessing. In Alta California, there was no permanent status for a person who was not a legal citizen of the Mexican Republic, and no father would allow marriage of his daughter to any man who was not a confirmed Catholic.

"You can become these things," Josefa said when he talked about them, but her sad eyes told Fitch more than her words. Her father had so much to gain by a favorable relationship with the governor that any request from Jose Echeandia would be difficult to refuse. How simple to trade a daughter in exchange for land and a lifetime of favors. Fitch knew it was a likely occurrence in this part of the world.

"I will talk to your papa," he said.

Then Josefa said something that puzzled him. "I will talk to mama."

3. Enrique in San Diego

Enrique found the low tide of early dawn good for his crew. Arduous hours of lifting weapons and munitions and trade goods from the hold of the ship to the deck and then letting heavy pieces down the side to waiting lighters was exhausting. The three cannon gave them the greatest problem because of the difficulty of balancing them on lighters as they were rowed to the beach. Enrique's bare-waisted Kanaka crew, all huge men out of the Sandwich Islands, leaned hard into the oars as promising waves pushed them toward the beach.

Fitch hung over the rail of the Maria Ester, both watching the action and contemplating how he could possibly take Josefa for himself without doing great damage to her papa. He considered Joaquin Carrillo a good and worthy man.

Soldiers at the beach transferred muskets and munitions directly from boats to military carretas and pack mules. Fitch jumped into one of the boats going ashore. He watched the pack-mules, wheel goods, and soldiers climb the slope up the beach toward the pueblo, the presidio and the mission. It was like watching a funeral procession. This kind of land-sea pageant happened often in the process of trading goods.

He was tempted to find Josefa now, but other matters needed attention. By following the river bank, he skirted the pueblo and finally fell in line behind the last of the loaded pack mules.

It was early afternoon. An unusually talkative guard met Fitch at the presidio gate and accompanied him across the assembly ground toward the padre's quarters.

"This priest is a strange one," the soldier said. "Do you know him?"

"No," Fitch answered.

"He's not like the others. He is Dominican. They say he was relieved of duty in Baja, and they sent him here as presidio chaplain. He has no association with the mission."

Fitch smiled. During one trip, he had hauled a full shipload of prisoners from Mazatlan in Mexico to Monterey in California to serve in the military. Alta California was the Mexican government's dumping ground for undesirables, but he had not expected the church to find it convenient to banish one of its own to this faraway territory.

Padre Menendez was a skinny little man with a perpetual grin, thinning hair and pallid skin. His nostrils and whiskers were discolored with snuff. The guard left, and the priest waved Fitch into his apartment. With the heavy door closed, the sitting room was almost dark. He motioned Fitch from there through a sparsely furnished bedroom and into the open air of an untidy walled yard in back. The priest walked with knees slightly bent, shoulders and head ducked forward. "Now, Señor Fitch," he said, "How can I help you?"

"I am a friend of Joaquin Carrillo's family," Fitch started. "I have come to see you because I want to join the church."

"You are not a Catholic?" the priest asked. The religion was such an intrinsic part of life in this far place that it rarely occurred to those living here that another faith could exist.

"No, Padre," Fitch said. "I have applied for Mexican citizenship in Acapulco, and now I hope to marry a California woman."

Padre Menendez frowned, then suddenly looked at him knowingly. "Ah, yes," he said. "So you desire instruction in the catechism?"

"Instruction?"

"Si."

"There is little time now," Fitch said, explaining his plans to sail.

"You must know that becoming a member of the Church is not so easy," the priest said. "There is a commitment required."

"I realize."

"Since you sail from pueblo to pueblo, and each place has a church, perhaps you can learn something as you go along, so you will be ready for the faith, the baptism and the responsibility of a church wedding when you return."

Padre Menendez seemed to have an endless list of suggestions, and Fitch tried to listen patiently. At the end of a long explanation, the priest suddenly frowned and asked, "You would marry Josefa Carrillo."

Fitch felt alarmed. "You have heard?" he asked.

"No," the small man said. "I only guessed. But I cannot believe that Joaquin Carrillo has given permission."

24

"I wanted to talk to you before asking him."

The little priest folded his hands in his lap and shook his head uncertainly. He said, "If this wedding comes to pass, I can only suggest that it be done quietly."

"I can't imagine a wedding or any other event taking place quietly in this small place," Fitch thought. However, he let the priest's remark pass. "I will plan to see you when I return, he said. "I'll ask Señor Carrillo to keep you informed about my plans."

As Fitch rode back down the trail from the presidio, he was aware of an unusually fine breeze across the land toward the bay, and he cursed it. He knew he should not wait until morning if the winds were right. A strong wind away from land that would take them far out to sea could save days in their southward journey. At the edge of the orchard, he galloped his horse until he reached the corral of Casa de Carrillo.

Two sweating horses in the corral told Fitch that Carrillo and Virmond had been out today overseeing the movement of goods to and from the mission. Inside, he found Virmond had gone to the bedroom to rest and since neither Josefa nor any of the Carrillo children were in sight, he assumed that all enjoyed the afternoon siesta in their rooms.

Only Carrillo sat in the courtyard. His eyes did not leave the cup of chocolate in front of him. Whatever had happened, Fitch knew it involved Josefa and him. He came directly to the table and sat across from Carrillo. Carrillo served him a cup of chocolate.

"The wind feels right for sailing tonight," Fitch said, "but there is much to do before leaving. Do you have room in your hidehouse for some mission goods?

Carrillo jumped to his feet. "Si. I will also round up more men in the pueblo," he said.

"Wait, Señor Carrillo," Fitch said.

Carrillo stood, legs braced, as though expecting to be pushed. Fitch remained seated.

"Don Joaquin," he said, "you are an intelligent man, and you must already know what I am going to ask you."

Carrillo picked up his cup and walked across the patio to the pit fire and with a long-handled spoon, dipped more chocolate from the open iron pot. He dallied over the task much too long. When the cup was full, he held it with both hands, staring at its contents, pondering. At last, he said, without turning, "Your wish is much more complicated than I can tell you," he said.

"I have talked to Josefa," Fitch said quietly.

"I should not have allowed you to be together."

"It was inevitable, Don Joaquin."

"You should have spoken to me before trying to reach an understanding with my daughter. You have hurt her deeply."

"Since she would live with me for the rest of her life, I wanted to know her feelings before I asked you for her hand."

"Did she tell you that she has other suitors?

"I understood that Governor Echeandia wants to marry her."

Joaquin turned, clearly relieved that he did not need to pursue this matter himself. "Would you expect me to ignore the governor?" he asked.

"I hoped Josefa's feelings might be important to you."

"She is too young to know her own mind. She has not considered what a governor offers with marriage."

"He is a sick man, Don Joaquin. If she marries him, she may never give you grandchildren."

Joaquin's face turned into an angry mask. His voice came in a fierce whisper. "How dare you interfere with my wishes!"

Fitch stood and paced the yard. Finally, he exploded. "Have you considered what I can give your daughter? If it's riches you want, I bring goods to the pueblo by the shipload. I have a partnership interest in the Maria Ester. If it's money you want, I already have as much as your governor."

Joaquin Carrillo left the courtyard, walking along the portico, disappearing into his room. Fitch thought the conversation had ended, but moments later, Carrillo returned carrying a sheet of foolscap paper in one hand. He shoved it at Fitch. It was a note dated that very day, and it was signed by Governor Jose Echeandia.

"Has he been here today?" Fitch asked.

"He sent this message by a soldier."

Fitch had learned to speak quite good Spanish, but reading was tortuously slow.

"Most Respected Don Joaquin Carrillo," the salutation read. "It now appears…we can soon talk…about the granting…of rancho lands in this section of Alta California. From…many evenings together, I know you are no ordinary man satisfied with ordinary means. If you are interested…" Fitch could feel the hurt welling up in his chest. He looked at Carrillo before continuing to read. "I, too, desire a fine casa that a governor's wife would be proud to oversee, and it is no secret in this pueblo, and I hope not with you, that…it is your…Josefa…whose hand I seek." The signature was an elaborate swirl.

Fitch knew that Carrillo could not read. He asked, "Do you know what this note says?"

"Si," he said meekly. "Josefa read it to me."

The thought of Josefa reading this message word by word to her father left Fitch sick. He wanted to reach out to her. She must be distraught. "Where is she?" he asked.

"The children are with their teacher. I do not want you to see Josefa now."

Fitch stretched his great arms across the table, feeling their weight. For awhile, he could not overcome the exhaustion that crept through him. The rigid ways of this land and its people were too much for an outsider. Josefa would be chattel, merely an instrument of trade, for a land grant. Finally, Fitch numbly said, "All right, I'll wake Virmond and gather my crew. We'll finish the padre's order before sailing."

Regardless of their differences, Joaquin Carrillo saddled a horse and did as he had promised. He brought a half-dozen men and boys to the beach to help transport merchandise from the brig to the beach. Neophytes from the mission would bring a second mule train to the beach to haul the manufactured goods and foodstuffs the priests ordered.

Fitch worked alongside his crew and the men of the pueblo carrying crated goods from surfboats beached in the low tide all of the way to Carrillo's warehouse on the embankment. As he lifted the heavy boxes filled with farm tools, his mind was racing. Before the brig sailed, he must check all parts of it…sails, rigging, galley inventory and above all, the ballast, now that so much heavy cargo was removed.

But Fitch's thoughts also mixed with feelings of dread. He kept looking about him helplessly. How could he simply sail away without seeing Josefa? Even if she were now reconciled to her father's dictates about her future, he desperately wanted a chance to say goodbye.

The sun was beginning to sink toward the horizon. Fitch knew that Joaquin Carrillo watched his every move, and it made him angry. He passed Carrillo in silence near the warehouse door several times as they worked. If Fitch could think of any other words that might persuade Carrillo, he was willing to try them.

A large thatch-covered crate aboard the last surfboat was too heavy for one man to lift, but Fitch managed to swing a side of it up on edge where he could tug at it. He was soon aware that Carrillo stood in the water beside him.

Together, they heaved and lifted the crate into position, then carried it through the tide to dry sand. Keeping a precarious balance, they climbed the embankment and into the hidehouse. Both men were panting as they stacked the crate. Breathless, Carrillo stretched full length across a pile of hides, and Fitch slumped to his haunches against the wall.

Fitch watched Carrillo's heavy chest rise and fall as he breathed. No wonder the man had the largest casa and the most cattle in the pueblo. He was a working fool. Carrillo finally sat up, still breathing hard. He surprised Fitch with what he said. "Whatever you think," shaking a finger, "I am not a man who does not want the best for my children. To show you, my friend, Julio says, I think too much about them for my own good." He took a long breath before continuing. "Our Josefa was born during the early days in this pueblo while my wife and I still lived in a tule-roofed one-room casa. Almost from the beginning, she had the same sad eyes as her mother, and I swore that somehow I would make those eyes brighten. I wanted to become a wealthy man and give my wife and children everything. I've lost my wife, but I still hold that dream."

Fitch walked over and sat down on the hides beside Carrillo. "Do you think I might spoil your dream?" he asked.

Carrillo was silent for a time. He slumped forward as though resigned to events outside his control. "No," he said, "but I believe that the governor could give her more than any other Californio. But for a little while today…" He paused. "I saw Josefa's eyes smiling like never before in her life. Today, when she read the message from Governor Echeandia to me, they filled with tears, and I saw a lifetime of grief ahead for her. Her heart was broken. I know my Josefa favors you. How can I stand in her way?"

Fitch's heart surged. At the same time he felt a deep compassion for Joaquin Carrillo. This man's love for Josefa would cost him dearly. Fitch said, "I talked to Padre Menendez today. I am sure he will baptize me when I return from the north. If you permit our marriage, I promise you Josefa will be cared for and loved all of her days."

Carrillo reached behind some boxes in the corner and came up with a half-filled jug of brandy that he obviously kept handy when he was working at the beach. He pulled the cork and handed the bottle to Fitch. "Drink," he said. Fitch took a long swig. Carrillo enjoyed several long swallows. His eyes gleamed when he looked at Fitch. "I may never own a rancho," he said, "but you have my permission."

Fitch jumped exuburantly to his feet and slapped Carrillo on the back. "Will you make arrangements with the priest while I am away?" he asked excitedly.

Carrillo paused, then shook his head. "No, Amigo, we must not wait. Take her with you today."

When they walked out of the warehouse, a strong wind blew seaward. It was ideal for sailing out of the bay. Fitch could see that members of his crew held a surfboat for him at water's edge, waiting to push out. In the wind and fading light, Fitch was struck with the despair of the circumstance. Josefa did not know of her papa's decision. He must hold the ship and go to her.

A member of the crew kept waving and calling for him to come. It was then that he heard shouting from the beach. He turned and saw Carrillo pointing up the trail. A lone rider, scarcely visible, rode toward them at maddening speed. Even as the silhouette of horse and rider neared the beach, Fitch only hoped rather than believed what he was seeing. He stood knee deep in water, studying the trail. She rode into the surf. She was crying his name. Gentle, fragile Josefa...breathless, skirt flying in the wind, hair strewn across her slim face. Fitch reached up to her as she dropped into his arms.

4. Joaquin in San Diego

Joaquin guided his horse absent-mindedly up presidio hill, scarcely aware of his friend, Julio, behind him. The San Diego sun was warm, the sky clear and the hills a mottled brown, broken only by grey-black brush in the crevices. Thoughts of Josefa occupied his mind. It was a torment he could not escape. Although he had given Josefa permission to marry, he felt rage when he realized that this first seed of his groin would have left home against his wishes. What kind of papa was he? Then his heart would fill with love and fear, a strange hollow feeling creeping through him when he thought of his beloved child floating on the great Pacific Ocean. Oh, Dios, esta, prohibito!

"I am a land person," he said, turning back to Julio. "No one would get me on water so far out that I could not see the trees!"

"It is nothing," Julio said, "These foreign traders sail their ships in storms so bad that the water washes across the decks."

"Oh," Joaquin mourned. "My poor child."

But Joaquin confessed that he felt some relief, knowing that the uncertainties about her marriage were now settled. No matter how much the governor complained, he, Joaquin, could only shrug his shoulders.

"It is in God's hands," he muttered.

"What is that?" Julio asked. But Joaquin did not explain.

Rabbits scampered across the trail at the bend near the presidio chapel and disappeared over the embankment under a clump of lavender blooming ceanothus. Near the top, Joaquin looked down the river's bank to where women from the pueblo washed clothes. In the distance, across the canyon, a small Indian party skinned a deer.

Upon arrival at the presidio, Joaquin unstrapped the case that held his violin. Today, they found their comrades in back of the barracks sitting in the shade of a crumbling adobe wall. One soldier lightly strummed his guitar and sang of women and love.

One of the men passed Joaquin the communal jug of wine, and he took a long drink, then handed it to Julio. Since Joaquin brought the promise of more music, the men offered him a place on the wall beside the man with the guitar.

Joaquin started to play, then paused. "I am just not able," he said.

"You sounded find," the guitar player said.

"The violin is in tune, but I am not."

The guitarist nodded uncertainly.

One of the soldiers in the group leaned across to Joaquin. "What do you hear about Pio and Andre?" he asked.

"My cousins? What about them."

"I hear that Governor Echeandia granted their petitions."

"Petitions?"

"I hear that Pio Pico received a grant for part of the Jumal Rancho and he and his brother, Andre, also received the great Santa Margarita y Los Flores. Thousands of acres!"

Joaquin sat dumbfounded. Pio made a living by buying from the trading vessels and keeping a small store in the pueblo. Recently, he was elected representative to the California diputacion, a five-man territorial governing team under the governor.

"Are they the only two men who asked for land?" Julio asked. His closest friend must surely have seen Joaquin close his eyes. Maybe he even saw the hurt lock Joaquin's throat. Julio had forgotten about Joaquin's longstanding application for a grant. It was small comfort when Julio then touched Joaquin's shoulder, realizing his mistake.

Someone else finally broke the silence by saying, "That Chilean, Jose Estudillo, got the rancho to the east of the river." Estudillo was treasurer for San Diego and the surrounding territory, well educated and owned a large home in the pueblo. Joaquin knew the governor had purposely ignored his request for land.

When the wine jug again reached Joaquin, it was empty. He turned to Julio. "I'm going home."

He walked around the barracks, carefully strapped his violin case on his horse and swung into the saddle. As he rode toward the gate, an invalid soldier hailed him. This old man, crippled and bent with the years, was one of several in the garrison . He was no longer suited for full military duty, and he had no family to care for him. So the army fed and housed him and he performed such duties as his health permitted, including distribution of dispatches arriving by overland rider and by ship. Joaquin turned his horse and rode to the man.

The old soldier handed him two letters and a small package. "Not even the governor receives this much mail," the soldier said, laughing, showing his jagged teeth and bare gums.

Joaquin tucked the letters and the small flat package into the pocket of his loose blouse. "Hey," the old man said, "are you going to open them and tell us the news?"

The old man knew that Joaquin could not read, but he hoped he would go back to his comrades, and among them, they would all stumble through the words of the dispatches until meaning emerged. This was the usual way among them, but Joaquin was not in the mood. His girls could read to him.

He touched spurs to his horse and headed down the trail. His thoughts were somewhat muddled. First, he felt embarrassed about his whole life. It seemed to him that most of it was wasted. What the hell else could happen to him? Why, today, would he receive more mail than he normally received in a year.

He thought about the land where most of his cattle grazed and watered, and he thought about the old mission orchard where the priests had allowed him to build his casa years earlier. If the governor gave away the mission lands around the pueblo, he might actually give away the Carrillo home and the mission lands provided him by the priests. "God," he whispered, "you test me too much. Please, I am afraid."

******

He pulled the letters and the package from his big jacket pocket, anticipating the excitement ahead for the children. How he wished his wife, Ignacia, was with him to enjoy the event. In this moment, he realized one of the letters must be from Josefa. He looked at the waxed closures. One letter along with the package had come overland. Sure enough, the other letter arrived by a small sailing ship in the bay the night before. He hurried from the corral and through the back gate into the courtyard of the casa. He found Oupay working at the earthen oven. She moved quietly. She placed pans of bread inside the oven upon smooth upended rocks, and then promptly closed the opening. Francisca sat on the tile floor grinding corn meal on a stone metate. One of Oupay's daughters turned a large piece of beef over on the open pit fire, fat dripping, flames flaring. Rosa came in from the garden laden with a basket of fresh beans, corn and tomatoes.

Joaquin could not explain why his children were so special to him. All of his girls read well. His wife had insisted upon that. Although it might be harder for his girls to find good husbands if they were too well educated, Joaquin understood how much ignorance could limit them. While other girls in the pueblo appeared satisfied to cook, sew and embroider, his daughters read whatever they could persuade Padre Menendez to loan them from his library, and any books neighbors bought from the trading ships.

"Maybe Rosa has too much of a mind of her own," Joaquin once said to his wife.

"No, no," she had insisted. "You wait. You'll be proud. She has the mind to overcome everything.".

With that assurance, Joaquin came to see Rosa as a picture of beauty and strength, much like her Mexican-Indian grandmother in Loreto. She stood straight-backed, and walked with the grace of a military officer's wife. Rosa was the perfect mix of all the best of all of her forebears, he told himself.

"Come, my Rosa," he said, "We've got mail."

Rosa dropped her basket. "There must be something from Josefa!" she said.

Joaquin handed her the dispatches. She looked at each quickly. "Si. Si." she said.

"Children," Joaquin called. "Come to the sala. We have a letter from Josefa!"

Oupay and her children took over food preparations. In the sala, Joaquin beckoned each child to a place. Rosa sat on the small handwoven rug in their midst. They watched her every move as she carefully broke the wax sealing the first dispatch. She glanced at the page and at her papa who waited so anxiously on the pillow-covered straightback bench. Then she smiled and read: "Dearest Papa, sisters, and brothers: How my heart breaks when I think of the distance between us. How much I long to see all of you..."

Francisca immediately cried aloud. Only Joaquin and his sons appeared brave, but Joaquin could not swallow. Rosa took a deep trembling breath and read on, "but I am so happy with Enrique. You must know that. He is a wonderful man. The Maria Ester is anchored in Matzatlan today, taking fresh supplies aboard. I will leave this letter for delivery by the next ship.

"Oh, how our ship bounces on the waves. I have been so sick. If it were not for Enrique, I would be frightened to death. But he says that I will grow so accustomed to the movement that I may be dizzy only when I go ashore. Each night I pray for all of you, and only hope that you have forgiven me for leaving. At Callao, I will become Enrique's wife, and he says that we will be back in the pueblo one day. Goodbye, my beloved family. May God take care of you."

For a few minutes Joaquin and his family sat huddled together in tears, just as they had done three years earlier when he lost his wife. In these minutes, they hurt together, explicably bound to one another.

Joaquin finally looked up. He raised his hands from the shoulders of young Julio and Ramon, and wiped his own tears. "Well." he said, "she is alive. She is happy. What more can God do for us? Read the other letter, Rosa."

So, Rosa wiped her eyes and broke the seal of the second letter and spread the sheet of paper on the low table before her.

"Who is it from?" young Juan asked.

Rosa glanced at the signature at the bottom of the page and her eyes widened with surprise. "It is from Romualdo Pacheco!" she said softly.

Joaquin felt his pulse quicken. How he admired this young officer. How he wished his own life and, yes, the lives of his boys could be as admirable as that of Romualdo.

"Lieutenant Pacheco," Joaquin said. "Well, he has not forgotten us."

Rosa glanced at the signature again. "Papa, he is a captain now."

"A captain! He must be the youngest captain and presidio commandante in California."

"I remember the first time we saw Romualdo Pacheco," Rosa said. "He rode his horse through the pueblo dressed in a new blue wool uniform with a coat that had bright red cuffs and collar. The coat hung to his thighs. We don't see new uniforms often."

"Read the letter, Rosa," Joaquin said.

"Greetings, Sergeant Joaquin Carrillo," Rosa began. "I am writing you from Santa Barbara where I am now commandante and where your many Carrillo cousins are either comrades or friends in the pueblo.

"Mi amigo," he continued, "we have not met since Governor Echeandia sent me to do duty in Monterey, and then Santa Barbara. Now, you are retired from service. But I have not forgotten you or your family. How I wish you were back at my side. You were, indeed, a trustworthy sergeant. I especially recall that evening when our survey party returned from the desert. You led our exhausted group directly to your hacienda, and though you were as tired

34

from the trip as any of us, you invited us to stay for supper. How relaxed and happy we were after so many strenuous days of searching to find the new route from Sonora and Tucson to San Diego…"

"And we found it!" Joaquin interrupted. "A much shorter route!"

His children watched him as he silently remembered his time of glory. Rosa then read ahead under her breath and suddenly looked at everyone in surprise. She repeated the words: "I recall how impressed I was to see Rosa reading from a large volume she had borrowed from the priest. She could hardly hold the book."

The family laughed because he described something all of them had talked about many times. She continued reading. "In a package with this letter, I send a small book of poems for Rosa that I recently purchased from a trading ship. I hope she enjoys them."

With this, Rosa reached for the package and quickly opened it, preserving the coarse paper in which it was wrapped since it was such a rare and useful material. "Oh" she exclaimed faintly, inspecting the leather binding of the thin book. It was handsewn and handbound. The type on each page was hand-pressed, two pages at one time, and it had been made in Mexico City. The family patiently waited while she carefully turned each page.

She paused to read an inscription on the flyleaf written by Romualdo. "Perhaps this momento may be one of many we share."

She glanced first at her papa and then at Francisca, eyes filled with wonder. "My own first book," she said. Joaquin watched her press it to her heart. He found himself feeling unexplainably joyous.

Again, Rosa turned to the letter. "Within the month," she read, "I expect to travel by ship to meet with Governor Echeandia. I hope that I may see you and your family while in the pueblo."

It was nearly dark as Rosa finished reading the letter. Francisca lighted candles and shifted to sit beside their papa. The boys huddled closer on the floor to face Rosa, deep in thought. For a time, they were one mind, one body; a portrait in muted light.

Young Julio broke the silence. "Josefa is floating on the ocean," he said. He was clearly frightened.

After another silence, Rosa whispered, "Romualdo Pacheco is coming here!"

Then Joaquin made a pronouncement. The family had heard some variation of it many times. He sounded so wise. "There are the good days and the bad days in every family," he said. "I would say the good overcomes the bad today. It is time for us to thank God for watching over us so closely. He must see greatness in us, for he gives us so many trials. It is our destiny, Children, to serve God in high places."

5. Rosa in San Diego

As soon as Rosa heard that Romualdo had arrived in the pueblo, she stayed near the garden gate watching the river trail that led to the presidio. He did not come to the casa that day. She continued to anticipate his arrival by the hour...sometimes by the minute. The next day her papa received a message requesting that he come to the presidio.

When her papa returned, he shook with excitement. He called Rosa into the sala. "He wants to marry you, My Little Rosa," He was nearly in tears.

"Marry me?" She took a deep breath. She ran out to the bench under the ramada in the courtyard, now pleading under her breath for some sign from the ghost of her mama. Instead, she felt her papa's hand on her shoulder. "Do you think I can be a wife?" she asked.

"You will be more than a wife." her papa said. "You will be a very special senora in the California territory. It is your destiny. You will be important to many people."

Rosa knew that her papa admired Romualdo beyond all other men. As far as he was concerned, he had arranged a perfect union. For Rosa, the meaning of marriage formed in illusory images including a church sanctuary with golden altar and a priest in crimson robes; and finally, a divine bed blessed by the whispers of the Mother of Jesus. She found herself trembling. Her voice became shaky.

"When will I see him?" she asked. "Should we not talk and plan together?"

"The senoras of the pueblo will take care of everything," her papa said. "Keep in mind, Romualdo is a very busy man. He is consulting with the governor."

Rosa found herself in shock when the governor, himself, announced the wedding. Word spread quickly throughout the pueblo district that the wedding would take place within the week and that Romualdo Pacheco's bride, the sixteen year old Rosa Carrillo would accompany her husband to

Santa Barbara. There had not been either a wedding or a fiesta for some time, so everyone in the pueblo fell into a festive mood, preparing for the event.

The fruits of the San Diego summer suggested sweets of every description, and women in the pueblo happily pursued delicacies using both corn and wheat dough. The prospect of good things to eat were never better, not only because of summer crops, but also because of the presence of the ship, Ayacucho. Its goods included plenty of brown sugar, chocolate, spices and foodstuffs from faraway places.

But Rosa knew she was not herself. Her friends, and even Francisca, told her she was acting differently. They saw her on the plaza playing hide and seek with the children, and later, someone saw her swimming naked with her younger brothers at the mouth of the river. One day she rode Chocolata, her favorite horse, farther along the beach and nearby foothills than ever before.

And then Francisca found her lying in the high grass of the open fields near the river where she aimlessly day dreamed. "You do not act like a woman who expects to marry this very week!" her younger sister argued.

"I know," Rosa said, "but I am doing my best."

"Would you rather not marry?

"I have dreamed of marrying Romualdo many times."

"Then why…

Do I act like a child?"

"Si."

Rosa looked sadly at her sister and shook her head. "I think it is because I am a child. I am trying to get all of the child out of me so that I can become a woman."

Francisca, standing above her in the grass, looked so sympathetic that Rosa was embarrassed. "I understand. I really do," she said.

"I think I will be lonesome too," Rosa said. "We were born in papa and mama's bedroom. These fields, this river, this orchard are home. What do I know of other places?"

"I remember," Francisca said, "when papa took all of us to Mission San Luis Rey for a special fiesta. Do you remember?"

"Si," Rosa said. "We were gone five days."

Francisca laughed at the memory. "My legs were chafed and my bottom was covered with saddle sores by the time we rode home. But think of Josefa. She is so faraway we may never see her again."

Rosa caught her breath. "Please don't say that," she scolded. "She is our sister. She must return. Mama said we have a special destiny. I believe it."

The women in the pueblo became so preoccupied with shaping and sewing the yards of white satin and layers of lace that they sought out Rosa only as fittings were required. The Ayacucho carried all of the fabrics needed. Groups of women, a half-dozen at one time, stitched lace in layers to a satin base, enjoying hours of gossip together.

Their papa spent his time discussing business with either James Scott, the supercargo aboard the Ayacucho, or John Wilson, the shipmaster. He not only sold his own hides, but also those belonging to the mission. Rosa loved to hear these seamen speak Spanish through the lilting accent of their native Scotland. She sensed joy in their speech and in their everyday lives. One day when Capt. John Wilson came to talk business with her papa, he brought a package.

"This is for the bride," Rosa heard him say to her papa in the courtyard. "It's our wedding gift."

"Gracias, Senor," her papa said. He beckoned Rosa from her room and introduced her. Francisca had just combed Rosa's black hair full down her back in preparation for braiding.

For a moment, Wilson simply stared at Rosa, nodding his own head of thick sand-colored hair "I am at a loss for words," he said to her papa." Then he turned to Rosa. "Lassie, you are breathtaking."

For a moment, Rosa thought, his tightly sculpted face flushed, even through its leathery coloring. Regaining his composure, he gestured clumsily toward the package on the table. "For you, Lassie," he said. "Open it now if you like."

Rosa excitedly pulled away the wrapping and unfolded the most delicate silk mantilla she had ever seen in her life. A tightly-sewn pattern of crimson and yellow lay over a bed of green leaves, all in silk thread. "It is from Canton," Wilson said.

She held it to her breast, then draped it over her shoulders and head. The women sewing her wedding gown gathered around. "I shall treasure it all of my life," Rosa said.

"Why not wear it for the wedding?" one woman suggested.

"I will," Rosa said softly . She glanced briefly at Captain Wilson, and his intent blue eyes enveloped her. She quickly turned away.

Somehow, the mantilla changed everything for Rosa. She felt she became a woman. She thought womanly thoughts, realizing that for now, the entire pueblo focused upon her. All of this attention was for her. in spite of the fact that she played no part in the planning. She knew that the women of the pueblo would talk about the mantilla for years to come, and it would always be slyly noted that it came as a wedding gift from a man other than her husband.

Once during a plaintive mood, Rosa again slipped away from the casa and sat alone on the rocks near a pool of water in the dry river bed. It was difficult to escape the sun and the dry heat, but she found the shade of a giant oak tree with massive twisting white barked limbs stretching far out over the river embankment. She carried the small book of poems Romualdo had sent her.

Rosa knew that Romualdo intrigued nearly all of the women in the pueblo, both young and old, married and unmarried. When she grasped the flattering realization that of all the women he might have chosen in California, he sought her as his wife, she felt a certain awe.

Still, since his arrival in San Diego, he had not come to see her. He met with her papa at the presidio more than once, and the two men made many arrangements. She was not even sure what was planned.

Rosa once complained to her papa, but he said, "Time is short. My Dove, and he has important affairs to settle with the governor. Every minute, he is planning for the good of the territory. There is simply no way for him to visit you. Try to understand, there is a revolution in the making."

Her papa's words hurt, and when she considered leaving San Diego, she again felt an unexplainable lonesomeness. How she envied the deep love that sent Josefa sailing away with Enrique without concern for home, past or future.

She climbed down a bank to the shallow pool in the river bed and dangled her feet. She opened her book of poems. For now, this book was her only promise of love and connection with her future husband. She recalled some of the verses. each so different. She prayed that the words of the poetry revealed the inner man of Romualdo Pacheco. She read again:

"In the soft light of campfire,
I see a vision of your face,
the reflection of flames dancing in your eyes,
and I find courage for tomorrow's battle…"

The lines of another verse clung in her mind because they seemed the very essence of this erect, firm, unshakable soldier she would marry.

"There is a point in the distance…
A place I relish, which compels my march,
My eyes see little around me…
Only that distant place."

40

Rosa was aware of an absolute stillness around her…no birds, no breeze in the grass or trees, no movement in her own life…only time imperceptibly passing. At first. the rustle escaped her. the rustle in distant dry grass…footsteps. Then the footsteps came in fast strides. They were strong steps like those of a soldier. Certain, firm, confident steps.

His voice was quiet when he parted the brush above her and peered down. "Buenas dias, Rosa."

Then Romualdo dropped from the rise down to where she sat. On this warm day, he wore only a lace-fronted white shirt and blue uniform pants, but his beard was meticulously groomed and his dark face shone.

"Romualdo," she said, catching her breath. "How did you find me?"

"Francisca pointed the way," he said.

He found a seat on the bank looking slightly up at her. "I have wanted very much to talk to you since arriving in San Diego,"

Seeing him in only partial uniform, she recalled his warm playful visits to their casa before he left San Diego. But she also felt his strength. Men like Romualdo Pacheco hold our world together, she thought. Soon she would be responsible for setting his table, keeping his home, bearing his children, and entertaining his guests. Then, to Rosa's surprise, he became only a boy, just as she was only a girl. His usually sharp eyes appeared misty and dreamy. He was happy to have her companionship, and knowing that, her worries about the future vanished.

After a moment, he said, "I need a special kind of wife, Rosa, and I knew long ago that you were the one."

"I'm not sure I can be all that you want me to be," she said.

He looked at her silently for a moment, and then as if sharing a secret, he said," I feel unsure about many things."

He was not a man who smiled often, but now he smiled. Rosa did not recall that he talked that much either, but he certainly talked now.

"I saw more of you when you were thirteen years old than I have since," he said, looking forthrightly into her eyes. "but even then, I liked the girl I saw."

He stopped and seemed to ponder. "I remember one time when you came running into the courtyard after riding your horse along the beach, and you were breathless. Your face was radiant with color, and you smiled at me, and I wanted…" He stopped, searching for words. "There was another time. You were cutting melons and offering pieces to each of my men after our survey reconnaissance in the desert. None of us had tasted anything so sweet or so thirst-quenching in weeks. Never before had I experienced such feelings as I did in your presence. How can you always be such a fragrant flower?"

He kept recalling earlier times, revealing his feelings about her. "Once," he said, "you danced alone at a fiesta on the pueblo plaza, and I still think of you in your twirling colors. Were you ever so aware of me?" But he did not wait for an answer. "Then I saw you reading, and I became convinced that you were preparing to become the wife of a very ambitious man."

Rosa smiled, impishly now..."a man who sees only a distant place?"

Romualdo looked puzzled for a moment.

She said, "There is a verse in the book you gave me. Do you recall it? 'There is a point in the distance...'

"Si." he said excitedly. "Rosa, you do understand!" And then, he too, recited, "a place...that compels my march..."

He looked up, seeming embarrassed, prepared to hide behind the mask of a soldier where he could be comfortable, but she did not let him. Instead, she touched his shoulder and asked, "Where are we going, Romualdo Pacheco? Where are you taking me?"

When she looked into his eyes, her heart and mind filled with dreams. "We will have a grand hacienda," he said. "High on a hill overlooking all of Alta California. You will be the senora of the hacienda, and I will be commandante-generale of the whole territory. We will hold fandangoes and fiestas for our vaqueros and our neighbors. You must see the land I have petitioned for a grant. It is the paradise of the California territory."

In the quiet moments following, Rosa found herself staring excitedly into space. She felt the surge of Romualdo's ambitions sweeping her into an indescribable destiny. Her heart beat fast with so many thoughts.

She saw her life unfolding before her with the beat of soldiers drums and many guitars. She would never be uncertain again, she told herself. Life would never become clouded. She would share Romualdo's bed, bear his children. She would help her husband hold the world together. No wonder her papa loved Romualdo so much. He was her papa's enlightened image. When Romualdo reached to kiss her, she lay joyously back in his arms.

The wedding took place at Casa de Carrillo the next day and the fiesta followed in the pueblo square. Late in the evening they rode to their wedding quarters in the presidio.

6. Rosa on the Mission Trail

When the first sunlight crept over the brown hills to the east of the presidio, Rosa guided her horse from the local river trail to the place where it joined El Camino Real, the long-established trail that connected all of the California missions. Romualdo rode ahead of her until the trail widened, and then he reined back beside her. A four-man escort from the presidio accompanied them, two riding well ahead and two behind. Farther back, a muleteer attended a dozen pack animals loaded with muskets, ammunition, lances, food supplies and Rosa's clothes, jewelry, and personal things. The muleteer also led a string of horses available for changes of mount.

Rosa's papa had saddled Chocolata, her favorite horse, a lively dark brown animal she named and helped break. She enjoyed the surge of Chocolata's strength while climbing hills, and his sure-footedness in loose rock where the trail descended. Riding farther and farther away from the pueblo, it occurred to Rosa that Chocolata was quickly becoming her last connection with home.

But for a time, her mind was possessed with thoughts and feelings of their wedding night. When, at last, they escaped the fiesta in the square and found their way along the steep trail by torchlight to the presidio apartment reserved for them, she was exhausted. In the coolness of the dark room, it was enough simply to be in Romualdo's arms. But soon she felt the excruciating pain and joy of their oneness melting her tiredness into deep sleep. Later, she awakened, scrambling and searching desperately for Romualdo's arms. Even now, on the trail, looking across at her husband's thick black hair, heavy brows, mustache and dark, handsome face, she felt stirrings. Now she knew love as she had never before tasted it.

Her mama had believed Rosa would always enjoy a perfect existence, that her life would be filled with continuous joy. Rosa thought about her life in Pueblo San Diego. It was true, what her mama said. She enjoyed good friends, good times. Nothing complicated or hurtful came her way. Now she was married to Romualdo. She was truly blessed.

The pack animals slowed them, even on the wide trail, but Rosa enjoyed the easy pace, the comfortable change occurring in her life. At first the trail kept them inland among the gently undulating golden hills of summer. Most streams were dry so they took water wherever they found it. A collection of huts framed with poles and covered with heavy tule and grass usually first identified the Indian rancherias along their route. They saw women and children working in their gardens, grinding grain and cooking over open fires.

The children, most of them naked in the mid-day heat, ran to the trail to see the soldiers and to stare at Rosa. The heat forced the soldiers, including Romualdo, to remove coats and fold them behind their saddles. Rosa wore an ankle-length light lavender skirt with elaborate gold embroidered hem, and a short-sleeved, round-necked blouse outlined with layers of lace. For travel, her hair hung in a long braid down her back and her head was covered with a wide-brimmed hat. The day was too warm to wear either a mantilla or jewelry, but she realized she still made a colorful sight for these children who had probably never visited a Mexican pueblo.

At first, Rosa rode side saddle, but soon, she lifted her skirt and threw one leg over the horse to straddle him. In the late afternoon, they made camp near a stream. Unlike her mother during her trek with her father from Loreto, Rosa knew she could not start a campfire with a flint and tinderbox. Fortunately, the soldiers in this escort group did it all.

By the time the sun was overhead the next day, Mission San Luis Rey de Francia, the largest of the missions in the Alta California chain, appeared in the distance, and soon, the bells in its double-tiered campanile rang across the hills. At one place in the trees and brush, the mission came into view as one great whole, and Rosa saw small bands of Indians moving along the trails among the hills in response to the call of the bells. They were neophytes of the mission who worked as herdsmen, but for the last few leagues, Rosa saw Indians working in vineyards and orchards.

The mission buildings, taken together, occupied more space than all of Pueblo San Diego. From her place on the hill, Rosa thrilled at the sight of the white facade of the church with its elaborately shaped arch outlined in gold. It stood in simple majesty against a clean blue sky.

A long two-story building with lattice work balcony paralleled the church. The balcony was supported by a line of columns. Near the church, a hundred or more round-topped tule huts provided housing for Indian neophytes.

"What is all of that below the mission," Rosa asked.

"The lavanderia," Romualdo answered.

Rosa could make out an archway built into a long adobe wall, and a tiled stairway leading to a tiled pool of water in a sunken garden. Now, she realized, there were women at the bottom of the stairs washing clothes.

Romualdo pointed to the rolling hills in the far distance beyond the mission and said, "Those hills are part of a rancho that stretches from the beach to the mountains. It is the land granted to your cousins, Pio and Andres Pico. It is called the Santa Margarita y Las Flores."

"There is no way to hold so much space in the mind's eye," she said, then added, "My papa suffers everyday because he was not included when the governor was considering petitions in the district."

"I know," Romualdo said. "I spoke to the governor on his behalf, but, for some reason, he holds a grudge I do not understand."

With the mission in sight, and knowing they would stay there for the night, Rosa felt a sudden whimsy.

"I will race you to the church!" she called, and with that, she spurred Chocolata to a run along the trail into a valley and then up the long gradual slope toward the mission. Romualdo pursued her across a stream in the valley and struck off along a narrow path into what appeared impenetrable brush.

By the time Rosa reached the great stretch of flatland, the site of the mission, Chocolata frothed at the mouth. She searched the slope for sight of Romualdo. Not seeing him, she trailed her horse among the great oak trees near the church. Halfway there, she stopped and smiled. From behind the massive twisted trunk of a giant live oak, Romualdo stepped out and waved to her.

Before she reached him, she was surrounded by curious Indian children. The escort soldiers soon joined them to ride through the gate of the quadrangle to a large round fountain of running water. What a welcome sight. Rosa felt dust and grime all over her. She moistened her handkerchief in the cool water and rubbed it over her neck and face and arms. Less delicately, Romualdo and the soldiers dipped their heads into the cold water and shouted with elation, scrubbing their arms to the elbows.

A half-dozen other soldiers assigned to the San Luis Rey escolta appeared in the compound to welcome them.

When Rosa turned from the fountain, she was surprised to find a group of Indian women and children surrounding her, smiling and curious. One child, a girl, came close to her. She wore a simple sack-like brown dress and sandals.

She touched Rosa's blouse and said, "Bonita, Senora."

"Gracias," Rosa replied, leaning close to the girl to see her necklace of shell fragments. Other young women moved closer to touch Rosa's clothing. Rosa found their curiosity warming.

But now, the church bells rang again and an old padre with thick black beard and a scar over one eye appeared in their midst and scolded the Indian girls. "It is time for mass," he shouted gruffly. "Get to the church now! Father Peyri is waiting."

Rosa and Romualdo entered the long nave of the church by a side door and stood close to the altar. A small group of young Lusieno Indian boys sang a Gregorian-style chant in haunting tones as they came down the aisle from the back of the church following an old Indian man. When they finished their singing, they, too, stood near the altar. Other boys acted as acolytes, lighting candles.

"He talks to the Indians in their own language," the Padre whispered. "Please remember that Father Peyri arrived in California in 1798. He built this greatest of all the missions and developed the mission ranchos. He is an extraordinary man of God."

Rosa soon heard that this mission had 26,000 head of cattle and almost as many sheep. She also heard that nearly 3,000 Christianized Indians made Mission San Luis Rey and its ranchos their home.

After the service, Padre Barona showed them to a guest apartment in the quadrangle and left them for siesta. Alone, at last, on the third day of their marriage, Rosa yearned for the passion of their wedding night. They were in a room with European furniture including a bedstead and mattress so high that a stool was provided to climb into it. It was such a luxury after sleeping on the ground the night before.

"This is the room where the governor sleeps when he visits San Luis Rey," Romualdo told her.

But Rosa scarcely heard him. His lips touched hers. She felt the uncontrollable joy of his touch. Her body throbbed. Every force of her being compelled her to Romualdo's arms. She felt her own mother's virgin pains and passion of the Baja journey. She moved in the rhythm of her life-mate. In this Casa de Dios, this House of God, she cried aloud and prayed against the bare shoulders of Romualdo, wanting the seed of their love to be fertile.

"It will be a male child," she whispered afterward. Romualdo kissed her cheeks, neck and breasts, over and over again.

"No child," she said breathlessly, "can be conceived in a house of God without divine blessing."

During the morning hours, Rosa and Romualdo strolled through the mission orchard and gardens. Romualdo stopped often to study the remarkable irrigation system where water filtered through rocks from a spring to the gardens, the lavanderia and finally the orchard. Along the way, Padre Antonio Peyri appeared.

Although he was at least sixty years old, he stood strong and straight in his robes and brim hat, face full of color, as vital in appearance here as in his vestments in the pulpit.

"I am glad that you could visit us, Captain," he said. "I was pleased to hear of your marriage." he said.

"The governor sends you greetings," Romualdo said. "He asked me to report to him how the soldiers assigned here serve you."

"They serve us well," Padre Peyri said, "but I hope that you will also advise him that thousands of our mission cattle and sheep graze on the Rancho Santa Margarita y Las Flores. It is our largest rancho, and it serves the needs of great numbers of mission neophytes. It would be a serious error to pass it into private ownership…"

"I will report that, Padre," Romualdo said, "but it is my understanding that this land has already been granted."

Padre Peyri appeared shocked. His eyes grew wide with anger and his voice hoarse. "This governor is Satin in the flesh!" he shouted. "Can't he show any respect for God's work? It has taken me thirty-two years to develop this mission and its ranchos. When, at last, the likelihood of civilizing this corner of the world appears possible, a man without decency or understanding sweeps away the livelihood of our neophytes and threatens the life work of every California missionary."

Romualdo looked helplessly at the priest. "I promise to deliver your message, Padre."

Padre Peyri, still trembling, shook a finger at Romualdo. "Without our missions, Captain, there is no reason for Alta California. We are its foundation. Indeed, the governor does not merely threaten us. He threatens God!"

For a moment, the padre's shoulders slumped as though he were clearly defeated. Then, he pulled himself erect. "If you and the senora will visit with us in the sala tonight," he said, "I promise that we will not talk about this again."

7. Rosa at San Gabriel Mission

Rosa stood quietly while the old Gabrieleno applied his paint to a canvas cut from a ship's sail. A young Indian girl worked beside him pouring paint into small ceramic containers and stirring the contents. The weathered and crippled old Indian man worked on the portico near the door of the Sacristia at Mission San Gabriel.

While Romualdo met with Padre Jose Sanchez, el Presidente of the mission chain in Alta California, Rosa amused herself in the mission courtyard. Now, she was transfixed by the work of this Gabrielite.

The Indian artist worked with a strange mix of colors created from boiling various vegetable, plant, and earth matter in linseed oil. He even used the powdered substance from fired brick, and the oil from hulls of black walnuts.

"Where did you learn to paint?" Rosa asked him.

The man did not look up from his work. "The priests gave me the brushes," he said. "God gives me the paints and guides my strokes."

She watched his callused hand as he dipped his brush into the paint, wiped it on the side of its container and deftly applied it to the canvas. The feeling of the earthlike colors in the summer light, the massive size of the human figures in the painting in proportion to background and the literal translation of the event he depicted left Rosa holding her hands tightly to her breast. In this moment, she became the mother he painted. She felt the hopeless agony of this woman holding the broken, bleeding body of her son. For a moment, Rosa almost saw the blood of Christ's punctured hands and feet dripping on the tiles of the portico. She winced unthinkingly.

The old Indian stood and motioned her down the stairs to the underground sacristia. His paintings covered the walls. "I think you know my feeling," he said.

He took her to the far wall and pointed to his first work. "You see," he said gently, "in this painting, the white chief tells the Indian, Jesus, he must die."

The old man hobbled along the wall to the next canvas. "Here, you see, the white chief's soldiers make Jesus carry a cross. If he doesn't do it, they will flog him."

The human figures in the paintings were mostly brightly dressed primitive silhouettes. Rosa could not understand why she was so affected. She began to feel the deep suffering of the Indian Christus as the old man led her through his moving scenes of the Passion. She witnessed Jesus falling under the weight of his burden. She experienced the grief of the Indian and of Maria, his mother, when she saw her son along the route. She felt relief when the Indian, Simon, lifted the cross to help Jesus. She shared the tears of Veronica who wiped the face of Jesus. She cringed as they nailed him to the cross, and she cried openly as she watched Jesus die. She wondered how many times she had passed the dark foreboding paintings of the Stations of the Cross hanging in the presidio chapel in San Diego without experiencing their meaning.

When they returned to the portico, she saw Romualdo and a straight-backed, dark-bearded priest walking across the courtyard. She turned to the Indian, still feeling drained.

"Gracias, Senor," she said to the Indian, "I shall always remember this day."

When Romualdo introduced her to Padre Jose Bernardo Sanchez, the priest looked at her intently. "You have been crying, child," he said.

"They are good tears, Padre."

"But why?" he asked with concern.

She thought for a time and then shook her head without answering. She cried, she knew, for the dying Indian Christus; and for churches shaken to ruins in the wrath of earthquakes and washed away by relentless floods. For a split second, she thought of the mission lands that would be taken from the church and given to individuals as political favors. All of the bad things in the world came together in one dreadful thought.

It was early in the day, and she had seen nothing of Mission San Gabriel. "We must ride," Romualdo said.

8. Rosa and Adriana at Buenaventura

Rosa rode Chocolata with increasing joy. He was stronger and better conditioned than she thought possible. Her loving experiences each night with Romualdo kept her constantly remembering their extraordinary night of intercourse at Mission San Luis Rey. For her, it remained a spiritual time that promised an extraordinary life for her first-born. This memory merged in an excruciating way with the larger than life paintings of the elderly Indian at Mission San Gabriel.

With the onset of dreams, day dreams and the reality of other missions along the El Camino Real, her mind whirled. There were the Mission San Fernando shops for carpentry, woodwork, weaving, along with the shed for agricultural tools and the wine press room. At Mission San Juan Capistrano the passioned sculpture of the Christ merged with the earlier earthquake destruction and tallow vats around her. Inside San Juan Mission, Rosa found herself enthralled with the colorful paintings on the adobe walls and the many wooden chandeliers topped with black candlestick holders. These many visions of church continued to blur together until they arrived at Santa Buenaventura.

It was here that Rosa met the ragged, half-naked nine-year-old Indian child. While their contingent rode into the partially walled mission compound, neophytes gathered to greet them, but Rosa could not take her eyes from the child whose dark hair fell across her forehead and half-way down her back. She waved to Rosa as though no one else existed. This unkempt little girl fit too well into the broken state of the mission.

Romualdo halted and gathered his men. Rosa stayed close to him. "The head priest here is blind," he said. "They no longer have soldiers on duty as guards. So, we are on our own. We'll prepare a fire on one of the outdoor spits and use our own rations. I'll see the priest or his assistant. Make camp now in the courtyard."

Rosa stretched her cramped legs by first walking through the badly kept gardens. With some discomfort, she became aware that the child followed. At the base of the slope in front of the mission, the bay came into view. To Rosa's surprise, she also saw an Indian rancheria down near the beach. As she followed the path in that direction, the child skipped alongside her.

"Do you live in the rancheria?" Rosa asked.

"Here," she said, pointing and twirling in the dust, apparently meaning the entire area.

An Indian woman coming up the path from the rancheria greeted them. "Is this child's family at the rancheria?" Rosa asked.

The woman shrugged slightly, finally saying, "She does not have a family."

"No family?"

Again, the woman shook her head.

Rosa passed the rancheria to walk through the sand to the water. The child followed, shrieking with delight, running into a low breaking wave. Rosa sat down in the sand and quietly watched this little creature who delighted her so much. Finally, she beckoned the child.

At water's edge, she stripped and bathed the child. All the while, the little girl looked intently at her, touching her hair and cheeks. Her eyes were filled with more love than Rosa could ever remember experiencing from one so young. She decided the child must have a proper meal. As they walked back up the slope, Rosa felt a small hand slip into her own.

"You are asking for trouble," Romualdo said, watching the child cling to Rosa.

"I want her to have a proper meal tonight.

Romualdo shrugged.

The child snuggled closely to Rosa as they sat near the fire. The soldiers prepared a meal from food carried on the muletrain. She fell asleep in the early evening, now stretched across Rosa's lap. "I'll put her to bed," Rosa said. "Where does she sleep?"

"I've never asked," the priest answered.

Rose felt the defiance her mama had warned her to deal with carefully. She grew angry with the priest. How could she defy a priest? She had heard many times. She must defy, but with love.

"Help me, Padre."

Romualdo watched uncomfortably. With the child in her arms, Rosa followed the priest into the mission to a small bedroom. She laid the child on the straw mattress.

"What is her name?" she asked.

"I've heard her called Adriana." The priest hesitated, then asked, "Would you consider taking her with you?

"I love the child. But we are just married. We will have children of our own soon."

"Still…" the priest said. Then he showed Rosa a room where she and Romualdo could sleep. She happily accepted.

When Rosa awakened next morning, she was shocked to see Adriana sleeping against one of the columns of the portico outside her room. "Adriana," she asked, almost in tears., "Why aren't you in your bed?"

"Are you leaving me?" Adriana asked. Her face was red and covered with tear stains. It was clear that she had been crying for hours.

Adriana brought the child into her arms. Through her own tears, she could see the priest talking to Romualdo. Romualdo saw Rosa and walked quickly toward her and the child. He stood for a moment. He seemed completely confounded when he saw both Rosa and the child in tears.

"We're leaving soon," he said. "Grab some breakfast." He looked at Adriana. "You, too, Child. But first, I want you to see the mule you will ride."

Rosa took Adriana's hand and pulled her close as Romualdo reached out to both of them.

9. Rosa in Santa Barbara

From the moment the daughters of Don Carlos Antonio de Carrillo, Rose's blood uncle, and the daughters of Don Juan Noriega de Guerra, her uncle by marriage, appeared on the presidio parade ground, the compound throbbed with their happiness. Rosa and Romualdo had arrived in the late evening of the night before. Even from the door of the commandante's headquarters, Rosa heard her cousins' lighthearted laughter on the other side of the grounds, and watched their spirited and daring stroll...talking, gesturing and flirting with the soldiers. As they came her direction, she too, found herself laughing. Rosa's Indian child ran from the back of their quarters to see the excitement. Soldiers appeared from everywhere...the bachelor's barracks, the corral and even the guard posts to walk with the girls, flattering and kidding them along the way. When one soldier strummed his guitar and began singing, the girls screeched with delight.

"Buenas dias, Rosa!" one of the girls called, and all of them waved.

Their delightful presence was infectious. The guitarist still played and the men continued singing as the girls entered the quarters. Even dour-faced Lima, the Indian woman who worked for Romualdo, smiled ever so slightly. She beckoned to Adriana to bring out cups while she scurried about the fire pit and work table in the yard preparing tidbits to eat. According to Romualdo, Lima became a different woman with Rosa's arrival. Not only did she like Rosa, but she took Adriana as her own.

The girls' chatter flowed with energy and questions.

"We hope you'll be happy in Santa Barbara," Encarnacion said.

"Have you heard about the bailes planned in your honor?" Natalie wanted to know.

"I think all of the senoritas in the pueblo must be jealous of you. How does it feel to be married to the commandante? asked little Manuela in all seriousness.

Rosa didn't try to keep up with the questions. She simply expressed her feelings. "I am pleased to have so many wonderful cousins and aunts and uncles," she told them. "But the bailes and fiestas must wait until I make more clothes."

"I am happy beyond belief," she heard herself saying. She had not dreamed that Santa Barbara's sweep of sandy beach and circling bay would be so magical, nor the climate so glorious.

They talked through a current of laughter, gathering at the table under the ramada in the yard behind the apartment. "Very soon," Rosa said, "I plan to start a flowerbed and an herb garden." All shook their heads with approval. As she sat down, she reached out for young Adriana's hand and pulled her gently to the bench beside her.

There was a brightness in the day; a lightness in the way the breeze caressed the women's cheeks. Both Romualdo and her family in Santa Barbara were spoiling her. With each passing day she fell more deeply in love with her husband and her own life.

"What can we do for you?" Margarita asked. "Do you need anything? Are there any problems?" Margarita was only slightly older, and Rosa felt an immediate kinship with her.

Rosa laughed. "Well, there are all of these soldiers," she said kiddingly.

"No?" Encarnacion said, wide-eyed. She was so petite, so animated. "They would not dare flirt with the commandante's wife."

"Not that," Rosa said, "but they try too hard to please me. I am weary with saying 'thank you' and 'no thank you'."

There were other Carrillos in Santa Barbara, and Rosa met them several at a time. All were at least grandchildren of one of Rosa's great uncles, the long deceased Jose Raimundo Carrillo. This man had escorted the great Padre Junipero Serra with the settlement and construction of the first Alta California missions.

Romualdo had been gone most of the day. When he returned, he looked both weary and worried. "What is it?" Rosa asked.

She served him dinner and then rubbed his shoulders as he sat at the table. "A rider came through the pueblo today from Monterey, he said. He is carrying a message from Mariano Vallejo, the commandante. The messenger is headed for San Diego to see the governor. He told Guerra and me that the soldiers in both Monterey and San Francisco are preparing for a rebellion."

"Vallejo has a reputation as an outstanding soldier," she said.

"You know him?"

"Our family and his family made an arrangement at Francisca's birth that she and Mariano Vallejo would marry when she became sixteen."

10. Mariano Vallejo at Monterey

"I am not happy with what I see on the grounds," the young commandante at the Monterey Presidio told his second-in-command, Alferez Jose Fernando del Campo. He turned from the grill-protected window of his quarters, smoothing his carefully trimmed full black beard to the contours of his broad face. "Have you heard anything?"

"The complaints. Always the same," his second in command said.

"That isn't what I mean."

"I have been feeling things for days. The men are talking too seriously among themselves."

Marino Vallejo had been only Alferez or ensign at the San Francisco Presidio, but Governor Echeandia had ordered him to Monterey. "Damn," Vallejo uttered.

He sucked in a long breath and crossed to a chair by his work table. His office was bare except for the table and two chairs. "When I rode across the grounds this morning, I could feel their defiance. As though I were personally to blame."

Vallejo had only recently celebrated his twenty-first birthday, and although he was almost born to his place in the military at this very presidio, he never learned his father's patience in times of trouble. He had already earned a good reputation as an Indian fighter, and took great pride in the loyalty of the garrison under his command.

Campo said, "I tried to speak to several of the men on my way here. They actually turned away when they saw me."

"I know conditions are bad," Vallejo said. "I understand their anger. But how can I help them when my messages to Echeandia go unanswered? We know the central government doesn't care. These soldiers were brought here and forgotten. We have few muskets, no ammunition, and I don't trust the condition of those old cannons. There is no way we could defend Monterey.

"If a revolt occurs," Campo said, "you should not feel badly. It won't be the first time."

He referred to the problem a year earlier when Romualdo Pacheco had returned from exploring north of San Francisco Bay and found Monterey Presidio nearly deserted. Vallejo still served in San Francisco at the time.

Vallejo walked back to the window and looked out on the presidio square.

"Look at those men. Not one of them has a decent uniform. They wear rags, their food is bad, and they can't depend upon getting paid."

"Yes, it's been three months since any of us were paid."

Vallejo's mind raced to other things. "How many months did it take Pacheco to round up the soldiers after they deserted the presidio last time."

"They straggled back for months."

Vallejo was not only a native of Monterey of Spanish descent, but the son of Don Ignacio Vallejo who arrived in California with the first land trek in 1769 under Don Gaspar de Portola.

Vallejo had asked Campo to come to headquarters because he had been the first among the officers to hear about a possible uprising on another occasion. That time Vallejo had immediately called in and interrogated several likely leaders, but the task was not undertaken with enthusiasm. Since nothing came of the earlier plot, it was happily forgotten. At best, Vallejo only hoped to stay ahead of events. He could not overcome conditions without money to meet payrolls and to purchase supplies.

"What do we do this time?" he muttered to himself.

"They want to be out from under Echeandia," Campo said. "Some of them would like an independent California."

It was an all too familiar idea. The soldiers thought that if California had its own independent government, the territory could solve its own problems. Continued dependence upon a remote and unresponsive central government left them without a system under which to live and raise their families. Vallejo doubted the wisdom of revolt, but it often occurred to him that he only accepted the bad conditions because he enjoyed the privilege of rank and prospered as a native son.

Before the day ended, he talked to others whom he thought he could trust. Among them, Juan Jose Rocha who, like so many other soldiers in the company, was banished from Mexico and assigned to the Alta California military because of a crime he had committed. At Monterey, Rocha seemed to find his place and gradually advanced to the rank of sergeant in the artillery. He was generally trusted by the officers of the company. Vallejo also talked to Sergeant Andres Cervantes, another trusted soldier. All felt uneasy, and believed a revolt was likely, but none knew of a move in that direction.

The day's discussions left Vallejo even less sure about what to expect, and in bed he rolled and tossed until well after midnight. When he finally convinced himself that he could not resolve the problem that night, he fell into a troubled sleep, dreaming that he was engaged in a battle. Soldiers fired their muskets, and he heard shouting as he ran for shelter. An artillery shell exploded near him, and then he suddenly awakened and sat up in bed. Someone was banging on the door. He stood up and pulled on his britches. The banging continued; and without warning, a group of soldiers burst through his locked door. One carried a torch that lighted the room.

"In Christ's name, what is going on?" Vallejo demanded.

"It is all right, Commandante. Be calm and nothing will happen," one of the men said.

The soldiers lighted the candles in the room with torches, confiscated Vallejo's weapons, and one of them told him to finish dressing. From his quarters, they escorted him across the quadrangle of the presidio to the one-room calamozo and closed the door. As soon as the iron door locked behind him, voices in the darkness of the large cell next to him called out. Both Sergeants Rocha and Cervantes were also prisoners. A short time later, the rebels brought in the acting comisario, Manuel Jimeno Casarin.

"The revolution has started," Casarin said.

"I can't blame them," Cervantes commented. "Maybe it's time for an independent California."

In the darkness, Vallejo pondered the words of these officers who served under his command. Days later, some of the them took him from his cell. "We are sending you to San Diego where you can't cause trouble or get hurt," they told him.

11. Romualdo at Santa Barbara

The Funchal, a small trading brig sailing coastal waters, anchored off the beach at Santa Barbara, and a lone man rowed ashore. By the time he reached the beach, a number of people arrived and helped him pull his rowboat to dry sand. By this time, too, the guard in the presidio bastion had notified Commandante Romualdo Pacheco, and he rode down to the beach.

The man was shipmaster Stephen Anderson, a Scotch trader. Most people in the pueblo knew him from other stops. Most of the time, he carried his Peruvian wife and his many children with him on board, and, normally, he brought all of them ashore, but not today.

As people gathered around, Romualdo rode up in time to hear Anderson say, "No trading this trip. I am here only for a short visit with your commandante."

He was a fat little man, red faced and puffing. Romualdo sent a soldier to get a presidio mount for Anderson. Amidst talking and excited children, he and Pacheco rode up the trail to the presidio and across the quadrangle to Pacheco's quarters.

Pacheco invited Anderson into his quarters. "I am here, Captain, only long enough to deliver these papers and explain as best I can what's happened."

Pacheco waited while Anderson gulped the brandy Rosa served him.

The poor man was extremely nervous. "You say you are not trading?"

"No, I have a full load of hides and little trade inventory. The priest at San Luis Obispo traded me out of nearly everything." San Luis Obispo was an accessible inland mission between Monterey and Santa Barbara channels.

"I am sorry to be the purveyor of ill tidings," Anderson said, "but I promised that I would stop here to tell you that a revolution is in progress at Monterey and in the north."

Rosa appeared from the back patio again and poured more brandy in their guest's glass, then quietly stepped into the bedroom. Romualdo waited for the shipmaster to down his drink.

"I was anchored at Monterey when the soldiers took the commandante and all of his officers as prisoners. I was delayed for several days, but finally permitted to leave after I promised to deliver these papers to you."

"What are they?" Romualdo asked. "They're copies of the terms the rebels demand of Governor Echeandia."

"He has received them?"

"By now, it is likely, They dispatched them several days before they allowed me to leave Monterey. Then I stopped in San Luis Obispo before coming here.

"Who is in charge at Monterey? Who is leading the rebels? Is it Solis?"

"It is Solis," Anderson replied. Pacheco remembered his troubles with Joaquin Solis while temporarily stationed at Monterey. He knew this man's potential. Solis had arrived in California from Mexico four years earlier along with a shipload of criminal convicts banished to California as punishment for their crimes. Among these prisoners, Solis proved himself a strongman, a leader, and a survivor who made affairs go his way. With determined energy, Solis settled open land and declared it his own. In Monterey, he took an Indian woman as wife and found a challenge equal to his brute ways in both the land and in the ambiguity of a government in disarray. God knows, Pacheco thought, this unruly rawboned wildman would have made a great officer in the Mexican military if he had ever lived within the system.

"By public manifesto," Anderson said, "the rebels actually summoned Solis to take command, and they have proclaimed him commandante-general of the California troops. I have brought you a handmade copy."

"It will take more than a proclamation by a few rebels for Solis to hold power for long," Pacheco said.

"I agree," the trader said. "But he is doing a good job of organizing so far. The first step he took was to call together the leading rebels and prepare a pronunciamiento. Since then, he has been spreading the word and gathering additional support."

"How did you get this assignment of coming to Santa Barbara to tell me?" Pacheco asked.

"As soon as the pronunciamiento was ready, Solis called a meeting of all the foreigners in Monterey, including me, and read it to us and asked for our support."

"Are you supporting him?"

"Most, like me, have no choice but to appear cooperative."

"Who are these foreigners?"

"Hartnell, Spence, Cooper, Stearns, McCulloch, and a few others."

Pacheco knew William Hartnell very well. He was married to Maria Teresa de la Guerra, one of Don Jose Guerra's daughters. He was an Englishman who came to California as an agent for a trading company with offices in Lima, Liverpool, and Edinburgh. David Spence worked for the same firm until he established his own business in Monterey. He was married to Adelaida Estrada, the daughter of Jose Mariano Estrada, a recently retired military officer. Pacheco also knew John Cooper, an American trader and rancher in Monterey.

"Who are Stearns and McCulloch?" Pacheco asked, wanting as much information as possible against uncertain events.

"Abel Stearns comes from Massachusetts, but he has been living in Mexico for the last few years. He is an ambitious man. He works with John Cooper. McCulloch comes from Lima. He works with Hartnell, but I think he is in Monterey only temporarily."

"You are most helpful," Pacheco said. Soon Rosa and young Adriana appeared with midday dinner. Rosa served a bottle of the wine given them when they stayed at San Fernando Mission.

"I am glad to help, Captain," Anderson said. "I am a foreigner here. A neutral. You asked why I happened to deliver this message to you. It is very simple. The rebels detained my brig, and my family is on board. When I volunteered to act as a messenger, they released me."

"What do they expect of me?" Pacheco asked.

"When I left Monterey, the rebels seemed convinced that they had already won their victory...that they needed only to get the word out. They sent messengers overland to San Luis Obispo, San Antonio, San Miguel and to the missions' escoltas to the north as well as the San Francisco presidio." Pacheco was surprised by the organized way Solis apparently conducted himself. He could not remember when soldiers had displayed such energy or initiative. But this kind of action could only succeed because the government was weak and living conditions were so difficult for the common soldier.

"Where are they getting money to operate?" Pacheco asked.

"The Monterey ayuntamiento, the pueblo council, accepted the rebel plan, announced it to its citizens, and urged its acceptance by people in other settlements. Tiburcio Castro, the alcalde of Monterey, turned over municipal funds to Solis and added more to the rebel treasury by imposing a tax or loan, whichever you want to call it, amounting to thousands of pesos on foreign traders...including me," Anderson declared.

"How would you say things are going?" Pacheco asked.

"Before we sailed," Anderson said, "I heard that Solis planned a trip north to the presidio at San Francisco. I'm sure he'll seek support in San Jose and all of the mission settlements along the way. Cooper told me that he heard an understanding already existed with a similar rebel group at the San Francisco presidio, but I think it will take Solis awhile to cover all of that territory and convince others."

With darkness, Anderson wanted to return to his ship, and so Rosa insisted that he take fresh fruit, freshly cooked meat and other provisions to his wife and children who waited on board.

Pacheco ordered two horses and rode with his guest to the beach where he aided him in getting his row boat beyond the breakers. He watched the trader rowing the boat into the darkness of the sea, aimed at the brig's silhouette and the light of a dim lantern hanging high on the mast.

The sky was clouded and there was a cool breeze, but it felt good to Pacheco. He trailed his horse through the sand at water's edge in the direction of the cliffs, hoping that the darkness and the breeze that played about his face would help him get his thoughts together.

The prospect of battle in no way pleased him. It was at times like this that he knew he was not honest with the world. He was not a soldier. His success had come by serving Governor Jose Echeandia. His talent, he thought, lay in his ability to survey and organize the geography of California into useful trails. Of course, he disciplined himself and tried to act the part of a model officer, but he feared the prospect of battle. In some ways, he actually admired a man like Solis, so able to defy authority and so apparently fearless. Romualdo, untested in battle, did not want to face the vengeance and animal instincts that drove such a leader.

12. Joaquin Carrillo in San Diego

Soon after receiving the dispatch from Monterey, Governor Jose Echeandia hung a public notice both in the San Diego plaza and at the presidio.

Joaquin Carrillo and his drinking companions at the presidio called the soldier-teacher to read it aloud and explain it. In a few words, it revealed the Solis revolt, then said that Echeandia had called together a council of seven officers at San Diego to consider Solis' accusations. The bulletin reported that the council was highly satisfied with the way the governor conducted affairs.

Echeandia then stated that unless Solis and his followers laid down their arms and freed the authorities at Monterey, they would be deemed traitors.

Word passed throughout the district that the governor planned a march to Santa Barbara in preparation for battle against Solis. He would take soldiers from the San Diego presidio, but he would also call soldiers and paisano recruits from the mission escoltas and pueblos, including Los Angeles.

One day, drunk and garrulous, Joaquin Carrillo declared his intention of riding with the San Diego Company and joining his long-admired commandante and son-in-law, Romualdo Pacheco. Just the thought was exhilarating after so many years. He hurried home from the presidio to tell his daughter, Francisca. She listened without expression, somewhat sadly, he thought, but she surely understood that an old soldier must do his duty. But she was thinking something else, he soon realized.

"Papa," she said, almost faintly, "have you considered that they may not take you?"

"Will not take me? What do you mean? They need men to defend the government. I am a man and a soldier, and I am ready."

Blurry-minded and with a mouth dry from drinking bad wine, he felt almost wild with excitement about marching again. He wanted desperately to do something that could make him feel proud. His drinking was much heavier. He knew it, but he could not stop himself these days.

"I am going to see the commandante at the presidio," he said. He stood, wavered and stumbled.

Francisca helped him regain his balance, and then spoke as a daughter who deeply loved her papa. "Papa," she said, "let the commandante see you as a soldier. Go to him early tomorrow morning wearing your uniform. Let him see you as he should see you."

Joaquin fell back on the bench with pillows in the sala and thought as best he could. He felt weak. Francisca was right. "I am drunk," he said half aloud. The whole pueblo drinks too much lately.

"The commandante must see you sober," Francisca said quietly She sat down beside him on the bench and lifted his head to her lap. He breathed so heavily. "Oh, my dear hija…" he said, feeling deep love for his youngest daughter.

13. Romualdo at Santa Barbara

Commandante Romualdo Pacheco was seized by his own Santa Barbara garrison at dawn of what started as a beautiful spring morning. Like everyone living in the presidio, he and his second, Alferez Rodrigo del Pliego had heard the firing of the musket in the yard and stepped outside to see what was happening. There, a sergeant along with a corporal and a squad of soldiers, seized both of them and forced them into the headquarters office.

Neither Pacheco nor del Pliego resisted. They were far outnumbered and completely surprised. Somehow, Pacheco had mistakenly thought the morale of his garrison was high and that his men and their families were happy in Santa Barbara. All of them had decent casas and good gardens around the presidio, and they enjoyed excellent fishing and hunting. Certainly, the padres were generous with meat from the mission herd.

"I am sorry, Commandante," Sergeant Rodriquez said. "We need not hold you nor Alferez Pliego long. Troops from Monterey should arrive soon, and I hope you will then join us in overthrowing Echeandia."

Rosa and Adriana along with Lima appeared after attending mass at the mission. "Will you permit my wife and the servants to leave the presidio?" Pacheco asked.

The men nodded. Pacheco kissed Rosa and told her to take Adriana and Lima and go to either Guerra's or Carlos Carrillo's casa. "Are you sure?" Rosa asked. "I could stay and cook for you."

"No, please go now," Pacheco said.

"So," Romualdo said to the men after the women were gone, "all of you have fallen under the spell of the criminal, Solis. You think that by taking Alferez Pliego and me prisoner, you can somehow convince the governor to forget the government he has sworn to uphold and that you can control the whole territory?"

The men looked to Sergeant Rodriquez, clearly not knowing what to say. A small soldier Pacheco did not recognize stepped forward and said, "The

Santa Barbara garrison has joined the Monterey and San Francisco companies in a demand that Governor Echeandia resign."

"Who are you?" Pacheco asked.

The little soldier appeared angered by the commanding way of Pacheco and very unsure of himself. "My name is Soto," he answered.

"And you are from the Monterey Company?"

"Si."

"Serving Solis?"

"Si," he said, stepping back.

This soldier had undoubtedly told Pacheco's men about the pattern of revolt followed in Monterey and urged them to take control in the same way. Pacheco was surprised to see Sergeant Rodriquez assuming leadership in this situation. In general, he was a reasonable man and a loyal soldier. He was also a family man.

In the afternoon, Lima, the Indian servant, returned to the apartment.

"The senora sent me to prepare food," she said without emotion. Romualdo thought about this for a moment.

Whether Rosa intended it or not, sending Lima made clear to him what he must do. "Si, you must prepare a good meal for all of us."

With this, he immediately assumed the role of host. "Lima," he said, "first, bring wine for our guests."

Lima was unshakable. If she understood what was occurring, she managed to appear indifferent. It was Pacheco's guess that Rosa had talked to her, and that she knew exactly what was expected, and, further, that Lima would serve as Rosa's liaison and spy.

The Chumash Indian woman silently poured wine for all of the men, and then soon returned to pour again.

"I understand your position," Pacheco said to the men in measured tones, "and I understand your discontent."

He continued talking. At first they were silent, but gradually they loosened up.

"It is too bad that we must hold you, Commandante," one said. "But we have no choice."

"I am sorry too," Pacheco said, "but we can be comfortable. I will not run away because when you think of it, there is no place to go. Right? And, like you, I would not leave my wife nor my post unless it was absolutely required."

Some of the men nodded and appeared to relax with these words.

"Who will play cards with me?" Pacheco asked. The men looked surprised. "Why not?" he urged, shrugging and smiling. "What shall we do until you are relieved of your duty? What shall I do if the men in my own company will not gamble a few pesos with me?"

They gathered in the patio and Pacheco dealt the cards. Soon all were talking and laughing.

"I have lost again," Pacheco said, feigning disgust, then laughing. "So, this is the reason you are holding me prisoner. You are robbing me one peso at a time. Next, you will want to play for my brandy!"

"Si," one of the soldiers said with relish, and so Pacheco poured brandy for everyone and left a newly-opened bottle on the table so that the men might help themselves.

Sergeant Rodriquez announced that he must leave matters in the hands of the corporal while he attended to other matters. At midnight, Pacheco retired to his bedroom, leaving the men to sleep wherever they chose in the sala.

The next day was long and weary for Pacheco. The size of the guard dwindled to not more than four men at a time, and the faces changed. With each new face, Pacheco rekindled his hosting posture, and, at last, Sergeant Rodriquez reappeared and accepted a drink for himself and his men. As they raised their glasses, Pacheco proposed a toast. "To the unity of our garrison and to the Republic of Mexico!"

"Compadres," Pacheco said, "I am very concerned about something." They looked at him, some frowning, one pretending to drink from his now empty glass. Pacheco glanced at each of them and said, "Even before the arrival of Soto, the messenger from Monterey, with his message of false hope, I received a dispatch from the governor informing me that reinforcements from San Diego and Los Angeles are on the way to Santa Barbara and Monterey. The governor intends to stop Solis and his followers. What will the governor and the military see when they arrive here? A handful of soldiers holding their commandante prisoner? Or a united garrison prepared to fight for the republic? Can Solis and his rebels save you? Can you trust a leader who was banished from Mexico because of his crimes? Please consider these things, senors. Do you want to wind up a traitor to your country like Solis?"

"We must provide for our families," one soldier said.

Romualdo lifted his shoulders and held out his hands, palms up. "You are providing well for your families. There are no naked and starving children in Santa Barbara as Solis tries to pretend. If there are, we can rescue them this day!"

"But what of our pay? The government has no right to withhold our pay."

"I agree," Pacheco said. "But you know the government, senors! You are military men. The government works its way slowly. One day all of our back pay will arrive, and we will be rich men."

Some of the men laughed. Amiable kidding continued throughout the day and into the night. New men arrived to guard Romualdo and Pliego, and Romualdo, with Lima's help, continued to provide food and drink. After a time, Romualdo began to wonder about the seemingly inexhaustible supply of food and wine, but then he realized that with Lima's frequent coming and going, new stocks also arrived. His beloved Rosa kept a steady supply line.

One of the men had a guitar and played love songs while the others played cards. At last, everyone was asleep again. Romualdo could have walked out. Instead, he went to his bedroom and fell into a relaxed sleep.

When he came out the next morning, the soldiers had left his quarters. Without ceremony or explanation, Romualdo was free. Moving casually about the quadrangle of the presidio and then out among the casas of the soldiers in the pueblo, Pacheco sought out those men he felt were probably most loyal to him. Later that day, he marched them to a place in front of the presidio barracks and called to the rest of the men who were inside of the barracks to fall out.

"I am commanding you as soldiers of the Santa Barbara company to return to your allegiance and duty on behalf of your country. You may think about this matter until evening muster. I will personally call the roster at that time."

There was a long silence. It was obvious that many of the men were glad to hear the commandante provide a clear choice for them. Six men disappeared by roll call time, including Sergeant Rodriquez, and Pacheco assumed that they had traveled north to join the Monterey insurgents. So had Soto, the rebel from Monterey.

That evening he ordered Alferez Pliego to enforce a new discipline, drilling the men and inspecting the condition of their mounts daily. He began conducting a severe daily inspection of the barracks and established a regular reconnaissance along the coast as far north as the mission at La Purissima. At the same time, he sent four soldiers south toward Buenaventura to watch for the arrival of support troops.

An overland dispatch delivered by a soldier from Commandante Ignacio Martinez in San Francisco warned Romualdo that Solis had been at that presidio, succeeded in persuading the soldiers of that garrison to relieve Martinez of his command, and Solis had recruited many of them to his cause.

Martinez also reported that he thought Solis gathered more followers and ammunition at San Jose.

Days passed into weeks. Pacheco did not share this latest dispatch with any of his men, although it was quite possible that the soldier who brought it had talked privately to some of them. He felt very alone. How long could he expect to keep peace among the men without signs of support from the south?

Rosa and Adriana returned to their presidio quarters, and they did everything possible to maintain an appearance of complete normalcy. Pacheco tried to estimate how long it would take the governor to organize a contingent at San Diego and begin marching in the direction of Los Angeles, Buenaventura and Santa Barbara. By even the slowest movement—transporting ammunition and supplies by muleback, herding some beef ahead of them so that fresh meat was available and gathering up the soldiers of the escolta at each mission, Pacheco was sure the governor should have already arrived in Santa Barbara.

Pacheco noted every small gathering of soldiers, listened for word that might indicate discontent, and offered words at morning roster to encourage a sense of support. He marched the men on horseback along the beach to the south every few days to make certain the animals were in good shape. In between times, he kept the men busy repairing breaks in the presidio wall.

Finally, late one afternoon during a training march along the southern beach trail, he saw his messenger riding at top speed toward them. Pacheco halted the troops and waited. Dusty and breathless, the young soldier brought his horse to a halt alongside him. "The governor will arrive by nightfall," he said.

"How far away is he?"

"Not more than two leagues, Commandante."

"Does he have a large force?"

"Si," the soldier said. He smiled broadly. "I could not see the end of them on the trail."

Thank God, at last, Romualdo thought, feeling a surge of excitement. He directed one of the corporals to take one squad ahead to meet and guide the governor to the presidio. He turned his mount and called out to the company, "We will ride back to the presidio and make ready to welcome the Governor and Commandante General of California!"

The troops let out an enthusiastic cheer. With that, he studied the men for a moment, saw that they were ready to follow him, and took up the lead back to Santa Barbara.

14. Joaquin Carrillo in Santa Barbara and Dos Pueblos

"Sergeant!" Captain Romualdo Pacheco commanded. He whirled his horse at the edge of the embankment in the direction of the fast riding soldier behind him. "Send two of your men down to the beach to check the caves for rebel scouts!"

"Si, commandante, pronto!" the old sergeant answered. He pointed to two men and gave them directions. "And watch the bushes above you," he instructed the men, "that you don't get a surprise."

Pacheco called again to the sergeant. "Hey, come ride with me."

The older man nudged his pony, brought him at a gallop to Pacheco's side. "How does it feel to be on duty again, Sergeant?" Pacheco asked.

Joaquin Carrillo took a deep breath of cool misty sea air. "At last!" he said, "I am alive again!" He slapped the rump of his horse with delight.

"And I need you, Sergeant," Pacheco said. "I need a sergeant I can trust without question. You are of the old school…disciplined, tough, accustomed to the punishment of the trail. Even when my own bones ache, you seem able to keep going. Most of all, I admire your courage!"

What Pacheco did not express was his own belief that men like Joaquin Carrillo could stand up to the violent coercion of a strong man like Solis better than he. He dared think that he could borrow courage from his father-in-law.

Governor Echeandia had ordered Pacheco to take about two platoons of soldiers to a place near the coast north of Mission Santa Barbara called Cieneguita and set up a line from the beach and inland to await the approach of rebel forces.

Before leaving the presidio, Pacheco read a proclamation written by Echeandia which had been dispatched by rider to Solis. The Governor ordered the rebel insurgents to surrender, and offered as a condition, full pardon and liberty to all participants except the leaders. Pardon for the leaders would be sought through the central government in Mexico,

Echeandia promised, but Solis and those closest to him would remain in prison until that pardon was forthcoming. He warned the rebels that in opposing him, they were in rebellion against the republic, and their actions would lead to bloodshed and their own ruin.

Echeandia seemed to feel the strength of his position more than ever. Pacheco was surprised that over thirty paisanos in Los Angeles had joined Echeandia's small force as he traveled from San Diego. En route, he commanded the soldiers of the escoltas at Missions San Luis Rey, San Juan Capistrano, San Gabriel, and San Fernando to join him. Then, he enlisted more than one hundred Indians from Mission San Gabriel, all carrying bows and arrows. The group riding with Pacheco today was a territorial mix of soldiers, paisanos and Indians.

Echeandia and Pacheco both sent riders with messages to Missions Santa Inez and La Purisima ordering the escolta at each location to send all men capable of bearing arms to Santa Barbara. They also ordered all spare cattle and supplies at these missions brought to Santa Barbara, both to feed the troops and as a strategy to prevent the insurgents from having a source of food supply for waging their battle. Pacheco now wanted to pull the renegade followers of Solis as far from their own supply lines as possible.

That night the call of "Viva La Republique!" echoed throughout the canyons from the beach to the tops of the foothills that dropped abruptly to the bay near Cieneguita.

"It is good to feel the spirit," Joaquin said to Pacheco.

In a sense, Pacheco thought, it was good to have a cause the men could support. Sometimes, they became bored and discontented for lack of any focused action. He sent several small reconnaissance patrols out ahead of the main line to report back any movement of rebels from the north.

At dawn the next morning, a patrol brought in a Monterey soldier carrying a message directed to Governor Echeandia from Solis. Pacheco left Pliego in charge and rode back to the presidio where the governor now occupied his quarters. Rosa stayed with the Guerras while Romualdo was away.

"That insolent bastard," Echeandia said, after reading the message. "He is telling me to give up the governorship according to his plan! That mother fucker will die in Hades first! Where did the messenger come from?"

"I have the messenger with me. He waits outside. He tells me that Solis and the rebel forces are camped at Santa Ynez."

"A day's ride from here," Echeandia muttered.

"Longer," Pacheco said, "if he moves a large garrison."

They didn't really know how many men might have joined Solis on this march. A message from San Jose some days earlier informed them that many men who joined Solis at San Francisco never reached Monterey, but instead, deserted him in San Jose. A few deserters would encourage more. Pacheco was encouraged.

"What if we beat him to it?" Echeandia pondered. "What if we ride to Santa Ynez?"

"If we can draw him farther this direction, he won't have anything but the open ground for hiding," Pacheco reminded his old professor. "And he would soon run out of food and ammunition without a close back-up supply."

"Si, you are right," the governor said. "You must think that I am very naive about soldiering, Romualdo, and I am. We will stay with your plan."

Pacheco felt sure about the loyalty of his own garrison now. They talked about nothing but the prospect of battle with Solis. He felt certain, however, that Solis probably still hoped the Santa Barbara company would oppose Echeandia and join him. Perhaps Sergeant Rodriquez had even encouraged that hope.

Governor Echeandia gave the messenger a return dispatch. In it, he vehemently declined to consider the rebel plan, and ordered the rebels to present themselves unarmed at Santa Barbara.

Many days passed while Pacheco held his troops at Cieneguita. It rained heavily for several days, and the men were soaked. So were supplies, including musket powder.

Pacheco, with Carrillo, rode the length of the line he had established and considered what he might do if he were Solis. It would be so easy, he discovered, for Solis to flank their line and cut them off. So far, they were lucky. During an early morning in April, two of the men of a reconnaissance group rode hurriedly into base camp. "They are near," one of them called breathlessly. "They have drawn lines at Dos Pueblos!"

"How many of them?" Carrillo asked.

"Perhaps a hundred," the soldier estimated.

Pacheco sent a message to Echeandia and Guerra. He suggested moving the women and children of the pueblo into the presidio. He also wrote: "In the event of a battle, we cannot escape injuries unless we retreat to the protection of the presidio walls. We can now see enemy troops from high ground, and they outnumber us…"

The messenger returned with notes for Pacheco from both men. Guerra wrote: "The Brig Funschal returned to our bay after some trouble with weather. I am sending all women and children of our family out to this vessel anchored a half league off-shore, including Rosa and your Indian child.

Echeandia informed Pacheco to take whatever action necessary. As he suggested, the people of the pueblo were moved inside the presidio walls. Soldiers and Indians already manned the walls if fighting became necessary. Families living near the mission, Echeandia wrote, took refuge inside the mission courtyard.

With the pueblo cleared of people, Pacheco decided that nothing could be gained in face-to-face combat or within firing range of rebel muskets. He would stretch rebel supply lines farther. He ordered all troops and artillery back to the presidio.

At dusk the next morning, soldiers on the wall reported seeing Solis' men on the high ground between the mission and the presidio. Pacheco ordered a volley of artillery, more for the impact on the rebels than with any expectation of doing harm.

Echeandia sent out another order demanding that the rebels lay down their arms and turn themselves in at the presidio. Solis sent an immediate return message stating that his men were ready to fight and would not surrender until they were given their back pay. In this message, Solis had altered his entire tactic. No more demand that the Governor resign or accept rebel demands.

An uneasy darkness fell across Santa Barbara presidio, the pueblo, the mission and the Brig Funschal tossing at anchor in the channel. The governor still occupied Pacheco's quarters. The soldiers' barracks, as well as the presidio grounds were overrun with men, including Indians. Families made small camps against the walls in the quadrangle. Romualdo and Joaquin, both weary, took turns resting in a lookout tower on the wall.

15. Rosa Aboard the Brig Funschal

Rosa lay on her blankets below the deck of the Brig Funschal holding her young cousin, Manuela, in one arm and Adriana in the other.

The women and children of the Carlos Carrillo family and the Guerra family shared an open space among stacked cowhides and bundles of tallow. The heavy, leathery smell was sickeningly putrid to all of them. The rocking of the ship where it stood anchored in the bay led to seasickness that kept most of them running to the deck and the ship's rail.

The old wooden hull brig creaked as she bobbed and pulled at anchor. Waves raised and dropped the ship unmercifully.

Rosa soon discovered she was not effected by either the unpleasant smell or the movement of the ship, but she was up most of the night attending to the children. She had talked to her papa only briefly after his arrival in Santa Barbara. She had not seen him so happy since her wedding, and, best of all, he was not drinking.

"You will be careful, Papa?" she asked when he took her into his arms.

"Si," he assured her, looking elegant in his well-worn uniform. "There is much to live for."

Romualdo had welcomed him with open arms. "We will ride together, Sergeant!" he said, and Rosa felt assured by her husband's kindness. Somehow, Romualdo understood her papa and appreciated him.

She shifted in the darkness, unable to be comfortable. Finally, she laid the two sleeping children in her place and climbed out of the hole to the deck. Her cousin, Margarita Dana, already stood at the rail looking toward the dark shore.

"Sick?" Rosa asked.

"No," she said, "but I cannot sleep."

An increasing wind blew across the deck and brought the women closer together for warmth. Margarita shared the blanket she carried. They wrapped themselves tightly together. Later, they found a protected place on the deck that was not too wet with the night's moisture and sat down.

"Perhaps we are safer on the ship," Margarita said kiddingly, "but I don't feel safer."

"The water frightens me," Rosa said.

"One does get accustomed to it. I have sailed with William along the coast. At first, I was sure we would be swallowed."

"I hope all of this ends soon," Rosa said, "so the governor will go home. I want to be with Romualdo." She smiled in the darkness as she thought about it.

"Do you feel at home at the presidio?" Margarita asked.

"Si, for now," Rosa answered. "But some day I hope we have a great rancho with cattle and horses and plenty of room for our children."

"I would like that, too," Margarita said. "Do you think the land will be opened?"

"Romualdo says that it will be opened if the governor can get complete control. Echeandia plans it, and he has plenty of support in the south."

"Oh, to have a hacienda," Margarita said dreamily.

"We will," Rosa said confidently.

Together, they dreamed of having large families and living in California casas on land extending beyond the farthest hills. When weariness finally overcame them, they went below deck again and found a place among the other women and children. But Rosa soon decided the smell was unhealthy. She gathered her blankets as well as her young cousin, Manuela, and her Indian child, Adriana, and found a place on deck to sleep. Toward morning, she jumped up. She thought she heard musket fire, but she could see nothing through the mist.

16. Sergeant Joaquin Carrillo at the Santa Barbara Presidio

A large group of rebel soldiers appeared along the trail riding in the direction of the presidio. They held their hands high above their heads as they neared the wall, and it was apparent that they did not carry weapons. Joaquin stood on the wall with Romualdo.

As the men neared the outside of the wall, one shouted, "We have come to surrender."

"Where are your arms?" Pacheco called from the wall.

"We hid them near the mission."

"How many of you?

"Twenty-six, Sir."

"Come to the gate with you hands behind your heads," he ordered. He turned to Joaquin, "Sergeant, go down to the gate and lead a body search."

Joaquin ordered the gate opened, and assigned a half-dozen men to search every rebel for knives, pistols or any metal items that could do damage.

Romualdo came down from the wall. "Who is your leader here?" he asked.

No one responded. "No one of you led the group here this morning?"

Finally, a small man in uniform answered. "Our leaders are on their way back to Monterey, Capitan. The battle is over."

"Are all of the other men riding back?

The little man smiled. "I don't think many are riding. Our horses were weak without forage. Some are lame. Every man is on his own."

"Why have some of you remained behind?"

"It was our choice."

"Where is Monterey's commandante?"

"He was sent to San Diego by ship."

"San Diego?"

"Si."

Pacheco surveyed the landscape for stragglers and confirmed the count. "The battle is over," one rebel said.

"Why have some of you remained behind?"

"It was our choice," another soldier said.

Joaquin stared at the ground for a moment. Is this whole affair ended? he asked himself. No battles? No one injured? Had Solis and his men really turned around?

It was in that moment that a single rebel stepped out of the brush outside the wall with pistol aimed at Romualdo. The deadly bullet passed over heads of both rebels and presidio soldiers. Joaquin saw the rebel shooter. He saw his aim. As though in a mad trance, Joaquin reached out to his beloved commandante and dropped with him to the ground. He covered Romualdo's body with his own, letting out a broken anguished cry. Blindly, covered with blood, he raised up and ran toward the rebel who had fired the shot. He did not let go of the man's throat until he had choked the last of life out of him.

Exhausted and with uncontrolled crying, Joaquin then broke through the men who surrounded Romualdo's body. He dropped to his knees and gently held his son-in-law. Romualdo was dead.

17. Mariano Vallejo in San Diego

The Schooner Brookline dropped anchor in well-protected waters off the beach running along Point Loma near Pueblo San Diego after many days of rough sailing from Monterey. Mariano Vallejo stood on deck, a leather travel bag at his feet stuffed with personal effects. He had never felt so unsure, never dealt with so many ambiguities since joining the military at fifteen years old. Fighting back feelings of guilt and embarrassment about being taken prisoner in Monterey by his own garrison and fearing that this whole episode would destroy his career, he tried unsuccessfully to find some satisfaction in the calm of the bay and the brightness of the January day.

The San Diego sky domed the water in satin blue, and the incoming tide soon pushed their surfboat toward shore in an almost effortless roll. For days now, Vallejo and Alferez Rocha had paced the deck, discussing and cursing their failure to prevent an uprising which they had actually anticipated for months. Vallejo admitted to himself that he had been blind to the desperation of his men.

Solis and the rebel leaders found it only too convenient to put Rocha and him on a vessel going south to San Diego where neither of them could interfere with the uprising.

"Where is the governor's house?" Vallejo asked the first paisano he saw on the beach.

"He lives on the high ground of the presidio," he was told.

From the rise above the beach, Vallejo studied the landscape of early morning. The beach and ground immediately below them was covered with hide houses. Most of them, Vallejo was sure, owned by foreigners and traders who referred to the area as "Hide Park," the place they stored their hides and tallow.

The paisano pointed them in the right direction, and they began the walk toward the pueblo. Following the river bed, they walked among the trees. Now, in the distance they saw a cluster of adobe casas. Vallejo and Rocha made their way into the pueblo, attracting much attention from women, children and a few Indians, asking directions as the proceeded. Vallejo knew that many people considered him haughty and indifferent. It was probably at times like this when preoccupied with problems that he seemed all the more so.

At the center of the pueblo they found the dusty plaza and a few shade trees. Children and animals were everywhere. Several girls in their teens flirted with Vallejo. One with wide dark eyes, dragging her companion with her, followed the men at some distance. Both were giggling and whispering to one another.

"Hey, why don't we have girls like these in Monterey?" Rocha said, smiling back at the pair.

At first, Vallejo ignored them, then finally motioned to them. Both laughed. "Tell me" he called, "where is the trail leading to the presidio?"

The bolder and more beautiful of the two came to him smiling, eyes aglow. She was a vibrant girl.

"I will show you," she said.

They walked across the plaza, and as they did so, Vallejo noted two unusually fine homes, both of them new, one not nearly finished.

"Who lives in these casas?" Vallejo asked.

"This one is the home of Jose Maria Estudillo," the young girl said. "It has just been blessed. The unfinished casa is that of Juan Bandini. It will be so beautiful when it is finished!" Vallejo knew both of these men from attendance at meetings with the governor when held in Monterey.

They passed a cluster of smaller adobe casas and entered an orchard where an exceptionally large fortress-like casa came into view. It was the most clearly established and well-lived-in place in the pueblo. Along the top of the casa wall protecting the property, large pots had been placed every few feet, and in them grew immensely large red flowers with heavy variegated green leaves. Vallejo paused to look more carefully.

"Do you like our flowers?" the girl asked.

Vallejo didn't usually pay much attention to such things, but these plants grew rank and large in their pots, making such a colorful show that he examined the leaf and flower of one of them.

"Geraniums. My papa bought them from a trader for me." What a compelling girl, he thought.

"Do you live here?" Vallejo asked. He admired her flowing black hair falling loosely around her shoulders.

"Si," she said.

"What is your name, and who is your father?"

"My name is Francisca. My father is Joaquin Carrillo. He has gone to fight the rebels in Santa Barbara and Monterey."

"Of course," Vallejo said. "That explains why I see so few men.

"Si, nearly all of the men are gone."

Suddenly, something else was clear. He said it aloud. "You are my fiancee!"

She looked at him long and hard. "You are Mariano?"

Somehow, he felt stripped of all dignity. He, commandant of Monterey presidio, stood helplessly while half of the men in California fought to regain his post. This was his introduction to the senorita he expected to marry?

Francisca was clearly caught up in the moment. She looked deeply into his eyes. "Are we still engaged?"

She was unbelievably daring, he thought.

"Under the circumstances, do you want to be?"

She looked down. He thought her cheeks flushed. Then, again, she looked into his eyes. "I have waited all of my life to meet and know the man my parents promised I would marry. I feel so proud of you."

Rocha had walked ahead toward the presidio. They were alone.

Mariano faced her, touching her elbows with both hands. "With both of your parents gone, we must make our own plans.

Francisca was radiant. He took her hand.

"We can loan you horses," she said. Please come back for supper."

18. Francisca San Diego

It had been sometime since they prepared a meal for guests, Both Francisca and their Indian servant, Oupay, went about dinner preparations with special joy. Francisca raked the hot charcoals in the earthen oven in the courtyard, placed pans of bread and other baked goods on raised bricks inside of it and quickly covered the opening.

Francisca led Vallejo and Rocha directly to the sala upon their arrival, and poured wine for them. The younger children swarmed in and out and around them, and Vallejo picked up Francisca's youngest brother, and held him on one knee.

He told Francisca that he had visited with her neighbors, the Bandinis. "I was surprised," he said, "to learn your sister, Rosa, is the wife of Romualdo Pacheco."

"It is a good marriage," Francisca commented. Then she asked, "What do you hear about the rebellion? I worry about our papa."

"I've heard nothing, I had hoped the presidio here would have news."

Since the evening was cold, Francisca served the men at the inside table without joining them. In truth, his resonant voice, strong square face and large unstinting smile excited her. She tried to be more adult than she had been earlier.

When he and Rocha prepared to leave, she felt disappointed because she had talked so little to him. Both men bade her good evening with courteous bows. Vallejo lingered a moment and kissed her hand.

"Thank you," he said, "not only for a fine dinner, but for making this such a special day for me."

In the days ahead, she saw him often, and the Spirit of her mama offered her encouragement. "Take your time, Little One, Wait for the right time."

"How long can I wait? Francisca asked.

"He will help you."

Mariano visited the Carrillo casa daily, staying for long periods, He gathered the children and read to them. He took Francisca for long walks. He was forthright and talkative.

But as soon as word reached San Diego that Solis had retreated and Romualdo Pacheco had been killed, Vallejo and Rocha rounded up horses belonging to the presidio in preparation for riding back to Monterey. Before leaving the pueblo, he visited the Carrillo casa one more time. This time he was alone.

They kissed for the first time. It was long and gentle and then lovingly passionate. She had waited since birth. "I'll return soon." he promised.

She stood by the courtyard gate until the men disappeared at the turn of the Royal Road leading to all of California's missions. Her little brothers stood beside her. With her mama dead, her papa fighting rebels and both Josefa and Rosa gone, she had never felt lonelier in her life. She wanted to cry, but her younger brothers were watching.

A few days later, her papa appeared at the corral gate with two other soldiers. Her brothers reached him first. She followed. His arms hung at his side as all of them attempted to hug him.

"Papa," she cried.

He gave no sign of recognition.

19. Josefa and Enrique

Exhilarated by at last reaching San Diego Bay, Josefa leaned against the ship's rail, covering her newborn son against the breeze with part of her rebozo.

From the ship's mate of the Brig Leonor came the call to drop sails and man the windlass, and for the next several minutes the deck filled with the small crew scurrying about wrapping canvas and adjusting rigging. The windlass made a terrible screech as the anchor dropped.

Enrique appeared at the rail and slipped his big arm around her waist. She leaned against him. Josefa ached to go ashore, see her papa, her sister, and her little brothers. It had been one and a half years since she sailed away with Enrique.

"Do we dare go ashore, Enrique?" she asked.

"Yes, of course," he said. "Things may be forgotten after so long."

Josefa knew her husband well now, and realized that he faced every problem frankly and unhesitatingly. By his side, all things seemed certain.

When she, overwhelmed with joy, appeared in the courtyard of Casa Carrillo, her papa took her into his arms, crying aloud. He was drunk, and overcome by the sight of her. Then Enrique arrived. When her papa saw him, he suddenly roared like a mad animal, and in the moments that followed he vented all of the pent-up anger and embarrassment and shame that had clouded his life in the pueblo since Enrique and she had left San Diego. The death of Romualdo made everything more difficult for him. He seemed to have forgotten that he had sanctioned Josefa's marriage to Enrique.

"You shamed this family!" he told Enrique. "You...you kidnapped my child! You took her from our family.! You and Satan destroyed all of us."

Enrique, towering above her papa, stared in disbelief. How easily he might have avenged himself, but he did not. Francisca began crying, tugging at her papa, begging him to stop shouting. "Do not say words that will make you sorry," she pleaded.

Enrique turned to Josefa, "It is best that I go," he said. "We can talk about all of this later."

Francisca rushed to Josefa. "Go with your husband. Return to the ship as quickly as possible. There is more to this than you know!"

Enrique took their infant son in his arms and led Josefa from the casa to the still bridled horses they had rented at the beach. There was a desperate look in Francisca's eyes, saying more than words could ever express. Josefa cried uncontrollably.

"Follow us now for a visit on the brig before we sail," Enrique said to Francisca.

When they were back aboard, Enrique sent a crew member to bring Francisca aboard. As soon as she arrived, he took her to their cabin and left her with Josefa.

Francisca held her first nephew lovingly while she and Josefa shared quiet, tearful conversation.

"Have I been that bad?" Josefa finally asked.

Francisca rocked the infant silently. Finally, she answered, "There has been talk that the church would make Enrique stand trial when he returned.

"What?" Josefa asked incredulously.

"I do not know," Francisca said helplessly. "I do not understand the rules."

Josefa wondered if such a thing were possible. She had expected to remain in San Diego while Enrique traded along the coast to the north, but now, she resolved to sail with him.

Her long-awaited return to San Diego now left her feeling sick, desperate. Their conversation that afternoon related almost entirely to their papa. Francisca told her of her papa's return to temporary service during the Solis revolt, and how much it meant to him. When Romualdo was killed, he went mad. Some of the time, he lived in another world. Sometimes he strutted, boasted. Once again, he submitted a petition to the governor for a grant of land, but it was rejected. After that, he withdrew completely and started drinking heavier than ever.

"I was so happy when he returned from the fighting. Now, I am watching our papa die," Francisca said sadly, "and I cannot stop it."

When the winds came up, Enrique told them it was time to sail. Josefa wept until she felt drained of life itself. She stood at the rail watching her sister climb down the rope ladder into the waiting surf boat. It was not until the crewmen took the oars and pulled away that she saw Francisca's eyes brighten. At first, Josefa could not hear Francisca's shout. She cupped her ear and leaned out over the rail, straining. A wave washed against the side of the boat. It rocked the rowboat. Francisca shouted even louder.

"I am engaged," she called, smiling.

20. Josefa and Enrique

At San Pedro, Josefa's world crumbled further. Enrique went ashore first, but quickly returned to the ship so angry that he was kicking things about the deck when she came out of their cabin.

"What is it?" she asked, alarmed by his unlikely behavior.

He handed her a paper he held in his hand. It was a summons given to him by a military messenger almost immediately upon reaching shore. It was signed by Padre Jose Bernardo Sanchez, head of Mission San Gabriel, el presidente of all of the California missions and ecclesiastical judge of the California territory. Josefa could scarcely breathe. The summons demanded that Enrique present himself at Mission San Gabriel for trial on very serious charges.

Henry Virmond, owner of this trading fleet, had left Matzatlan several days ahead of them aboard the Maria Ester, promising to meet them here. When they arrived, they saw Virmond's brig and anchored as close to it as possible, allowing for drifting, but Virmond was ashore.

"I left a message for Virmond at the trading store," Enrique said. Not long afterward, Virmond rowed a small boat to the Leonor. There was much to lose by turning back, yet they knew that in ecclesiastical matters such as this one, even the governor of California would support the church.

Virmond agreed to ride to San Gabriel, taking their marriage certificate from the sailor's chapel in Valparaiso to show Padre Jose Sanchez. With that assurance, she and Enrique felt they could immediately sail for Santa Barbara and then Monterey while Virmond did business in Los Angeles and at Mission San Gabriel. Eventually, Virmond would catch up with them in Monterey. But even while trying to satisfy what seemed very strange notions of the church, Josefa worried because Enrique had difficulty accepting the matter as serious.

21. Josefa at Santa Barbara

From the deck, Santa Barbara reached out to Josefa, so many white-washed houses capped in red tiles. A Mexican flag flew over the presidio and a cross at the top of one gable identified the chapel. A trail led up the slope to the pueblo through gardens, fields, and brush to the twin-towered facade of the mission. By the time the crew lowered the surfboats into the water, Enrique seemed to have put their San Diego and San Pedro experiences behind him. Josefa was exuberantly happy about the possibility of visiting Rosa. She prayed fervently about it. The July sky was clearing and the white-washed portion of the Santa Barbara settlement gleamed in the sun. If all went well here, Enrique planned to bring merchandise to the beach for sale and trade.

Since sailing away to marry, Josefa had embarked and disembarked in more bays and inlets than she could remember. She no longer suffered seasickness when on board, and when it was her turn to go over the side, she went down the rope ladder without a thought, her infant child swaddled firmly to her back.

"You are a true California woman," Enrique once told her. "Strong, but as feminine as any female I have ever seen." He kissed her as she crawled over the side.

The crewmen of the Leonor consisted of young Mexican Indians out of Matzatlan. Enrique hired boys who grew up playing along the beaches and in the water of the pueblos. They not only made good sailors, but worked well as boatsmen in the transport of heavy California cowhides and tallow between ship and shore.

Now, as their surfboat neared the break of the waves, the crewmen held their oars steady until the largest possible wave swelled behind them. Then, in unity, they heaved with their paddles in long pulls, catching the crest, keeping the nose of the boat moving toward the beach. They jumped out as the boat approached shore, and using the force of the wave, pulled the boat into shallow water. Enrique jumped into the water and lifted both Josefa and their child into his large arms, carrying them to dry sand. A crewman brought Adriana to shore.

Men, women and children from the pueblo ran toward the beach. In the quiet life of the pueblo, the appearance of a ship still created extraordinary excitement. Josefa watched her husband as he studied the trail to the pueblo. He clearly searched for signs of danger. He had visited this port many times, she knew. He and Virmond had traded with the mission priests and all of the men who had cattle, and he viewed most of them as friends. But he did not expect anyone to suffer the wrath of the church to protect him.

Josefa squinted against the light. The whitewashed bastions of the presidio reflected the light high above the casas surrounding the military post. The trail filled with more people coming to the beach on foot and horseback. Joseph searched every face.

Enrique remained with the crew, and for a time Josefa stood alone, greeting the smiling happy people as they arrived. The women and children gathered around her, greeting her warmly, curious about a woman who traveled aboard a trader. When baby Enrique cried, she sat down in the sand, and opened the front of her blouse to feed him. The young women, all talking happily, joined her in an irregular circle, some of them also nursing their babies. Children, barefoot and scantily clad, clung to their young mothers. The women told Josefa about the mission, the recent weddings and funerals, and the fiestas of the pueblo. All listened intently to her while she told them about life in Callao, Lima, Valparaiso, Matzatlan, and Acapulco, all places she had visited. Even San Diego and San Pedro were unfamiliar names to these young mothers, nearly all of them born in Santa Barbara. At last, children fed and everyone excited by the moment, Josefa was able to ask the question that was uppermost in her mind.

"Do you know my sister, Rosa?"

Of course, all of the women knew Rosa, the former commandante's wife. "Yes, this is her special day," one of them said. "And now, you are here!"

Josefa did not understand what the women were saying, and she was too overwhelmed to try to get their meaning straight. Instead, she said, "Oh, I must go to her. Where is she?"

"Come, we'll show you," one of the women said. At that moment, Enrique approached. He had overheard the women.

"I'll be busy for a while," he said. "Go ahead. I'll join you when I can."

The women and children surrounded Josefa as she followed the trail. All had something they wanted to say. Adriana seemd to enjoy the whole experience.

One woman pressed close to her and said, "Your sister is receiving the best of care. You may be sure of that."

"What do you mean?" Josefa asked.

"She is at the home of Don Jose de la Guerra. Dona Maria Antonia is attending to her personally."

"What is it? What is wrong?" Josefa asked anxiously. The women all smiled knowingly, and suddenly Josefa understood, too, and smiled. She almost ran now.

They scattered a few sheep and cattle as they hurried along, and skirted a corn patch that some of the women had planted.

Her companions dressed in much the same way as the women in San Diego—loose round-neck blouses with short sleeves, often trimmed in lace, and brightly colored muslin skirts tied in place at the waist by a separate wide band of silk or other fabric. All wore a colorful reboza and their dark hair, like her own, fell in one or two long broad braids down their backs. Most of them also wore earrings, bracelets and necklaces.

A child broke through the group of women and touched Josefa's hand. Josefa took it in her own and leaned to hear her speak. "Dona Maria Antonia Guerra wanted your sister to have a large comfortable bed and a well lighted room for the birth of the new Romualdo," the child said.

Josefa felt the thrill of the words and squeezed the child's hand. "Who are you? How do you know so much about my sister?" she asked.

"I am Manuela Carrillo," she said. "Dona Maria is my aunt, and when she decides upon something in the pueblo, that is the way it must be."

Josefa had known of Maria Antonia and her husband, Jose de la Guerra y Noriega, all of her life, and it was comforting to know that Rosa enjoyed the favor of this prominent family as well as the other Carrillos in Santa Barbara.

At the iron grill gate of the large adobe, Josefa bade her many companions adios and with Manuela's hand still in her own, she proceeded to the large covered porch. The door opened before she arrived, and it was Don Jose Guerra, himself, who greeted her. He received her with all the courtliness of Old Spain, and although she was taller than he, she felt comfortable in his presence. This man, she knew from descriptions by her papa, was born in Spain and descended from nobility.

In those moments before Dona Maria Antonia appeared, Josefa glanced about the sala at the paintings, candlesticks and vases that decorated the adobe walls. Actual cushioned chairs and Chinese silk rugs covered the tile floors. With all shutters open, the grillwork covering the windows made shadowed lines in the sunlight upon the whitewashed interior walls. There was a mix of furniture, nearly all of it imported—an ornately carved oriental chest of drawers, an American dropleaf table that had come around the horn and a wall shelf displaying Rose Canton porcelain.

Maria Antonia greeted Josefa as though she were her own child. She held her in long embrace and then admired Josefa's baby boy, sleeping soundly in her arms. She took Manuela and Adriana to the outdoor kitchen for chocolate. Josefa quietly entered Rosa's room.

Rosa lay so still that it frightened Josefa. Her high cheek bones seemed almost to protrude, and all of her face was sallow. For the first time, Josefa felt the weariness of her long journey. Without a sound, she went to the bed and stretched across to the far side to kiss Rosa's cheek.

Rosa opened her eyes, blinking, not at first recognizing her sister. Then tears welled up. Josefa did not constrain herself longer. She, too, cried freely. How long she had waited to share such a time.

Exhausted, she stretched out on the unused side of the bed with Baby Enrique beside her. A young Chumash Indian girl brought Rosa's newborn child to her. Josefa lay in silence beside her sister, overwhelmed with joy. Their babies lay on each side of them, and Rosa reached out and found Josefa's hand.

Do you remember?" she asked.

"Si," Josefa whispered without opening her eyes. It was something both their mama and papa said. "God gives us moments."

22. Enrique in Santa Barbara

Before leaving the beach, Henry Fitch inspected hides and tallow offered by three soldier-rancheros running small herds of cattle on open range not used by the mission. He also received a message from Don Jose de la Guerra who represented Missions Santa Barbara and Buenaventura in trading. In light of events at San Pedro, Fitch was wary about trying to trade with the missions, but he decided he was foolish. The missions still produced much of the trade goods available in California.

It was late in the day when he rented an old horse from a child who stood nearby, waiting hopefully. He headed for the back of the Guerra home. Indian workers were laying tile on the roof of a storage building. A carreta, filled with leather pouches of grain, waited to be transferred to storage. Women and girls, both Indians and members of the Guerra family, seemed to be everywhere, preparing food in an outdoor oven, weaving, sewing and embroidering in the patio. Fitch shook his head in wonder, smiling when he saw a young Indian mother seated in a New England rocker on one side of the porch feeding his very own son the milk from her breast. The custom was common, he knew, and he no longer questioned it.

He walked through the gardens of the Guerra home to the front where the casa and porch formed a wide U with heavy tiled roof. When Fitch first traded along the Pacific Coast, he viewed adobe construction as a poor alternative to the fired brick and shiplap construction of New England, but time altered this feeling. He gradually came to respect the insulating qualities of the great thick walls in all kinds of weather. Then, too, the accessibility of material for adobe bricks made homes possible for every underpaid soldier and paisano in California. Using huge beams across open ceilings added strength and massiveness to these structures, so magnificent in their simplicity when built well. Guerra brought together the best of the world in his casa.

Most casas had adobe or dirt floors, but he used fired tile, and the wide porch that wrapped the home protected the walls of the casa from the direct effects of rain.

Fitch saw Guerra at one corner of the property. He was supervising two Indians cutting oak planking. One stood on a high platform at one end of a two-man saw while the other worked on the ground at the other end of the saw.

After a few pleasantries, Guerra said., "Come, Maria Antonia will soon serve supper."

They sat in the shade of a large oak tree in back of the house where an Indian woman served them generous slices of meat with tortillas made from coarse stoneground corn. Guerra did not take the meat, but peeled and quartered a peach from a bowl in the center of the table. After hearing that Rosa was the mother of a newborn child, Fitch knew they must stay over night. But now, in this quiet corner of Guerra's property, he felt he must talk about his predicament with the church. Guerra could help so much.

"While we are together, I feel the need to talk to you…" he started.

But Guerra interrupted with miscellaneous talk. Enrique tried again. This time, Guerra stood erect with his wine glass in hand. "Permit me to propose a toast to you, Captain Fitch, upon your return to Alta California. I have a list of the needs of both Missions Santa Barbara and Ventura. I'll also give you a list of our household needs. I would consider it an honor now if you would accompany me to my office.'

From this point, Guerra was all business. He gave Enrique a tremendous order. Then said, "I must get back to my work, We have a guest room for you for as long as you want to stay."

Enrique suddenly realized there was good reason why Guerra didn't want him to talk.

Two nights later, Henry Fitch, with Josefa and their infant son close to him, moved to the sound of oars stirring the water as crewmen rowed them back to the brig. Quietly, perfunctorily, the surfboats were hoisted into position, and Fitch called for sails that soon caught a fair breeze. Far at sea, the wind held the sails taut, the weather remained fair, and some of the time they moved almost silently through the summer waters.

When the course was set, Fitch went to quarters. Josefa sat pensively on the dropped in the candlelight. He sat down beside her.

"You could have remained with Rosa," he said quietly.

She turned her large sad eyes to him. "I never want to be separated from you, Enrique."

Their child was asleep in his crib, and they soon laid down together. He was exhausted by the day, but a wondrous wildness ran through him as he drew Josefa close to him.

The old wooden-sided brig creaked with the motion of the water, and he could feel the tension leave Josefa's body as she fell into sleep.

23. Enrique at Monterey

Sergeant Jose Palomares, juez de policia, read the summons in the headquarters office of Monterey presidio: "The foreigner, Henry Fitch, has committed the most heinous of crimes against God and the church, abducting the innocent daughter of a Mexican citizen, removing her from family and country and committing the most damnable offenses against her. I demand, in the name of the Mother Church that this man be captured upon arrival at Monterey and delivered to San Gabriel Mission to stand ecclesiastical trial. Signed Fr. Jose Bernardo Sanchez."

Henry Fitch scarcely heard the accusation.

"Damn it!" he said. "What have you done with my wife and child?"

"They will be placed in proper care," the sergeant said.

From the moment Fitch touched the beach at Monterey, the militia moved relentlessly in their determination to hold him. He told himself to deal with the situation in a cooperative way, but their antagonism and harsh physical treatment changed everything. Fitch was much larger than either Palomares or the guards who stood by the open headquarters door, and they took no chances. He stood hobbled in a leg-cross.

"Can't I make you understand that I am married to the Senora?" Fitch said in frustration.

"Where is your marriage certificate?" Palomares demanded.

"By now, the priest, Sanchez, at San Gabriel, has it. My employer took it to him."

"You must realize that you have committed a most serious crime. You come to our country to trade with us, you take our money, you steal our women, and now, you want us to simply overlook it. You do not even respect our church."

"I am a member of the church," Fitch argued, only gradually realizing that no matter what he said in his defense, it fell on the deaf ears of a sergeant determined to obey orders. So, he took a deep breath and remained silent.

It was a long walk across the presidio grounds to the jail cell between guards and hobbled by a leg-cross, but his mind was absorbed with concern for Josefa and his child. She had tried to follow him after he was captured, but they restrained her, and he heard her screaming. Her calls to him as the soldiers hustled him from the beach and through the pueblo turned him into a raging madman...fighting the soldiers, striking one, grabbing another by the throat. Outnumbered, he fell in exhaustion, feeling a sharp pain in his hip and lower back. In the prison cell with shackles removed, Fitch discovered that he could scarcely walk.

Suffering with every step, Fitch found his way to a mat on the dirt floor and sunk painfully to it, stretching his long frame to its full length. He asked himself how he came to this place and this life. Against excruciating flashes of pain, he recalled childhood play in New Bedford, envisioned a familiar one-room schoolhouse, and a white Congregational church with spire. There was the excitement of boyhood working along the harbor on Buzzards Bay, then becoming a member of a crew of a trading ship out of Boston that took him around the Horn and into the sea-going trade of the Pacific. It was all more dream than reality now. Had there once been a childhood in such a distant place for him?

A deep dread gripped him. Where was the strong, fiercely independent, confident man standing at the helm of his ship, the man he thought himself to be? He stared into the darkness, trembling in the damp cold. In the cracks of the cell wall, he watched day pass into night and an eternity later, a struggling dawn. An indifferent jailkeeper offered him a plate of food in the early morning, but Fitch could not rise from the mat to take it, so the jailer passed him by. In the afternoon, a stream of sunlight found its way through an opening between the roof and the top of the rock wall of the cell, and although hurting, Fitch awakened, finally alert and thinking clearly.

He must find out about Josefa. He knew of her strength, and he felt sure that if there was a way for her to get to him, she would do it. He thought about the Brig Leonor in the harbor loaded with cargo for trade, some of it already sold by advance order to men with ranchos in the vicinity. There was also his crew of men, undoubtedly wondering about their own plight with their shipmaster in jail. Fitch could only hope that Henry Virmond succeeded in dealing with the priest at San Gabriel. Surely, reason would prevail.

Thinking of Josefa again, he leaned desperately into the sharp pains in his hip and back, managing to face the wall. By bringing his knees slowly to his chest, he felt some relief. At last, he turned again until his weight was upon his knees. With the wall as support, he came slowly to a standing position, and then gradually stretched his long arms above his head.

"My God," he muttered, "I've never been so helpless!"

In short painful steps, he made it to the iron door of the cell. At some time while he slept, the guard had shoved a bowl of coarse cooked cereal with beans inside the cell. Fitch ate all of it with relish. He studied the cell minutely as if some miraculous opening might appear, yet knowing full well that this situation must be overcome by keeping faith in those close to him.

He still leaned against the rock wall when he heard the noise in the corridor of the jail, heard the sounds of jingling keys in the metal door of his cell and then saw the outlines of an unfamiliar man.

"Henry Fitch," the man said, "my name is John Cooper. I live in these parts."

"I'm moving very slowly, Mr. Cooper," Fitch said, "but you are a welcome sight, and you sound like someone from home."

"I grew up in Boston," Cooper said, "and sailed out of there for this place six years ago."

"Then you are from home."

"Yes," he said, "but it's a long way back." Then he said, "Mr. Fitch, your wife and child are well cared for in our home."

Fitch felt his body relax with Cooper's words. "Then I am already deeply in your debt," he said. Cooper looked about the cell and shook his head.

"As I said, Mr. Fitch, both of us are a long way from home. The ways of these people can be as kind as any in the world, but they can also be cruel."

He reached into the deep pockets of his big seaman's coat and brought out packages of food...cooked meat, tortillas, and summer fruits. Then he recovered a jug of wine hidden inside his jacket.

When he realized that Fitch was suffering because of his back, he pulled the mat to the middle of the dirt floor and insisted that Fitch lie down. He pulled upon his long legs with full weight, then he bent them until Fitch's thighs touched his chest. Again, Cooper pulled his legs straight, and the pulling seemed to relieve something in his hip. Though small, Cooper was a strong man, and he moved with a deftness that made it clear that he knew what he was doing. He continued the manipulating, then gave a slight straight jerk. Fitch heard a snap, and at the same time, felt an immediate sense of relief.

"How's that?" Cooper asked.

"I don't know what you did, but I feel better."

"We released a pinched nerve," Cooper said. "It will be sore as hell for a couple of days."

Cooper helped Fitch to his feet. "I've found a true friend," Fitch said, and he meant it.

Cooper, Fitch soon heard, had come to California from Boston in 1823, the master of a ship called The Rover. Upon arrival in Monterey, he sold the vessel to former Governor Jose Arguello, but continued as shipmaster, taking it to the Sandwich Islands, the Philippines and finally to Canton, China. As the governor's partner, both he and the governor enjoyed financial success. Cooper's wife was the former Encarnacion Vallejo, the sister of the acting commandante at the Monterey Presidio, Mariano Vallejo.

"Is it true that Vallejo was shipped to San Diego during the uprising?" Fitch asked.

"Yes," Cooper said, "but he was back within ten days after the troubles ended."

"What is the possibility of bringing Josefa to see me?" Fitch asked after awhile.

"I'll look into it," Cooper promised. "Do you know that they plan to take you to San Gabriel?"

"It's damn foolish," Fitch said, "I keep hoping that Henry Virmond will arrive with word saying the ecclesiastical judge has set aside the trial. I really am married to Josefa, you know, and our child was not conceived out of wedlock.

"Well, they won't take you to San Gabriel until they hear from Governor Echeandia," Cooper said.

Fitch did not welcome this information. With Jose Echeandia's earlier amorous interest in Josefa and her rejections, the governor could now enjoy a first-class lover's revenge.

Two days later, Encarnacion prepared a special basket of food and wine which Cooper used to bribe the guards, and they slipped Josefa into the cell.

After Fitch had held her in his arms for a long while, he quietly began trying to persuade her to take the first available ship to Santa Barbara and remain with Rosa until he came for her.

But Josefa remained as determined as ever to stay near him. Cooper supported them by continuing to find ways to frequently bring her to see him. Josefa brought him additional blankets and food. One day, a benevolent guard slammed the iron door behind her as she entered the cell, and after such a long time of separation, Josefa and Enrique could not resist each other any longer.

Later, still holding and caressing her soft body, Fitch began laughing. "I think my back is well, Josefa!"

She playfully swatted him. "You are thinking about the wrong things," she said in sharp mock anger.

Henry Virmond finally arrived in Monterey with the Maria Ester. When he found Fitch in jail, he became genuinely depressed. He reported finding Padre Jose Sanchez at San Gabriel absolutely unrelenting, determined that Fitch must stand trial.

"If we ever get you out of this place, Fitch, I think you had better head for the Sandwich Islands and stay there," he said.

But Fitch found new hope, both in Josefa's visits and in his friendship with Cooper. When Fitch mentioned Cooper, Virmond responded with great enthusiasm.

"Yes," he said, "he is one hell of a man. We should have known him from the beginning. He is a trader with plenty of connections. I think we can do business with him."

When Virmond returned to the problem at hand, he said, "I tried to see the commander of this place, Mariano Vallejo, but I found out that almost immediately after he returned from San Diego, the governor ordered him to explore the northern coast near the Russian settlement at Fort Ross. He's been gone for weeks.

Two days later, Virmond visited Fitch again.

"They've heard from Governor Echeandia," he said.

"I know Echeandia's answer," Fitch said.

"Right. Palomares received orders to obey the church summons."

"So, I must go to San Gabriel. How did you get the word?"

"I visited Sergeant Palomares at the headquarters office. As the juez de la policia, he seems to have authority in your case. I told him about your back. I also told him that you could not travel overland."

Fitch smiled. "But I want to get to San Gabriel soon. What did he say?"

"We do not move prisoners by ship," Virmond said, mocking Palomares. He cannot ride horseback, I told him. In fact, he cannot even walk across the presidio grounds. Palomares was very suspicious. I told him his soldiers had injured you. Palomares said you acted like an animal when they captured you, and he has recommended that the judge show you no mercy."

Fitch laid his fist against the wall in disgust. Virmond continued. Nonetheless, I told Palomares, Fitch can neither ride nor walk...he must travel by ship. He said that if what I said was a plot to help you escape, we would be out of business along this whole coast."

Fitch said, "I want to see this priest, Sanchez, and settle the matter. I'll crawl to San Gabriel if I must."

"No," Virmond said. "I have arranged to stand your bond and to be responsible for your safe delivery to San Gabriel."

"Good!" Fitch said. "Have you told Josefa? When can we leave?"

"I'm not sure," Virmond said. "But I must tell you. Palomares made one other demand."

"What is it?"

"Josefa cannot leave. By keeping her, he knows you will go to San Gabriel."

******

Even after Jose Palomares in Monterey gave permission for Fitch to travel by ship, he remained suspicious. He delayed the trip for another month. At first, he told Henry Virmond that two soldiers must accompany Fitch on board the brig, but at the last minute, he renewed his threats to banish Virmond as a trader if he failed to live up to his promise. With that, he allowed Fitch to travel unguarded.

After reaching San Pedro and passing through the pueblo of Los Angeles, Fitch and Virmond found themselves riding across gently rolling hills with the sight of high mountains in the distance. The ground was brown with only a stubble of grass after a hot summer and dry fall. Yet, thousands of longhorn Mexican cattle and wild horses grazed across the land.

"These herds belong to the mission," Virmond told Fitch. "Beyond the mission is the Santa Anita Rancho. It belongs to a man named Tomas Yorba who received a land grant back when Spain controlled things. If this problem with the priest can be settled, we should ride to Yorba's hacienda. It's quite a place, and he is a good man to do business with. He runs big herds."

Virmond encouraged Fitch by his continued support. "If you can be heard by one reasonable man, the case will be closed," he said as they rode. "During my first visit with Padre Sanchez, I had the feeling that everything that was happening was both an object lesson and a test of power. Not even the governor, the churches worst enemy, defies Sanchez when it comes to ecclesiastical matters."

Leaving Josefa in Monterey as hostage of the government had seemed intolerable, but she had convinced Fitch there was no other way. With so many delays, the weeks of summer had passed into fall, and now as the mission came in sight, it was December 8, 1840.

Arriving at the entrance to the mission compound, one of the soldiers of the escolta informed them that Padre Sanchez was ill and could not be disturbed that day. After Fitch introduced himself, the soldier knew immediately why he was there.

"I will show you to your quarters, Senor," he said.

He directed them through the courtyard past the kitchen and the vegetable garden. They passed a great vat giving off a putrid smell as Indian neophytes rendered fat into tallow. Fitch was shaken when they reached the last room of the soldiers' quarters because it was a jail cell with an iron door.

The soldier motioned him to enter. Fitch paused, looked at Virmond.

"We've come a long way to settle this," Virmond said. "Maybe it will soon be behind us."

Fitch still hesitated, then walked through the barred door. He turned to Henry Virmond, saying, "This can't be settled overnight, My Friend. We have already lost money on this trip. I should have remained in Callao or Matzatlan. You go ahead now. Sell our goods and find a profitable load for the vessels. I'll join you wherever you are when I leave this place."

They shook hands through the bars and agreed to meet in San Pedro in a fortnight. If Fitch was not there by deadline, Virmond would leave a message at the general trading store at the port. So, once again, they parted.

24. Josefa at Monterey

Josefa truly appreciated the Coopers. Juan Cooper was a quick-thinking, energetic man. Problems were for solving, and most of his time was well occupied with meeting each new foreign trading vessel that arrived in port; expanding his growing herds on the Bolsa del Potrero y Moro Cayo, a rancho he had purchased in the Monterey district from its Mexican grantee; and still occasionally serving as a shipmaster for any company operating a vessel along the California coast.

Though his days were long, and Cooper was nearly always away from the casa, he passed along any information he picked up about Enrique. Fitch's case was on the lips of every passing seaman. Apart from the Cooper family, there seemed to be no one friendly to the cause of Enrique, and Josefa's days of simply waiting became intolerable. Gradually and privately, she conceived a plan.

First, she wrote a long letter to Governor Jose Echeandia, and Cooper dispatched it for her on the first ship going south. In the letter, she set aside all pride and implored the governor to help her. She wrote: "Dear Governor Jose Echeandia, the fiestas and the happy days of the San Diego district are far behind me, and for sometime now, I have known only dark days.

"As you know, the Church has torn my husband from me, and seems determined to punish him for reasons I cannot understand. If he is guilty of some crime against God, then I am equally guilty, and must share his punishment because I pleaded with him to take me away and marry me, and I went willingly. No one is interested in understanding these things, and they doubt that we are married and have a legitimate child. Dear Senor, you are the only man the authorities in Monterey will obey. I implore you to command them to free me, and permit me and my child to travel to San Gabriel. Be assured, I will remain forever grateful."

Without shame, she also wrote to her father asking him to forgive her and support her in her efforts to join Enrique. She bluntly reminded him that he could enjoy favor in trading his hides with Henry Virmond's company because Enrique was his son-in-law.

By the time she wrote Rosa, she felt depressed again. Only Rosa truly understood her unshakable love for Enrique. Her words came from the heart.

"My Beloved Sister, Rosa," she wrote. "I once deeply believed that love could bring nothing but happiness in one's life, yet as much as you loved Romualdo, and I, Enrique, we suffer terrible despair. In those rare moments when Enrique and I are together, nothing else in the world matters. Then reality returns. Have we really flaunted God and Church and family beyond repair and forgiveness? I pray every day. May God take care of you. May god help Enrique and me. Affectionately, Josefa."

Encarnacion Cooper, a round-eyed, round-faced and sympathetic woman, never gave up trying to comfort Josefa, but without word from Enrique, the pain continued. When the women of the pueblo declared a "wash-up," Josefa did not have the heart to participate, but Encarnacion insisted.

"It will be a change," she said simply. "And it is a gay time for everyone."

Women gathered at a damned up water hole along the creek that rushed down from the hills, everyone bringing everything in their household that needed washing. It was an annual affair. The women set up a camp, and with the help of Indian boys, constructed a long ramada of poles with tule and grass roof for protection from the sun.

During the morning hours, they washed clothes, gossiped, discussed prospective marriage arrangements on behalf of their daughters, teased one another and drew pleasure from simply being together. They came from miles around.

In the late afternoon, the men came down to the encampment. They brought meat to be roasted and an assortment of vegetables. They also brought guitars and violins. By the light of many small fires, the musicians played while others sang and danced. Many couples, young and old, were pushed to the center for their turn at dancing.

During this time Josefa realized that she and Enrique had never danced together. Nor had they even attended a fiesta or a social event. Every act of their lives together was one of moving desperation, and their love remained a desperate love. Again, she fell into tears. With her child in arms, she retreated to a mat and blanket. The next day the washing, the eating and the socializing continued.

Weeks passed, and although John Cooper's family surrounded her with love and warmth, Josefa remained lonely, trapped by a pervasive sadness she could not overcome.

But then, one evening, Cooper returned home, smiled at her, reached into the inside pocket of his coat and brought out a letter.

"It is for you, Josefa."

She took it with trembling hand, broke the seal and by the light of a candle in the sala, read: "Dearest Sister, My thoughts are with you and Enrique during every moment of your separation. It must be so difficult. I have pleaded your cause throughout Santa Barbara, and I have high hopes for you. Captain Jose de la Guerra y Noriega, himself, has written a letter to Governor Echeandia, and so has Carlos Carrillo. The governor must listen to these men. I have also written Francisca urging her to talk to Papa. We shall see, Dear Sister, whether or not the combined efforts of the Carrillo family can move the governor. I am happy to know that you are safe and with a good family. With love and affection, Your sister, Rosa."

There was another sentence below Rosa's signature. "Captain John Wilson, a friend of many here, will be in Monterey soon. Don Jose de la Guerra wants him to contact you and assist you on behalf of the family."

An overland dispatch reached Josefa soon after her letter from Rosa. It came from Henry Virmond in San Pedro telling her that Enrique arrived safely in San Gabriel. It did not tell her of his condition or treatment. She could only guess, imagine terrible possibilities and worry through sleepless nights. She soon found she did not give enough milk to satisfy her growing son, but Encarnacion happily fed Enrique on one breast while feeding her own infant on the other.

Josefa dived into the work of the household to forget her sorrows, but each day had to end, and though weary, her nights remained nightmarish. She feared that both Encarnacion and John Cooper must hear her crying in her room during the night.

Then during one overcast morning in the new year, Josefa stepped outside the gate to look down at Monterey bay. Among the pine trees along the trail, she saw John Cooper riding toward the house, and at his side was a military officer in full uniform. As they came closer, Josefa knew that she had never seen Cooper's companion. He sat erect on his horse, a large man when compared with Cooper.

Cooper called greetings as they approached, and even before they climbed down from their horses, he said, "Meet the commandante of the Monterey presidio, Mariano Guadalupe Vallejo."

Vallejo dropped from his horse smiling at her and walked directly to where Josefa stood, then bowed from the waist. "So," he said in a gentle voice, "you are the eldest daughter of Joaquin Carrillo."

"Si," she answered. Her heart beat with anticipation when the commandante mentioned her papa's name. She knew that Vallejo had been in Northern California for months.

"Please come in Commandante," Cooper said. Josefa walked ahead of them.

"May I prepare chocolate for you?" she asked.

"Let's bring out the brandy," Cooper said.

"No, I think that I would prefer chocolate," Vallejo said. "I have much work to do today."

Cooper led Vallejo to a chair near a small table in the patio in back of the house. Josefa busied herself across from them, at the outdoor adobe stove, but Encarnacion came to her almost immediately.

"He must be here to see you, Josefa," she said.

Josefa stole a glance in the direction of the men, and Cooper motioned her to a stool near them.

Vallejo handed her a sealed folded paper. "My dispatch from Francisca included this separate message for you," he said.

She wanted to open the letter immediately, but restrained herself because the young commandante still talked. "I also bring you another message," he said. "This one is from the governor."

Josefa started, then gripped both hands tightly in her lap. "I believe you recently petitioned to travel to San Gabriel to be near your husband" Vallejo said.

"Si," she said anxiously. "Si…oh, please…"

He looked at her intently. He reached out as though wanting to comfort her, reassure her. Then, he said, "All of the services of my command are at your disposal, Senora. I have the governor's permission to see that you receive safe passage to San Gabriel."

Encarnacion stood behind the stool where Josefa sat. Now, the Cooper children ran to her. Encarnacion took her into her arms. John Cooper touched her cheek and the commandante handed her his large silk handkerchief as great tears rolled down her slim brown cheeks. But somehow, through the tears, Josefa smiled as none of the Cooper family had ever seen her smile.

"Thank you, commandante," she whispered brokenly.

She opened the letter from Francisca, but could not read it through the tears. Instead, she helped Encarnacion serve the chocolate, then silently attended to the needs of some of the children. While the men talked, she found her way to her room, lighted a candle and sat down on the rawhide cot and tried again to read the letter.

"My dearest sister," Francisca began, "Your papa, your brothers and I send you greetings and hope the news you have received brings you pleasure. You would not believe the discomfort of the governor when he received so many letters and visits asking that you be permitted to join Enrique. I believe that Papa has almost forgiven Enrique.

Your letter asking for his help meant so much to him. The governor finally appeared at our casa with letters from the Carrillos in Santa Barbara. I might add, Dear Sister, that Mariano Vallejo, himself, influenced the governor. And why? Please do not be too surprised. As I tried to tell you at the last minute when you were here, Papa has entered into a final agreement assuring Commandante Vallejo that when I am sixteen, I may become his wife. He is such a handsome man and speaks so romantically. I think that I will love him. We pray that you may soon be with Enrique and that he will be free."

Josefa wiped her eyes as best she could and went to the patio, wanting more than ever to express thanks to her future brother-in-law, Mariano Vallejo.

25. Shipmaster John Wilson at Monterey

The entire deck of the Brig Ayacucho, swabbed from bow to stern, became a colorful country store within hours after it dropped anchor at Monterey, and two surf boats shuttled local residents continuously between the ship and the customhouse of the Monterey pueblo.

Shipmaster John Wilson and his partner, Supercargo James Scott, along with their Kanaka crew, gave the pueblo their version of a fiesta. "A Scottish fiesta," Scott told people.

Scott, a happy round-bodied man, kept his customers laughing with his mix of Scotch brogue and broken Spanish language. For today, the Senoritas and Senoras were all "lassies" and the men were all "lads," and the word "aye" substituted for "si" and they made deals in the bartering of fabrics, tools, furniture, hardware, fabrics, sugar, chocolate, jewelry, and spices in exchange for cowhides, tallow and some otter skins.

Wilson and Scott played it straight with officials in every port by paying inventory duty, and no official or his wife was overlooked in the distribution of pleasing gifts. So, the Ayacucho did a brisk business everywhere. In every port, the best musicians were invariably enticed on board with gifts and promises of the best brandy. While the women shopped, the men enjoyed liquid refreshments and talked trade with Supercargo Scott.

On this occasion in early fall, Wilson looked forward to welcoming Commandante Vallejo, himself, and knew he would be accompanied by John Cooper and his wife and Joaquin Carrillo's eldest daughter, dark hair swept tightly in a bun, silk mantilla covering her shoulders.

Wilson greeted each of them as they climbed the ladder and stepped aboard. The problems of Shipmaster Henry Fitch had spread with the trade winds of the Pacific, reaching every foreigner who did business along the coast of California. All wanted to help a fellow trader, but they knew not how and took fair warning from his experience in their own relationships with California women. The fact that Josefa was a Carrillo made Fitch's problem with the church much more interesting than if it had been otherwise. This family seemed to have influence wherever they happened to be living. But quite apart from family, Wilson was readily moved to sympathy when he saw the heavy-lidded eyes of Josefa.

When he was introduced to her, he said, "It is my pleasure to know you, Lassie. I know your parents, and I attended the wedding of your sister, Rosa. I also know your uncles, Jose Guerra and Carlos Carrillo, in Santa Barbara. I am at your service."

"Thank you, Captain," she said, and glanced at Vallejo, hoping he approved of Wilson.

Wilson knew she must wait for Vallejo and Cooper to make any arrangement, and that the matter would be settled slowly, and with some posturing, according to their custom.

Vallejo stood back, arms folded, a noble, somewhat aristocratic appearing man, while Encarnacion tugged Josefa into the milieu of happy female shoppers. The musicians kept those arriving by boat spirited and happy. The brandy was exceptional, and as Wilson poured, he jokingly told of the costly trade he made at Mission San Luis Rey to acquire it.

When he filled Vallejo's glass for a second time, he said, "Permit me to show you our vessel, Commandante."

Vallejo responded immediately, and Wilson was glad that he had ordered the crew to clean the ship so thoroughly. He showed the young commandante the galley, the crew's quarters, the hold where inventory was stored and then his own quarters on deck at the stern.

"When we have special guests traveling with us," Wilson said carefully, "I join my crew in the bunks below and turn my cabin over to the passengers."

Vallejo seemed to be waiting for such an opening. "I find your ship unusually clean, and I have heard that it is fast."

Wilson laughed, "Aye, 'tis that. The fastest vessel on this coast and the smoothest sailing in the Pacific. She is a stable vessel." Then he told Vallejo about his recent visit in Santa Barbara and Don Jose Guerra's request that he serve the needs of Josefa.

Vallejo looked directly into Wilson's blue eyes, and spoke in a most confidential manner. "I have similar instructions from Governor Echeandia and her family in San Diego."

"Then permit me, Commandante," Wilson said with weighted deference, to be of service to you in meeting our mutual obligation."

"When do you sail?" Vallejo asked.

"My crew loads hides from the beach tonight and tomorrow. Tomorrow evening we plan to sail to Santa Barbara. We'll remain there several days. Unless another ship leaves Santa Barbara for San Pedro before us, the Senora may stay on the Ayacucho with us."

Vallejo considered this information for a long moment, then said, "I will arrange for my housekeeper to be her companion until she is safely settled in San Gabriel."

The two men lifted their glasses as a token of contract.

26. Josefa in Monterey

The immediate future and fate of Josefa was settled, and as far as she was concerned, all of those who exercised an interest in taking her to her husband performed exactly in keeping with her wishes.

It was nearly dark the next evening when she and her companion, to her surprise, a young Indian woman named Tash, were escorted by Vallejo and Cooper to a surfboat on the beach and pushed out into the water by Kanaka crew members.

Captain Wilson greeted them on deck while one of his crew carried the women's bags to the cabin. Wilson often accommodated travelers on his vessel from among California families, and he kept especially embroidered pillow covers, lace curtains and other niceties to dress up the cabin.

Josefa was delighted and surprised to see her quarters. In fact, the Ayacucho was an especially beautiful sailing vessel, a schooner, much nicer than the square-sail brigs in Virmond's trading fleet. She touched the varnished mahogany walls of the inside of the cabin and marveled at the grain of the wood and the brass fixtures of the drawers built into the wall opposite the door. A double bed could be drawn down from one wall, and there was a wood-burning stove in the cabin and a kettle for boiling water on top.

Now, Josefa considered her companion, a beautiful girl about her own age. Although the intention of a companion was to provide her a certain comfort and protection, Josefa smiled slightly because she had the feeling that the roles could easily become reversed in this situation. Tash was dressed much the same as Josefa except that her short-sleeved dress did not have embroidery. She wore a brightly colored reboza, a cotton skirt and blue velvet shoes. Both her beads and earrings must be gifts, Josefa suspected, much nicer than household servants normally wore. And that handsome Vallejo had contracted for her sister's hand?

Josefa heard Captain Wilson giving orders to get the ship under sail, and she stepped out on deck for a last look at Monterey. The customs building stood out along the shore against the pueblo and pine-covered hills. Among the casas on the high ground, she picked out the Cooper house, whitewashed and clean, barely visible in the foliage.

With her back against the cabin wall, Tash's dark eyes bulged wide in her round immobile face. She obviously had never been on board a ship and probably had never been more than a few leagues from the rancheria where she was born. With anchor pulled to deck and sails set to catch the breeze, the Ayacucho almost bound out of the bay. Thoughts of Enrique blossomed in the sea wind and even visions of his face became clearer to Josefa. Hair blowing and eyes watering in the breeze, she raised her arms to the sky in ecstasy. Tash made her way back to the cabin, and Josefa left her to care for the baby. She remained at the stern, observing the white wake in the disappearing day. The sun wavered below the horizon and cast its final glory of colors. Later, there were clouds and then a break in the night sky revealed a heaven of stars. Leaning into the wind, Josefa felt a new strength. She sought the rosary beads about her neck and above the sound of the waves, called aloud her devotion to the Mother Mary. Still exhilarated, she went to the cabin. Later, Captain Wilson appeared at the door and handed Tash a tray with food.

"If you need anything, Lassies," he said, "ring the bell." He pointed to a large bell outside their door, then bade them goodnight.

There was only one bed in the cabin, and Tash remained dressed while Josefa put on her gown. Finally, Josefa realized why Tash did not undress. This will be another first in my life, Josefa thought…sleeping with an Indian servant. She tried to be easy about it. "We will let little Enrique sleep between us," she told Tash. "He should like that."

After Josefa was in bed, Tash blew out the candle and undressed in the dark. Josefa lay with her eyes open for a long time, seeing nothing in the pitch blackness, feeling the vessel roll from side to side and up and down. Baby Enrique slept soundly, but Tash moved around a great deal. Suddenly, the girl jumped out of bed, groping toward the door. The wind swept into the cabin. Josefa followed Tash to the stern directly in back of their cabin where the girl heaved and spit into the sea. Josefa could do nothing but hold her writhing body. At long last, Tash hung weakly on the rail.

"Do you feel better?" Josefa called above the beating wind.

"Si" she said, her body still shaking as they returned to the cabin. Josefa lighted the candle again and poured water from the kettle on the stove into a pan, and Tash washed her face. Then she began sobbing.

"What is it, Tash?" Josefa asked.

"I am so afraid," she said. "I am so afraid. The water is so deep."

As they sat on the side of the bed, Josefa held the Indian girl until sleep overcame both of them. Tash cuddled the baby constantly during the next three days and nights, never leaving the cabin. Each day when the sun fell across the deck, Josefa went out. Standing at the rail, she actually thrilled at the sensation of the ocean picking up the back end of the ship and dropping it again. She had learned from Enrique to enjoy the rising and falling and the wind in her face. But the side rolls sometimes threw her off balance. In those moments, she laughed like a child again.

One day she turned and found Captain John Wilson also laughing. "Aye, Lassie, I think you enjoy the sea," he said.

"Si," she answered, filled with joy, "but I also remember losing supper my first time aboard, even with the brig at anchor.

"It is good to see you happy," the Captain said. "I was beginning to think…"

"What?"

"That I would never see you smile."

"Life stopped for me when they took my husband away," she said, but you have helped so much. Gracias, Captain."

She could not recall talking to a man outside her family without other persons present, but Wilson's manner made it easy. His face and neck appeared sinewy and strong, and he carried himself so forcefully, often bouncing across the deck with both fists closed.

Wilson seemed to know he was scrutinized. "I have known your husband since he first arrived in the Pacific," he said. "He is a patient, giant of a man. Not a man people readily oppose."

Josefa believed all would be well when she reached Enrique, but she so much needed support until that time. Wilson carried himself with such certainty. She felt secure with him.

"How long have you sailed in the Pacific?" she asked.

"I came from Dundee in 1835."

"Is that in Scotland?"

"Aye, Lass. A long way from California."

"Enrique was not a Catholic when he came from Massachusetts. Are you?"

Captain Wilson appeared amused by her prodding. "No," he answered. "In fact, Dundee is a stronghold against Catholicism.

Josefa did not understand him. She asked, "Do you believe in The Church?"

He studied her for a long moment. "I have been away from formal religions for a long time...long enough to find a religion of my own."

"Your own?" she asked, unbelievingly.

"Are you sure you want to talk about such things?" he asked.

"It frightens me," she said, "but I do."

Captain Wilson stood with both elbows on the rail, staring into the gray-green moving depths below them. "Do you feel the rise and fall of the vessel, Lassie?"

"Si."

"It is an extraordinary movement, isn't it?" he asked quietly.

He remained silent for a time. Josefa closed her eyes, allowing herself to merge with the tilting sky, the falling away and cresting of the sea below her.

"Si," she said. "It is God's movement."

"And the wind fills our sails," he said, seeming almost unaware of her. "So as we shift the sails, even slightly, we move in our own chosen direction. We reach the place we want to go by being one with everything around us."

"Do you pray to it? This force around you?" she asked, feeling awkward, groping for words.

"No, I am part of it, so words are not necessary."

Here, in this moment, Wilson's mysterious explanation was easy for Josefa to understand. She drifted momentarily into a swaying ecstasy, trembling, too emerged to resist. But that night the thought changed. She dreamed of falling through a dark chasm, a godless frightening abyss, utterly helpless.

When they talked again, Captain Wilson was thinking about Enrique. He said, "I hope Henry Fitch realizes the priests in this part of the world do not understand his ways any better than he understands their ways, but this is their territory. These robed men control this part of the world. Their power cannot be ignored. They enslave converts and topple governors. They certainly could imprison him!"

"No!" Josefa cried, startled and shaking.

His voice became gentle again. "I'm sorry, Senora," he said. "Henry Fitch will work everything out. You'll see, Lass. We both know it."

Captain Wilson compelled Josefa with his words. She could not resist talking to him, yet his thoughts were fearful. Still, she did not know how it could be otherwise. She did not have his kind of ideas nor his practice in talking about them.

27. Rosa and Josefa in Santa Barbara

John Wilson had promised de la Guerra and the Carrillo family that he would drop anchor at Santa Barbara if Josefa sailed aboard the Ayacucho enroute to Los Angeles and San Gabriel. Day after day, Rosa impatiently waited the arrival of his brig. Because she could not see the bay from the Guerra hacienda, she urged several of the children of the pueblo as well as the soldiers standing watch in the presidio bastion on the far wall to call her when they saw the ship.

The children's first call proved a false alarm because it was the Pocahontas that first dropped anchor for trade. A few days later, however, a guard sent word that Wilson's ship had definitely arrived. One of the men in the presidio corral saddled a horse for her, and she raced to the beach. Baby Romualdo remained with Adriana today, although Rosa often strapped him to her back in the Chumash Indian rush holder her adopted daughter had made for her.

Crew jumped over the side, and pushed the surfboat through the water until it beached.

Rosa saw one of the large Sandwich Islanders lift Josefa out of the boat and carry her to dry sand. Another crewman carried a young and very pretty Indian woman who cradled a child in her arms.

Captain John Wilson followed both crew members, and while Rosa and Josefa greeted each other, he beamed. "Sure now," he said, "the Carrillo sisters together must be California's most beautiful sight."

Rosa turned to Captain Wilson and did something she had not expected to do. She took his hand. "You did it, Captain John Wilson! You found my sister and brought her to us. We are forever in your debt."

"And the debt is already repaid, me Lassie, by the pleasure of seeing you together," Wilson answered.

But when Rosa glanced at Captain Wilson again, she realized that she had never been so completely smiled upon or so lavishly consumed by a man's eyes in her life.

Josefa and Rosa walked arm-in-arm through the pueblo, Rosa leading her horse. Tash strolled a few steps behind with Josefa's son.

"Don Jose Guerra wants to talk to you," Rosa said. "I told him we would come to the casa when you arrived."

28. Josefa in Santa Barbara

Even during her first visit in Santa Barbara, the pueblo and the presidio had looked enough like San Diego so that Josefa felt immediately comfortable among the whitewashed adobe casas and cracking presidio walls. The mission buildings on the slope loomed large and distinct against the mountains. Soldiers, women, children and Indians moved as though in an easy dream toward the beach wanting to see trade goods come ashore.

"The people seem so happy here," she said.

"Why not?" Rosa answered. "Like Romualdo always said...there are plenty of fish in the bay, shell fish on the rocks and cliffs, rabbits, deer and quail in the hills. And everyone can have cattle, sheep and gardens. There is plenty for everyone."

Maria Antonia Guerra greeted Rosa and Josefa in her usual gracious way. Since Don Jose Guerra was away, but expected to return soon, Josefa was pleased to have this time with her aunt. Maria Antonia was a quiet woman, and her soft voice and her gentle touch were reassuring. An Indian servant took Tash and baby Enrique to a bedroom where the child could sleep.

Maria Antonia brought food to a small table on the covered porch, including a bowl of oranges. "A gift from the padres at Mission Santa Buenaventura," she explained. "Don Jose attends to the business affairs of both that mission and Santa Barbara."

The Senoras ate bits of beef and lamb from a common platter with miniature tortillas dipped in a tomato and pepper sauce. At the same time, they enjoyed the sweet flavor of tree-ripened orange sections. Maria Antonia provided generous-sized linen napkins with embroidered designs to cover their laps.

"It is good that we have this time together before my husband arrives," Maria Antonia said as they ate. "He will have advice to offer you, Josefa. It is good advice. That is all I can say." Then she laughed. "But I must also advise you, and this should be our secret."

Josefa thought for a long moment, and decided that she must speak her mind clearly in advance. "I do not want to disobey or disregard the good intentions of my family," she said. "I have permission from the governor to go to San Gabriel. Enrique needs me, and I will go. Any advice to the contrary would only make more difficult what I must do."

Both Maria Antonia and Rosa looked at Josefa in amazement. The older woman gently pushed back her chair and went inside. When she returned, she had three small glasses of red wine on a tray. "Well," she said, "you are a good wife." She raised her glass, and the sisters followed. Now, you must tell Don Jose of your intentions before he advises you. Can you do that?"

Later, Josefa found herself in Don Jose's study at the end of one wing of the house, and she followed her aunt's advice. The small, relaxed former commandante of the presidio listened quietly to her. This was a most uncommon circumstance, she knew, setting the rules in advance for the advice that an older man might offer, especially coming from a woman, and she, a very young woman.

She determined not to be defiant. She felt like a child forced to womanhood too quickly, but she remained determined not to allow any person to advise her away from going to her Enrique.

Don Jose Guerra studied her face with compassion. "You have all of the right instincts, Child, and I can see the deep wounds you carry in those moist dark eyes." He paused, then added, "I'm glad that you have explained your feelings, but please do not be indifferent toward The Church, or for that matter, even give the appearance of indifference. If the ecclesiastical judge finds Enrique guilty of the worst crime in this case, he could be sent to Mexico to rot his life away in prison."

Josefa winced, her head starting to ache.

"The judge will not approve your presence at San Gabriel," Don Jose said. "You must know that he may hold it against both you and Enrique."

Josefa took a trembling breath. "But he must know the truth from both of us," she said. "The judge is a priest. He will know we speak the truth. I will swear before God. He cannot deny us!"

"All right, Josefa," Guerra said softly. "You are a lovely child, and my own faith convinces me of Enrique's innocence. I will not suggest strategies to you. The Pocahontas sails for San Pedro tonight. Do you want to go aboard?" Guerra asked her.

"May I speak to Captain Wilson first?" she said. "He promised Commandante Vallejo to see me safely all of the way to San Gabriel."

"He also swore his services to me," Don Jose said, smiling. "Please let me arrange everything for you."

"Si," Josefa said. "I am so relieved, Uncle, to know I have your support."

29. John Wilson in Santa Barbara

It always paid John Wilson to visit Don Jose de la Guerra y Noriega before others in Santa Barbara. This time, Guerra immediately expressed interest in solving the problems of his wife's niece, Josefa. As reward, he offered enough hides in trade to more than justify their stop here. Then, as sindico for Mission Santa Barbara, he bargained with Wilson on behalf of the priests. He held one hundred premium otter pelts collected at the Mission by neophyte hunters. Every trader sought them because there was a demand for them in Canton, and even for those trading ships not traveling that far, they brought a good price in the Sandwich Islands from other traders sailing to Manila and Canton. Guerra offered a long list of items which the Mission needed. It included everything from flour sifters to broad-brimmed hats for neophyte sheepherders.

Wilson studied the list: brass candlesticks, chocolate, oregano, Pepper, carding combs, plowshares, castilan mattocks, door hinges, pots and kettles, gold brocade binding, alarm clocks, frying pans and small hand drills. Items not now on board the Ayacucho could be delivered at a future date. For his hides, Guerra accepted a letter of credit from Wilson and Scott against future purchases.

"And now," Guerra said, as if an afterthought, "I must rely upon you to personally deliver Josefa, her child, and the Indian girl directly to the home of Josefa's cousin, Senora Eulalia Perez, at San Gabriel.

"You may depend upon us," Wilson said, as pleased by the faith Guerra expressed in him as by the exceptional trading arrangement.

Wilson talked to Guerra about the arrangements made to take Josefa to San Pedro and then overland to San Gabriel, and Guerra agreed to bring Josefa and her Indian companion to the beach before the Ayacucho sailed. Soon, Scott arrived with a flask of brandy for the commandante. When the food was ready, Rosa and Josefa served them. Josefa was far more reserved now than when on board ship, and Rosa was even more distant. It was the way of California women in the presence of family. Any appearance of vivaciousness could be misinterpreted. Both Wilson and Scott understood the custom.

At the end of the evening, Scott gave Guerra a handpainted Chinese silk fan and a pair of decorative hair combs, presents for Maria Antonia and Rosa. In turn, Guerra handed Scott a list of items needed at the presidio. In the present state of affairs, the central government had not paid its bills for California military needs for some time. In this case, Wilson and Scott would fill the order as a favor to the commandante. In return, Guerra would purposely overlook recording their visit, so they paid no inventory duty. It was a simple arrangement which traders, pueblo administrators, the military and even the missionaries accepted as necessary. If any of them completely enforced existing law, all would be hurt. Such informal understandings made living far more gracious for all.

30. Josefa and Euladia at San Gabriel

Josefa could scarcely constrain the excitement she felt upon coming ashore at San Pedro. She had never heard of her cousin, Senora Eulalia Perez, the woman she would live with in San Gabriel. Maria Antonia Guerra told her Senora Perez was a woman in her sixties, a nurse and midwife, and she depended upon the services she offered for her living. Her husband had died a few years earlier, and her grown children had scattered throughout Alta California. She lived alone in one of the many small adobe casas clustered near San Gabriel Mission.

The Ayacucho anchored at San Pedro one day in November, and Captain Wilson and Supercargo James Scott gave immediate attention to escorting Josefa, her child and Tash to San Gabriel. Both men knew the trail from many trips.

They rented horses and a half-dozen pack mules at San Pedro in preparation for the long ride. The mules not only carried Josefa and Tash's personal bags, but Scott took food as well as gifts for Senora Perez, the mission priests and the local rancheros with whom they hoped to do business.

"We can stay at a place on the Domenquez Rancho the first night," Wilson told Josefa. "The second night, we will reach the Los Angeles pueblo. You could visit your Carrillo cousins."

"Must we take so long?" Josefa asked. "I can visit my cousins when Enrique is free. Please, Captain, we are so near."

At first, Wilson objected, then finally said, "Let's see how you feel after the day's ride."

He expected her to become too weary to continue, Josefa knew, but he did not know about the churning inside her. In the early afternoon, they approached the first overnight stop Wilson planned.

"Please, Captain, let's keep going, Josefa pleaded. "We can camp somewhere, anywhere, when it is dark."

Wilson shrugged. Scott did not object. Josefa took baby Enrique from Tash's back, slung him to her breast and rode happily along the trail.

Everyone in the family, especially her Papa and Don Jose Guerra, would be shocked if they knew she and Tash camped overnight with two men, but the Scotsmen proved men of honor. They arranged Josefa and Tash's sleeping place on the opposite side of a clump of bushes from where they slept.

At noon the next day they passed Pueblo Los Angeles on the opposite side of the river and followed the well-worn mission trail for miles through brush and trees across gently rolling hills near the river.

Josefa could not resist. She kept riding ahead for any clearing that might give her a view of the path ahead. Before dark, she pointed into the distance at a high adobe wall. "Look," she shouted with joy, "Mission San Gabriel!"

Senora Perez was a complete surprise to Josefa. She expected to find a reserved round little old lady, but after receiving directions from a half-dozen people among the cluster of adobes in the vicinity of the mission, she found herself face-to-face with a slim rawboned, sun-darkened woman chopping wood.

When Josefa stepped down from her horse and introduced herself, Senora Perez tossed aside her ax and gave a gleeful grin. "Joaquin Carrillo's daughter!" she said.

Then she looked beyond Josefa to where Wilson and Scott sat on their horses. Even in her sixties, it was immediately clear that Eulalia Perez liked men, and upon seeing the two seamen, she flirted scandalously. She took baby Enrique from Tash, both cuddling and talking to the child. Josefa felt overjoyed by Senora Perez' warmth, and tried to hid her discomfort when she saw the dirty hands that fondled her child.

Senora Perez shared beef with tortillas and beans with her guests, telling stories that kept all of them laughing.

"I knew your father when he was a child in Loreto," she said. "So, I am not surprised to know he has a fine casa and many beautiful children. He was a handsome boy, a strong boy, too, with more energy and bigger dreams than anyone in the pueblo." She paused. "So you have come to be near your husband. I am sorry that he must deal with Padre Sanchez. He is a good priest, but very strict."

"Why do you say that?" Josefa asked.

"He thinks I am a bad woman, but I tell him no one goes to mass or recites the rosary more often than I do. What does he expect?"

Scott chided her. "Perhaps it is not your attendance at mass that worries him, Senora, but the devil in your eyes."

Senora Perez lifted her shoulders in a haughty gesture and rolled her eyes, smiling at him. "So," she said, "I cannot help how I am."

With evening and the Senora's permission, the men took their bedrolls to a thatched shelter at the back of the casa. For Josefa, the baby and Tash, Eulalia arranged sleeping space on mats laid out on the adobe floor in her one large room.

The next morning Wilson told Josefa that he and Scott planned to visit the mission that day to do what trading they could. At the same time, Wilson volunteered to find out Enrique's circumstances. He suggested she wait until their return. Josefa was consoled by Wilson's promise and the feeling that Enrique was somewhere on the other side of the high wall. For now, she remained content to keep her presence secret, but it was a long day of waiting.

Wilson was a man of his word. That evening he and Scott returned to Senora Perez' casa laden with lemons and oranges from the mission gardens as well as a crock of honey from the mission beehives. They had fared well in trading, and both men smiled in a strange way.

When they remained silent, Josefa said, "Why do you tease me, Senors? What about my Enrique?"

"Aye..." said Scott. "What about her Enrique, John?"

"Oh!" Josefa said, stamping a foot angrily, tears welling up. Then both men came to her, exuding warmth and affection. During the weeks of traveling with her, they had come to treat her like a beloved sister and friend. She knew they did not intend to hurt her.

"He looks well," Wilson said simply.

"You saw him!" Josefa screeched.

"Yes, he is healthy, he misses you and..."

"You told him I am here?"

The men's eyes were flashing with the excitement they were able to share with her. "Aye," Scott said. They no longer contained themselves. They were delighted to bring her good news.

From behind, Eulalia struck up her guitar. Wilson reached for castanets hanging on the adobe wall and found the rhythm of the music. Scott began clapping his hands.

"Dance, Josefa," he urged, "dance!"

Bursting inside, she feigned an immobile face, assumed an erect posture, tossed her head to the right with face downward, and the El Jarabe began. It was a dance from the heart. At last, she could let out everything that had built up inside her during the months that had passed. Neighbors appeared from the other adobes, peeking in the window and the doorway. First, a paisano with violin appeared and then others with their instruments.

"What is the celebration?" a woman asked.

"I don't know," another answered, "but it has been too long since we had one."

Eulalia joined the group outside her door, beckoning to Josefa and the men. Others appeared, and the celebration began and continued into the night until all were too exhausted to dance longer.

Josefa lay awake later in the night, planning to see Enrique. Tomorrow, regardless of consequences, she would go to the mission.

******

At dawn the next morning, Wilson and Scott prepared to visit the owners and mayordomos of a few local ranchos. The San Gabriel and Santa Anita areas offered good opportunities for traders because large tracts of original mission lands already belonged to private owners. Before they rode away, Josefa came running out.

"Is Enrique locked up at the Mission?" she asked.

"His cell is his room," Wilson told her, "but the door is open, and he walks about the gardens in the quadrangle within the walls. Yesterday, he was helping the Indians repair the back wall. As you know, he isn't a man to sit around."

Guessing Josefa's intentions, Wilson said, "Go directly into the church through the big doors on the outside wall Then you'll see a door on the opposite side of the nave that looks directly into the mission courtyard."

As Josefa watched them ride away, she felt suddenly alone and unsure. Inside, Eulalia insisted that Josefa drink some chocolate and eat a piece of fruit.

"I will accompany you to church," Eulalia said, fully realizing what was on Josefa's mind.

Within the hour, mantillas covering their heads and baby Enrique in Josefa's arms, they crossed the dusty opening among the casas to a door built into the great wall of the church.

San Gabriel Mission was different from the others Josefa had seen in California. The long high wall reminded her more of a presidio than a mission. Massive bells hung in what appeared a relatively new companario.

"The old church fell in the earthquake way back in 1812," Eulalia said. "They rebuilt it stronger than ever."

Inside, both touched their foreheads with holy water from the font and crossed themselves. At the altar, they dropped to their knees, bowed their heads and repeated the parts of the rosary. Josefa was consumed by thoughts of Enrique and the meaning of her recitation was clouded by visions of his face.

She looked up often at the bright polychrome retablo with its many wooden statues: San Francisco de Asis, San Joaquin, San Antonio de Padua, and Santa Domingo. From the center above, San.Gabriel and La Purisima Conception looked down at her. Above the tabernacle she saw and prayed to the image of the Immaculate Conception.

"Dear Mother of Jesus," she whispered. "Hear this prayer for my husband."

When, at last, she turned, Josefa saw Eulalia at the back of the nave. Josefa studied the long narrow church in the dim light. Now standing below the high pulpit with its decorative balustrade, she was frightened rather than comforted by the church…frightened by its damp air, dark paintings, and lonely cavernous nave with high ceiling. With the church holding Enrique prisoner, she felt its terrible curse upon their child. She held Baby Enrique closer.

Senora Perez waited near a side room beside a large round hammered copper baptismal font. She motioned Josefa to a crude bench along the wall and disappeared out the door leading into a cemetery in the mission courtyard.

Josefa sat quietly, listening, tucking baby Enrique's legs under her mantilla. She heard Senora Eulalia talking to someone, perhaps an Indian neophyte, a soldier or a priest. The Senora's voice trailed off as she walked away.

Josefa stared blankly at a pair of thick doors attached to a nearby wooden confessional. They were rounded at the top with gothic tips at center, opening like a cupboard. At top and bottom, eye-like wooden and brass decorations stared back at her. One door stood ajar, and she made out a leather-covered seat with arm rests. Pierced tin screens on the side served as ears through which parishioners could unburden their sins to a priest. She actually prayed that a priest would not find her feeling the way she felt at this moment…guilty, angry, filled with despair. But in the same instant, all thoughts blurred. From out of nowhere, the shadowed image appeared. She gasped. Stood. Ran toward it, and it was real! At last…at last! Oh, Mother Mary forgive…

"Enrique," she said weakly.

He gently took her and baby Enrique into his arms, and he, too, cried brokenly. They stood through an eternity…together…one family. The crying inside was no longer grievous. Josefa was passionately happy.

Finally, Enrique called Senora Perez close to them. "You must take her home now," he said, "and keep her there until you receive word from me. I don't know how long it will take, but I'm sure things will be worse if we are discovered together."

He turned to Josefa. "I love you with all my heart," he said. "Let's be patient a little longer."

At that moment, all of them looked up into the face of a Gabrieleno Indian neophyte. The Indian turned quickly and walked away. After he disappeared, Senora Eulalia grabbed Josefa's arm, and they hurried out the entrance of the church and across the wide expanse toward her casa.

"That Indian is a servant in the priest's apartment," she said when they were well away.

The next morning, even before rising, Josefa heard Senora Eulalia's voice outside the door of the adobe, and Tash stood by the window. The Senora was angry and arguing with someone. Then she heard the men's voices. When Josefa looked out, she saw two soldiers of the mission escolta.

"Back, Josefa!" Eulalia said emotionally, and for a moment, Josefa stepped away from the doorway. Then she realized the folly of believing that staying inside the house was protection.

"What is this?" she asked, walking out to the soldiers. "Why are you here?"

"Senora, we are here to take you from this house."

"But, why?"

"It is the order of Padre Sanchez. You were supposed to remain in Monterey."

"I have permission from Governor Echeandia."

"But you do not have permission from El Presidente of the missions, and he does not want you near this man, Enrique Fitch."

"He is my husband!" Josefa screamed.

"He is a foreigner who has compromised the daughter of one of our citizens."

Senora Eulalia was taller than the man who talked and perhaps even stronger. She stepped up to the soldier and put her nose within inches of his face. "Who is the judge in this case?" she demanded. "You? What right have you to condemn this man?"

The Senora's defiance did quiet both of the soldiers. Finally, the larger man spoke directly to Josefa. "It is bad for the Senora to remain here. The padre presidente does not want you so close until this affair is settled. He has arranged for you to stay in Pueblo Los Angeles with another family."

Josefa considered what the soldier said. The neophyte at the church had wasted no time in telling Padre Sanchez about her arrival. There could be no secrets. She looked at Senora Eulalia.

"It is best for Enrique if I go," she said. "Los Angeles is not far away. Tash and I will pack our things."

When Wilson and Scott returned to San Pedro, they took Tash with them. They would put her on a trading vessel going north to Monterey.

31. Enrique

Fitch lighted the candles in his cell room, door open, body and mind pulsing with renewed resolve after doing several hundred pushups against the adobe wall in a tilted standing position. Breathing hard, blood rushing through him, he thought of climbing the mission compound wall in the night and being relieved of this hell which only innocents and madmen could call a church.

Josefa's love and loyalty was extraordinary medicine for a man trapped by foreign ways in a foreign land. Now, he wanted her. He needed both his wife and child. How long should he suppress this anger and frustration?

In part, he continued to control himself because Padre Jose Bernardo Sanchez, El Presidente of all the Alta California missions, showed himself a reasonable man trying to make a judgment under ecclesiastical law. They said the padre was ill that first day upon Fitch's arrival. They locked him in this cell to wait instructions.

At dawn the next morning, he heard a hoarse voice outside the metal door calling for the guard to bring the key. When the door swung open, there stood a colorless and tired looking man in robes. It was Padre Sanchez.

"Do not lock this door again!" he roared, and the soldier guard quietly wilted out of sight.

Fitch pulled on his denim pants and stood thoughtfully by the cot.

Somehow, this important priest was not nearly as formidable in appearance as Fitch's imagination had allowed. He was stout with light-brown hair and beard that almost matched his brown robes and wide-brimmed hat.

The Padre beckoned Fitch to follow him past the soldiers' quarters, the padre's quarters, the mission kitchen where Indian women began the day's work and then through the garden arbor and into the side door of the church. He asked Fitch to kneel at the rail that separated the sanctuary from the nave, and Padre Sanchez kneeled beside him. For a moment, Fitch could not believe what was happening. If the priest had asked Fitch to kneel before him in order that he might bless him or offer prayer, he would have felt the authority he associated with the church and the priesthood. Instead, Sanchez dropped to his knees beside him and prayed silently. When he stood again, he motioned Fitch to a bench near a side wall.

"I am told," Padre Sanchez said, "that you consider yourself a Catholic."

"I do," Fitch said. "Padre Antonio Menendez at San Diego conducted the baptism."

Sanchez thought about this for a moment, seeming to shake his head. Since arriving at San Gabriel, Fitch had learned that Padre Menendez, the Dominican friar from the lower California frontier, was considered an eccentric rebel in the church, certainly at odds with the Franciscans in Alta California. Having somehow conducted himself in an unacceptable manner in Baja California, Padre Menendez judgment was not readily acceptable to the Fernandinos. His decision to both baptize and confirm Fitch with minimum instruction was not viewed by Padre Sanchez as a credible action. On the other hand, the church baptized thousands of Indians, most of them not understanding their commitment.

"Are you finding fault with me because Padre Menendez did not follow procedures acceptable to you?" Fitch asked.

"Not exactly, Captain. I am concerned about your understanding of the Church. Do you know what is expected of you?"

Fitch felt the old anger well up inside of him. "If there has been an error, it is the church's error," he said firmly. Then, he immediately knew he had said the wrong thing.

"Captain Fitch!" Padre Sanchez said in a commanding voice. "The church belongs to God! It is subject to the laws of God! The servants of the Church may make errors, but the Church does not."

"All right," Fitch said, voice too loud, though he wanted to sound conciliatory. "I understand, and I accept that as truth."

Padre Sanchez had not risen to president of all of the missions by accident, Fitch knew. At least a quarter century earlier this man volunteered for service as a missionary in California. He received the Franciscan habit in the convent of Santa Maria de Gracia in the province of San Miguel Estremadura in Spain, and sailed from Cadiz to Vera Cruz, Mexico, joining the San Fernando College in Mexico City. With other friars, he set out from Mexico City for Acapulco where they boarded a ship that took them to Yerba Buena on San Francisco Bay in 1804.

In the years that followed, he served at Missions San Diego, Purisima and San Gabriel and conducted services at many other missions. In mission service, he made many expeditions to the rancherias of inland Indians, baptized hundreds of neophytes, and conducted himself honorably during a long life of mission administration.

His fellow missionaries considered him a gentle and devoted priest, and they elected him their president. During this decade while he headed the activities at Mission San Gabriel, morale among the neophytes was at its peak. All of this was information Fitch gathered while talking to the soldiers of the escolta and the mission Indians themselves. But he also heard that Sanchez adhered strictly to the formalities of the Church he loved and that he, like Fitch himself, angered easily. Sanchez remained totally indignant about Fitch's criticism of the Church.

"I think," Sanchez said, as if testing Fitch, "that you must have more complete instruction in the religion of the Church." He waited for some response, but Fitch remained determinedly silent. His fate depended upon this priest. "I suggest," he continued, "that you attend mass with the neophytes and that you say rosary every day."

There was no mention of a trial, and Fitch decided not to bring it up. The priest left Fitch on the bench staring at the retablo. It was the center top piece, San Gabriel Archangel, that attracted him. There was no mistaking that angelic face, Fitch thought, and the wings on the figure clearly established the Saint's status as both angel and messenger of God, but he also felt that perhaps this saint, more than the others, respected freedom, the freedom Fitch knew at sea. He looked about him until he found a statue of Christ and a cross, two meaningful images in his New England Congregational background.

During his years as a shipmaster in the Pacific, Fitch paid little attention to the churches. Now that he did so, he found himself comparing the structure of the mission with its thick adobe walls and no windows with the timber churches of New England with their plank floors, austere open wooden ceilings and simple altars. He fought a kind of depression even while admiring the many copper candlesticks, ornamented walls and dark paintings. Finally, he rushed out the door into the sunlight.

Each day, Padre Sanchez or an old neophyte gave Fitch instruction. "Jesus Christ founded the church in order to carry the message of salvation and assure all people of a place in eternity," Fitch was told. Padre Sanchez insisted that Fitch memorize the Apostle's Creed and the Nicene Creed. "These creeds sum up much of Catholic doctrine on the Trinity, creation, sin and salvation, the church, the sacraments and life after death," he was told.

"Among the sacraments," Padre Sanchez said, "we include baptism, confirmation and marriage. In your case, all of these sacred events have been handled in an irregular way."

"You saw our wedding certificate, Padre," Fitch said. "Was it irregular?"

"There are questions."

"What kinds of questions?"

"They will come out in the hearing."

"And when will that be?"

"In due time. Do you know that Jose Palomares is coming here from Monterey to pursue the case against you?"

Fitch heaved a sigh. How far would they go with this, he thought. Palomares was the fiscal who imprisoned him at Monterey. Fitch tried to shake himself free from the terrible feeling that a conspiracy existed to destroy him, to take his mind.

His days gradually fell into the mission pattern. Early each morning, the bells of the church rang to inform neophytes and all others within reach that it was time for mass. During the next half hour, Indians, paisanos and soldiers of the mission escolta gathered in the church and Fitch joined them. On Sundays, a neophyte choir provided an eerie chanting to the accompaniment of drums, primitive split-stick clappers, carved reed flutes and a little two-piece crane-wing bone whistle.

The music sounded strange to his Protestant ear, but the neophytes obviously enjoyed their own singing more than any other part of the service. Their day began with "El Cantico del Alba," the Canticle of Dawn, the traditional morning hymn to Mary. Then came morning prayers and the Doctrina recited in Spanish. They closed the service with the "Alabado," a traditional Spanish hymn of praise, a simple chant-like melody with many stanzas. The Indians still sang as they left the church to go to breakfast and then to work. It was a religious pageant rather than church service, the Indians caught up in the sounds of a hurdy-gurdy and hand bells, actually swaying to the rhythm of their own chant as they walked out the door.

Sometimes, the choir, along with the padre, chanted prayers in a simple psalm tone. The neophytes reacted emotionally in church, not only to the music, but to the ornament on the walls and ceilings of the nave and sanctuary, and they were audible in their wonder when Padre Sanchez appeared in colorful vestments. Fitch soon realized that Padre Sanchez kept an extraordinary collection of vestments in the great chest and closet of the sacristy. Some of them were older than the mission, itself, vestments originally shipped from the missions of Baja.

At one Sunday service, Padre Sanchez appeared in a chasuble of ivory satin with silk and metallic embroidery. It had a matching stole, maniple and chalice veil along with bright ribbons and accessories. At another mass, he wore red cut velvet. Each Sunday, there were stirrings and expressions of wonder among the neophytes when the priest first appeared in his colorful vestments. Sanchez was God, himself, in the eyes of some of these people.

During those first days at the mission, Fitch paced in the gardens. Finally, he joined the Indians within the walls at whatever work they performed.

During the evenings Fitch sat with the soldiers of the escolta and a few older Indian neophytes around the fire in the courtyard where there was talk about the mission's outlying ranchos. At one time, the whole valley of Rio San Gabriel belonged to the mission as well as another stretch of land referred to as the Canada Verde y Los Coyotes. Mission cattle, and, at times, sheep and pigs grazed this land. The mission also ran cattle in the localities called Serritos and Bolsa, both now part of a large rancho granted to Juan Jose Nieto while Spain still ruled.

Fitch began to see the mission priests in ways other than as religious men. Each of the missions was a cooperative community with a priest serving as central authority. Some priests were better administrators than others, but unfortunately, the neophytes enjoyed little more than a livelihood in exchange for their labors. Men like himself traded manufactured goods for the hides and the great stores of tallow produced at the mission ranchos.

Fitch was learning to appreciate the labor that went into preparing the products he and Oscar Virmond so casually purchased from the missions. A shipload of hides represented a mass slaughter of cattle. Neophyte vaqueros and soldiers of the escolta roped and tied the steers one at a time and cut their throats where they lay. A skinner cut away the hide and the slabs of fat. Some beef was salted down for future use, but most of the animal carcasses remained in the fields to rot in the sun, feeding the vultures and coyotes.

Large shallow brick-lined sinks in the ground at the missions served as cleaning and tanning vats for preparing the hides. Water poured into the sinks by gravity flow through primitive tile pipes connected to a settling tank that stored water. This water reached the mission from the river via ditches. After use in the tanning vats, the same water flowed to nearby gardens and orchards. The soaked animal hair was scraped from the hides by persistent and patient neophyte women. When a hide was clean and pliable, it was stretched on a flat area of clean bricks. Properly stretched and dried hard, each hide was finally stacked with others in a storage building to wait sale.

Padre Sanchez called upon Fitch to make a 3-day trip with the mission soldiers to review the mission cattle, sheep, orchards, and gardens of the far-reaching mission ranches. Enrique regretted the further loss of time, but enjoyed the open space.

Upon returning, he shared a meal of pozole with the Indians, then went to his cell room, his home since arrival at the mission. But the soldier, Alfredo, came by the cell and insisted that Fitch share his aguardiente, a poorly distilled brandy made from the pulp of the grapes after the wine had been drained. It tasted badly and burned all of the way down, but Fitch welcomed the friendship and the gesture.

"I have just reported our trip to the Padre," Alfredo told him.

"How is the old man?" Fitch asked.

"In good spirits, but he was much involved with his company. He hurried me away."

"Who is more important than you?" Fitch kidded.

"I think they are all here now."

"Who?"

"The board. The priests who will judge you and the military lawyer from Monterey."

Fitch stared unbelievingly at Alfredo and took a deep breath. "Jose Palomares?" he asked.

"That is the one," Alfredo said.

32. Enrique at San Gabriel

At dawn the next day, Henry Fitch carefully sharpened his long ivory-handled razor and shaved as carefully as possible in the heavy pottery washbowl provided him. He used hot water dipped from a huge iron cauldron heated on the brick fire pit outside the mission kitchen. His light hair had grown as long as Alfredo's, and now he braided it in a que down the back of his neck in much the same fashion as some of the soldiers. Sometime earlier, in order to get a change of shirts, he paid one of the Indian women to hand sew a new one for him, and she out did herself. Following the pattern of shirts worn by some of the Mexican military officers, she made it tight-fitting across his chest with full length sleeves. She did not spare the lace down the front nor on the cuffs.

The call came early, without warning, and Alfredo led him to the sala located in the building reserved as quarters for the padres and important guests. He found Padre Jose Sanchez seated at the head of a long oak table with square legs and huge supporting stretchers. Straight-back mission-style chairs were placed around the table, but with one exception. Father Sanchez' chair was a solid walnut gothic piece. Both the legs and the back of the chair were heavy with Spanish ornamentation. The chair's heavy arms and wooden seat were covered with a thick sheepskin.

Fitch recognized Sergeant Palomares from Monterey, now sitting as prosecutor. Fitch was directed to the opposite end of the long table facing Sanchez. Palomares was seated on his right. Padre Geronimo Boscana, old for his fifty odd years, small and frail, sat beside Palomares. Boscana had an unusually dark complexion for a man from Majorca. His eyebrows hung heavy over his eyes, matching his black beard. They said this priest, more than any other, pursued a scholarly interest in the California Indians. Some years earlier, he had written an ethnological treatise about the Indians living near San Juan Capistrano Mission. He was a close associate of Padre Sanchez, and as Fitch considered what might be the outcome of this session, he expected that Padre Boscana would simply agree with the wishes of Sanchez.

A third priest sat on Fitch's left. He was Francisco Gonzalez de Ibarra from Mission San Fernando. He was a tense man, old and tired. His bald head was bent so that Fitch could not really see his face in the dimly lighted room.

Palomares will feed these men all of the poison they are willing to consume, Fitch thought. He recalled, again, his first meeting with Palomares in the Monterey presidio office where this sergeant vented a strange hatred that had angered Fitch into a kind of despair. Hobbled by leg clamps, Fitch had responded by useless arguments that only made his case worse. Undoubtedly, Palomares was now fully organized against him, and he had probably already presented his case to Padre Sanchez.

Padre Sanchez spoke first. "Captain Fitch, we are aware that you come from a country where ways are different from our own. In this corner of the earth, we have an unusually heavy responsibility. We are trying to establish the Christian manners of Spain and the Catholic church. Simply because we are remote does not mean that our people can deviate from the forms and principles of the Mother Church and the King. No, on the contrary. Because the opportunity exists to deviate, we must be even more diligent and insistent upon proper behavior. Now, Sergeant Jose Palomares is here in the capacity of juez de policia in Monterey to present the charges against you."

"By whose appointment and authority does the sergeant speak?" Fitch asked.

"I speak for our government and our church," Palomares said immediately.

"He represents Governor Echeandia," Padre Sanchez said, correcting the sergeant.

From a leather pouch Sergeant Palomares unrolled several sheets of paper, wiped a hand across his mustache, cleared his throat and began talking. His words came out gravelly and muffled. "The charges of the church and state against Henry Dominic Fitch are as follows: as a foreigner on our shore, arriving by sailing ship, he kidnapped the daughter of one of our citizens."

Fitch broke in. "I didn't kidnap anyone!"

Palomares appeared startled by the disruption. Padre Sanchez held up his hand.

"Let's hear the charges, Captain Fitch. You may speak later."

Fitch ached for an opportunity to grab Palomares and throw him across the room. Palomares saw this anger and noticeably softened his voice. "He transported the girl, Josefa Carrillo, to a foreign country where he kept her for a year."

Fitch stirred again, but remained silent. Sergeant Palomares hurriedly continued. "He has presented irregular and questionable papers purporting to have married Josefa Carrillo, and there is a serious question about whether he received proper instruction for baptism and confirmation in the church."

Palomares took a deep breath before continuing. He looked about the table at each of the priests serving in judgment. "With all of these crimes, I still have not named the most heinous of all. Enrique Fitch, a foreigner with doubtful marriage papers from another country, forced himself upon Josefa Carrillo, and she has given birth to a bastard child."

With that, Fitch hit the table and stood facing Palomares with fists clenched. Palomare's face reddened, and he moved back.

"Padres," Fitch said, voice filled with anger and hurt he could not disguise, "if you have any intention of making a just and Christian decision, I insist that you hear me without these damning and false accusations. Sergeant Jose Palomares knows nothing! He was not there. Yet he speaks of my son as a bastard. If I did not love my wife, and if I did not want what would make her happy, and what is best for my child, I would not have returned to California to tolerate this imprisonment, this harassment and this condemnation."

"Please sit down, Captain Fitch," Padre Sanchez insisted. He addressed Sergeant Palomares. "Your charges have not been clearly objective. I want to consider this matter in an orderly way. You may speak, Enrique Fitch."

With that, Fitch told about first seeing and meeting Josefa. He recalled his discussion with Joaquin Carrillo, her father, and the arrangements made for his baptism at the presidio chapel by Padre Jose Menendez. He told of the ironic arrangements for the wedding, Joaquin Carrillo's brother's refusal to serve as a witness and the secretive movements in the night that brought Josefa into his arms on board the ship.

Padre Sanchez rolled out the marriage certificate that Oscar Virmond had delivered to him months earlier. "I have studied this document, Captain Fitch. It is not only torn and badly blotted in places, but it contains no statement of either the city or the church where the marriage occurred."

"Within two days after our arrival in Callao, we were married by Padre Pedro Orrego at the Sailor's chapel closest to the port," Fitch said quietly.

"Still," Padre Sanchez said, "your certificate leaves out information of the most common sort. It has not even been legalized before escribanos nor is there a visa from the minister of foreign affairs."

Palomares added, "Padre Orrego is not the curate of either Enrique Fitch nor Josefa Carrillo. He could not perform a legal marriage ceremony under these circumstances without a dispensation from the bishop."

The priests all clearly became weary of the tenseness of the proceedings. At last, Padre Sanchez said, "We will continue our discussions tomorrow morning.

33. Josefa in Los Angeles

William Richardson and his wife, Maria Antonia, had lived in the San Gabriel district on the fringes of the Pueblo de Los Angeles for only a short time. Richardson, an American, had become a Mexican citizen years earlier after leaving the English whaling vessel Orion at San Francisco. Soon after, he joined the Catholic Church and married the daughter of Captain Ignacio Martinez, at the time, commandante of the San Francisco presidio.

His growing familiarity with California coastal waters and the San Francisco Bay kept him in regular demand among foreign owners of trading ships, and opportunities now appeared even better in Southern California. Like all of the shipmasters along the coast, he knew of Fitch's troubles, so when Padre Boscana, acting for Padre Sanchez, asked him to provide sanctuary for Josefa and her child, he readily accepted, and his wife, Maria Antonia, lonesome in her new home with a husband who left her for long periods, was happy to have a companion near her own age.

The adobe casa in which they lived was only slightly larger than the Eulalia Perez casa. It consisted of two rooms...one a small bedroom, the other serving all the purposes of daily living except cooking. The cooking area was located under a tule shelter outside. Josefa thought many times about the comfort of her parent's home in San Diego as she moved from place to place. Maria Antonia, stylish but plump, was very spoiled, she soon discovered. In her childhood, she enjoyed the privileges of a commandante's daughter, but since William Richardson sometimes involved himself in business deals in which he was a loser, Maria Antonia's way of life had changed radically, and she was unhappy much of the time.

Richardson was away on a trip almost immediately after Josefa's arrival at their home, and this brought Josefa even closer to her hostess. Together, they washed clothes in the Los Angeles River, cooked and baked, and entertained other women living nearby, including Josefa's cousin, Estefana Carrillo. Estefana persuaded both Josefa and Maria Antonia to attend mass with her and Jose Antonio Carrillo at the plaza church.

Padre Boscana usually conducted the services at Plaza Church, an assistencia of Mission San Gabriel, and Josefa, anxious to hear about Enrique, frequently waited by the sacristy until she could speak to the padre. The old man was kindness itself, Josefa thought.

"Enrique Fitch is doing extremely well," he always assured her, and once he said, "I think we will miss him when he leaves. He works hard himself, and he has taught the neophytes how to perform some tasks." Then, he added, "And I will tell him about your new living arrangements so that he need not worry about you."

"I hope he is not required to suffer because I went to see him," Josefa said. It was not his fault."

"We know," Padre Boscana said. "It was Governor Echeandia's fault. Father Sanchez wanted you to remain in Monterey."

It was not until much later that Josefa heard about Padre Sanchez' anger about her arrival in San Gabriel. He not only ordered her away from Senora Eulalia Perez' home, but he wrote the officer of the presidio in San Diego demanding that the governor be arrested for disregarding an ecclesiastical order. Padre Sanchez did not pursue the matter, but he apparently hoped that the threat from the president of the missions might influence Echeandia's future behavior toward church authority. In Los Angeles, word began to spread that Echeandia might be replaced.

On a Sunday before mass soon after Josefa's first talk with Padre Boscana, he called to her and asked her to remain after the service.

The service in the plainly ornamented plaza church passed without meaning for her, and when it was over, she waited impatiently with Maria Antonia at the edge of the square. When every last parishioner had been greeted, Padre Boscana looked about him, saw them, and walked to where they waited.

"Is everything all right, Padre?" Josefa asked anxiously, but the Padre had already spotted baby Enrique in her arms and gently touched the child's face. Little Enrique readily smiled up at the priest.

"I am only a messenger today," he said. "Enrique Fitch's trial has advanced now to a place where Padre Sanchez wishes you to attend and give testimony. We will begin early tomorrow morning."

The thought of talking to a group of priests around a big table terrified Josefa, but she was determined to speak. It bothered her that Padre Boscana so obviously avoided calling Enrique her husband. She reminded him by saying, "I will do anything to help my husband. I want him free of this terrible injustice."

If Padre Boscana was moved by her words, he gave no sign. "Until tomorrow then," he said. He turned to Antoia Richardson. "I hope you can accompany her."

34. Enrique at San Gabriel Mission

Henry Fitch took his place at the long table, and the priests arrived soon afterward. Jose Palomares came in late, smiling from ear to ear. "I am pleased," Palomares said, "to see that we have someone else present today to give testimony."

Fitch looked sharply at Sergeant Palomares and then at Padre Sanchez. "There is only one person who can corroborate your testimony, Captain Fitch," Padre Sanchez said. Padre Ibarra brought another chair to the table and placed it near Padre Sanchez, well away from Fitch. Then he opened the door, and Josefa entered. She looked more feminine, more beautiful than Fitch had ever seen her. She stood tall and statuesque, wearing a black taffeta dress and silk mantilla with colorful embroidered designs laid over a tortoise-shell comb in her black hair. She stood quietly until Padre Sanchez waved her to the chair closest to him. She looked very frightened, and Fitch wanted to help her. He said, "It is good to see you, My Darling. How is our son?"

She smiled faintly, lovingly at him. "He is fine. He is with Maria Antonia in the garden. Perhaps..." then she stopped.

Padre Jose Sanchez called the meeting to order, and Jose Palomares was permitted to question Josefa. By his wording, Fitch realized, he hoped to trap her, to find differences in her testimony from that which the board had heard from him. At first, Josefa's voice was weak, uncertain, and one of the priests asked her to speak up. Palomares led Josefa step-by-step through the same series of questions he had asked Fitch earlier. As she spoke, her voice strengthened, and Fitch felt sure she was aware what Palomares was trying to do.

"When Enrique Fitch forced you to board the ship..." he started to say, but Josefa never let him finish.

"My husband did not force me! I sought help to get to the beach so that I could board the surfboat that took us to the ship in the bay."

"What did you do during those long days on board ship before you arrived in Callao?" Palomares asked.

"Most of the time I was seasick because I was not accustomed to the movement of the boat," she said honestly.

"Didn't it worry you that you had disobeyed your father?"

"My papa gave permission for my marriage to Enrique. He asked Enrique to take me away quickly.

Padre Sanchez interrupted Palomares questioning to say, "Let us move ahead. I am interested in determining the legitimacy of the marriage ceremony."

Palomares unfolded the marriage certificate that Sanchez had shared with him. "Senorita," he said.

"Senora," she corrected.

Palomares ignored her. "There are discrepancies in this wedding certificate that lead us to doubt its legitimacy."

Fitch found himself leaning sympathetically toward Josefa. He realized now that the arrangements for the papers were between him and the priest, Ortego.

"I have not seen that paper," she said. "It does not matter to me. What matters is that Enrique and I bowed at the altar of the church in the presence of a priest while the ceremony was read. We vowed our love until death. When the priest asked if we accepted each other in marriage, each of us said 'I do.' No paper, nothing said here can change that."

Josefa's sincerity made Palomares' seem pompous, Fitch thought, and that was good. Palomares interrupted her time after time, but she refused to allow any of his insinuations.

"In the eyes of God, we are man and wife," she insisted. "We were married in the great Mother Church."

When at long last, the priests seemed not to react to Sergeant Palomares, he shrugged and said, "It is clear that both of these people believe they have entered into marriage and that their motives are honest. It does not seem to me that this affair necessarily needs to be referred to the bishop, but legally, this marriage is null and void. Henry Fitch should be punished for his crime, and if they are to remain together, they should be legitimately married."

Fitch constrained himself no longer. "Based upon a technicality," he said, "Sergeant Palomares has tried to make our son illegitimate. Punish me if you must, but do not taint the lives of my wife and child."

Padre Sanchez folded his thick hands on the table and studied first Fitch and then Josefa. "I want to talk to Padres Ibarra and Boscana in private now," he said.

35. Francisca in San Diego

Francisca Benecia Carrillo turned sixteen without anyone speaking of it, and she took more and more responsibility at Casa de Carrillo. With their Indian helper, Oupay, she prepared meals, baked bread, selected vegetables from the garden and cleaned the casa.

For a time, Francisca thought life unbearable with the boys demanding so much. Often, through inner tears, Francisca still played and laughed and answered her brothers' silly questions.

She was proud to see Joaquin and Julio become men almost overnight. They tended the animals in the corral, and when it was time, they moved their papa's cattle to new grass and water. When they were only eleven and thirteen years old, she told them they would soon become the two best vaqueros in the pueblo.

When their papa's compadres had brought him back to the casa from the Cahuenga Pass uprising, he did not even recognize Francisca or the boys. He talked only to the spirit of their mother, and always in despair or anger. From the oven in the courtyard where Francisca baked, she recalled the daily ritual of her mama running her hands through her papa's hair and across his shoulders. Sometimes, she would hold a cup of broth to his lips until he had no choice but to take nourishment.

"Oh, Madre de Dios, I am soaked with the blood of our beloved Romualdo," Joaquin said over and over.

"No, no," Francisca whispered, her own voice filled with grief. "You must not think such thoughts."

In broken sentences, hour after hour, her papa talked, repeating himself over and over, his mind locked upon the horror of Romualdo's death. Francisca watched and listened and when alone, cried.

Through the difficult days, Francisca still gathered her brothers and took them to the cover of the ramada in the pueblo plaza where the soldier-teacher from the presidio conducted classes. The sad monotony was not broken by a letter from Don Jose de la Guerra in Santa Barbara

"As you know, Rosa is staying with us where we attend to her every comfort," Guerra wrote," but I cannot underestimate her anguish. She spends the early hours of every day at the mission church in prayer. Her young Indian companion, Adriana, remains constantly at her side, and sometimes persuades her to walk or ride along the beach. Her close friend and cousin, Dona Margarita Dana, also spends much time with her. I'm sure you know that in addition to infante Romualdo, she also carries another child due some months from now. For all of our attention, only her young son succeeds in bringing an occasional smile to her face, and in spite of her grief, she becomes more beautiful each day.

"There is not much more I can say at this time except to extend my family's condolences. You may rely upon me to keep you informed."

Rosa wrote only after Francisca sent three overland dispatches with military riders pleading with her for some word. The letters finally reached Rosa and she wrote a note. Francisca read and re-read it, only gradually realizing her sister's state of mind.

"How can life be so nearly perfect one day, and so tragic the next that we wish our own selves dead. I can only be thankful now that my beloved husband did not die without leaving me with heirs. Our son, Romualdo, is truly our gift from God, and to God, I offer him in lifelong service. Our next son is due in a few months.

During these days, school was a welcome distraction for Francisca. The soldier-teacher seldom held the children for more than an hour at a time without allowing some play. During these times, he taught Francisca by talking to her about history, geography and even California political affairs.

"Who is president of Mexico?" Francisca wanted to know.

"Santa Ana," her teacher said, "but he leaves the governing to others...the vice president and his advisers.

"Have these men caused our problems in California?"

"Perhaps, indirectly," he told her. "They are filled with new ideas. They want to reform the church, the schools and the military all at the same time." Francisca felt so good when the teacher talked to her as an adult.

Francisca could not decide whether or not her teacher always intended her to make a connection between the lessons he taught and what was happening in California, but he often said, "You will soon marry a Californio who makes important public decisions. Understanding what is happening will make you a better wife."

Mariano Vallejo continued writing her papa at least once each month, knowing that Francisca would be the one to read the letter to the family. On behalf of her deranged papa, she also faithfully answered these letters, adding her own message. In early January of the new year, Vallejo wrote an extra long and very serious letter.

Francisca sat down beside her sick papa in the courtyard and opened it. "It is from Mariano," she said. "Would you like to hear it?"

He offered no visible sign of interest, but the boys gathered around.

After a warm salutation, Mariano wrote: "I join with you and your family in sorrow at the loss of Romualdo Pacheco, a truly brave officer and commandante. Like Californios everywhere, I have expressed my deepest sympathy by letter to Dona Rosa, your daughter.

You may already know that your cousin, Pio Pico, was elected to this position. I had the great honor of conducting the ceremonies and installing him to this office.

"My duties as commandante at the Yerba Buena presidio require little effort. Everything was quiet when I left to come to Los Angeles.

"The above serves to provide you the news about what I am doing, but one thought above all remains foremost in my mind. My beloved Francisca has reached her sixteenth birthday, and as we formerly agreed, I now hope to set an early date for our wedding. I write to you now from the Los Angeles pueblo with high hopes. It is only a few days ride from here to San Diego. I humbly request Senorita Francisca's hand in marriage in early March, and anxiously await your word."

When Francisca finished reading, she was breathless. For a time, she almost forgotten about her papa's illness. She glanced at him expectantly, as she had done all of her life, waiting to hear from him. Now, she realized that he had not comprehended or heard a word of the letter. She turned to her brothers. They, too, looked helpless.

Francisca looked up from the courtyard to the light clouds in the blue sky and said dreamily, "When I was very young, Papa took the whole family to Mission San Luis Rey for a week-long fiesta. It was such a happy time for all of us. I don't remember much about the mission, but I will always remember the priest."

Francisca shook her head slightly, recalling the joyous festivities of Rosa's wedding.

For the next several days, she talked to neighbors about plans. They discussed wedding clothes, preparation of food and decorations at Casa de Carrillo. They happily shared ideas . Suddenly, Francisca felt blessed.

But then the appearance of the American ship, Pocahontas, distracted everyone in the pueblo for the next few days. At first, people assumed that Shipmaster John Bradshaw and Supercargo Thomas Shaw anchored at San Diego in planning to trade.

"Pio Pico and Juan Bandini have contracted with these men to move a number of rebels to Mexico," a neighbor told them. Then Francisca saw the real reason—a tall, slim man walking along the trail.

"Padre!" she called. "Padre Peyri, please wait."

Four young Luiseno neophytes rode behind the priest. When Padre Peyri halted his horse, they also stopped.

Francisca and her brothers were returning from school. Now, they stood beside the priest.

Padre Peyri dropped to the ground alongside Francisca and the children. "What is it, little one?" he asked.

"Our family," Francisca started, then searched for another way of saying it. Finally, "We...I have been needing to talk to you about my wedding plans."

"Oh?"

Padre Peyri lifted two of her brothers to his horse's back and trailed the animal while walking beside Francisca across the pueblo and into the old orchard to the Carrillo casa.

Francisca led the padre to a bench at the table in the courtyard where her papa was seated.

"How are you, Joaquin Carrillo?" the priest asked. Her papa gave no answer.

"He lives in a dream," Francisca said. "A terrible dream, and he is ashamed to leave it."

The padre looked at Joaquin Carrillo for a long moment. Then, he insisted upon taking him from the courtyard into the sala.

Francisca and her brothers sat silently at the courtyard table. In the sala, Francisca could hear Padre Peyri praying, and then, after what seemed an eternity, she heard her papa speaking brokenly. Francisca stood and crossed herself. The ghost of her mother appeared in the doorway of the sala, her face glowing.

"Francisca!" she said. "Gather squash from the garden. Mix corn meal for tortillas."

Francisca ran to her mama. "What is happening?" she asked.

"Padre Antonio is healing your papa," she said simply.

"Do you believe that?"

"I do believe," she said.

Francisca suddenly realized that Padre Peyri was now hearing her papa's confession, more words than he had spoken in months.

Later, her papa took his place at the table along with the padre. Francisca served the men in the sala and the boys in the courtyard. After taking food to the neophytres, Francisca ate and prayed in the pantry.

When she heard their papa laugh, she smiled through her tears. When they heard his violin, they knew he would soon be calling her and the boys to sing.

They did not find out until late in the night that Padre Peyri and the Indian neophytes who accompanied him were leaving California. The padre was leaving forever. The neophytes expected to return one day as priests. After much persuasion from the family, the padre agreed to stay at Casa Carrillo for the night.

At dawn, Francisca and Oupay served breakfast. Padre Peyri insisted they ride with him on a surf boat to the Pocahontas. He asked that they stay with him until the ship sailed.

The wind, the spray of salt water and the movement of the rowboat bouncing through the waves was the most exhilarating experience any of them had had in months. Francisca was overcome with delight when she heard her papa laughing.

"We're a little late," her papa called, "but happy birthday, Francisca!"

At last, we dare think about such things again, Francisca thought. She would remember this birthday for the rest of her life.

Shipmaster Bradshaw seemed to be waiting for them. He and his crew helped each of them through an opening in the deck rail as they came up the rope ladder.

"You are in time for tea," Bradshaw said. "I hope you will join me."

"That we will, Captain," her papa said. "But we are here, first and foremost, for another purpose."

"And what is that?" the captain asked.

"My daughter," her papa said, looking proudly at Francisca, "will soon be married. Do you have fabrics in stock for a wedding gown?"

Francisca could feel herself twinkling all over. She leaned her head against her papa's arm.

Padre Peyri smiled as he watched her. "I am really sorry that I will not have the pleasure of conducting the ceremony for your wedding," he said.

Later, while her papa negotiated with the captain, Francisca was distracted by the look of deep distress on Padre Peyrí's face. She watched him at the rail looking toward the pueblo.

She went to his side, and on impulse, she took his arm. The strong invincible Padre Peyri was crying. No wonder, Francisca thought. He was leaving behind the mission he established 34 years earlier. Thousands of Indians had been baptized by him since that first day when Padres Fermin Lasuen, Norberto Santiago and he had dedicated the ground and baptized an Indian child under the tule roof of a temporary open shelter.

At this moment, several successful ranchos of the mission remained under the care of Indians he trained. While some missions began to fail, San Luis Rey reached new heights under his persistent administration. Would the world ever know what this man had done, young Francisca wondered, still remembering that day years before when he had played with the children? In her eyes, he was already a saint.

36. Francisca at San Diego

Early in 1843 the Brig Maria Ester cast anchor, and Josefa and Enrique mysteriously reappeared in the pueblo. None of the family knew that Enrique was free. Josefa sent word by one of the Estudillo children saying that they had arrived during the night aboard the Brig Maria Ester and gone directly to the home of Jose Antonio Estudillo. Francisca ran immediately across the pueblo plaza to the Estudillo casa. She was breathless by the time she reached the gate.

Estudillo was the son of a California military pioneer. Now, this young man, his wife, and his mother, Maria Victoria, and her younger children lived together. He was a friend of Enrique Fitch as well as the Carrillo family. During the last two years he had served as local revenue collector and treasurer.

When Francisca arrived, it was the children of the family who opened the gate leading into the courtyard around which the adobe structure was built. Like other homes built by the more successful Californios, it was constructed in a U-shape around a large enclosed courtyard with rooms opening from outdoors upon a wide portico. Dolores Bandini, Jose Antonio's sister and the wife of Juan Bandini, heard the commotion of the children at the entrance and hurried to see Francisca.

Francisca's anxiety was too apparent for the usual amenities. Dolores led her along the portico past the sala and the children's rooms to the end of the bedroom wing where Josefa sat in a small American rocker holding her child.

"Francisca!" she said, jumping quickly to her feet and placing the baby in a small cradle at the foot of the bed.

"At last!" Francisca said, hugging her eldest sister. "Have they treated you badly, Josefa? Are you all right? Why didn't you come home, Josefa? "Why are you at the Estudillos?"

"The Estudillos are Enrique's friends." Josefa said "With papa so angry…"

"Things have changed. You will see. You will come home." Francisca said with determination.

"Please," Josefa said softly. "Try to understand. The last several months have been very hard for Enrique. He is like a wounded soldier. He must heal. There is time later for all of us to be together."

Then Enrique appeared from nowhere. He was even taller than Francisca remembered him. He was not like the men of Spain or Mexico. He did not bow from the waist. Instead, he swooped Francisca into his arms and kissed her cheek.

Jose Antonio appeared from the portico. "It is time for lunch." he said. "It is time to celebrate."

Before they could leave the small bedroom, Donna Victoria Estudillo, Senora Grande of the Pueblo, appeared, followed by numerous children and grandchildren. An Indian servant held a tray, glasses and a decanter of wine. The small room was so filled with people that they could scarcely raise their glasses in the toast which Jose Antonio proposed. "To our new citizens in the pueblo, Senor and Senora Enrique Fitch. Welcome!"

"Is it true?" Francisca asked Josefa, thrilled by the thought of having her sister home again.

"Si. Enrique plans to open a store in the pueblo." Francisca could see that Josefa was overjoyed.

Slowly, with everyone talking at once, all of them moved along the open portico toward the dining sala.

Francisca saw and wondered why Jose Antonio left the casa after his toast. He returned soon and her brothers were with him. Again, he turned and hurried out the gate, returning minutes later. This time, he strolled into the sala with someone else. Francisca gasped. Josefa broke into tears. "Papa," she gasped.

Francisca watched their papa draw Josefa into his arms. "My child," he whispered. "My child…"

In that frenzied moment, Francisca glanced across the room to where Enrique stood. Then, she turned again to their papa. With his arm still around Josefa, her papa walked directly toward the tall fair-haired man. Francisca knew it was not in her papa to apologize, but with every eye upon him, he did his best. "Thank you for bringing my daughter home. Please come be with your family."

Fitch extended his large hand, and Joaquin took it. When they separated, Josefa took Enrique's arm.

"Are you really free?" one of the children asked Enrique.

"We are free," Enrique said. He and Josefa told their story in bits and pieces all through the rest of the day.

Padre Jose Sanchez had rendered his decision: this case was Christi nomine invocato. Jose Palomares, acting fiscal, had not substantiated his accusations against Henry Fitch, the priest judged. Fitch's marriage to Josefa at Callao, though not legitimate in the eyes of The Church, was still not null. Their child was a child of their marriage. Padre Sanchez declared that Enrique should go free and that Josefa should be given up to him. However, before all that happened, the Padre required that they be "velados" the next Sunday, receiving the sacraments that should have preceded their marriage ceremony.

There was a penalty which Henry Fitch readily accepted. "Considering the great scandal which Don Enrique has caused in this province," the Padre proclaimed, "I shall require penance and reparation with a bell of at least fifty pounds in weight to be given to the new parish church in the Pueblo La Reina de Los Angeles.

37. Enrique in San Diego

On the plaza, in the cantinas and along the narrow streets of the pueblo, people gossiped about a sudden change in government. Governor Jose Echeandia had left the area without a word. In a sense, Enrique felt relieved. This distraction helped shift the gossip about Josefa and him.

However he found it frustrating trying to start a business. He walked the plaza studying buildings he might buy or share as a general trading store. He also rode along the beach searching for possible space for a hidehouse. It was here that he experienced some success.

Fitch was able to rent an old hide storage place. He was a frugal man. Even while confined to San Gabriel Mission, he hung onto money he had saved with this day in mind. By paying for hides in pesos rather than trading merchandise, he found he could make better deals. He hoped to regularly trade enough hides and tallow not only to make a living, but to accumulate an inventory of manufactured goods for a general store. He decided he must be patient, and keep his eyes open for opportunities.

But wherever he went in the pueblo, people wanted to talk about Pio Pico, Josefa's cousin, the man who replaced Governor Echeandia, and Enrique simply did not give a damn. He had had enough involvement in the intrigue of Mexican politics and the church to last a lifetime. Echeandia's sudden disappearance eliminated the terrible taint of a man who had caused them so much trouble.

While riding across the ranchos around San Gabriel Mission, Fitch had shared the fever of wanting a vast tract of California land, of building a large home and of running cattle and sheep. It was not an unusual dream. Almost every citizen in the territory wanted the same thing,

A great many soldiers and a few foreigners who ask for Mexican citizenship already occupied lands in an informal way, waiting for the day when they could petition for a grant to the land they occupied. Fitch talked to Joaquin about the pueblo, his business plans and his dreams of owning land.

Finally, one evening Joaquin cautiously said, "Have you found property for your home and store?"

"No," Fitch said. "I will probably have to be satisfied with only warehouse space for a time, and we will try to rent a casa."

Joaquin Carrillo shifted on the bench where he sat, seemingly embarrassed. Finally, he said, "There is room on my land for another casa. I would like to see you have your own place."

Fitch thought for a minute, then smiled. "We expect to present you with another grandchild before the year ends, so we must make plans."

"Then, please, I can help you build your casa."

During the days that followed, Fitch and Joaquin looked at the land near the Carrillo home and compared ideas. "I think," Fitch said, "I would like a home similar to my family home in New England."

"What is that like?" Joaquin asked, filled with curiosity.

"A two-story wood frame house with a wide porch around three sides of it."

"Where would you get the lumber?" asked Joaquin.

"Maybe I can bring it in by ship from northern California. There are stands of timber there like none other in the world."

"Si," Joaquin replied, laughing. That will give the pueblo something to talk about."

Then Fitch burst out laughing, and Joaquin looked puzzled. "I'll bet there isn't a sawmill anywhere in the California territory. I may have to get into that business too!"

38. Francisca

Although their correspondence was continuous, months had passed since Francisca last saw Mariano.

Since Josefa received so much help from Vallejo in Monterey, she actually knew him better than Francisca, and Francisca found pleasure in talking to her sister about her future husband.

"Is he really as handsome as I remember him?" she once asked.

"Ah, si," Josefa answered. "And so galante and noble in bearing. He is a true Californio, born in Monterey."

"And of true Spanish blood?"

"Only on his papa's side. Like ours, his mama is Mexican."

"In his letters, he wrote much about his campaigns against the Indians."

"Si," he has done much as an officer in the military," Josefa said. Then, she added, "He is a brave soldier."

Francisca thought about this for a moment and said, "Is he as brave as our papa? Or, as brave as Romualdo? I am very proud of them."

At last, the wedding date was set for March 5, 1843 Mariano Vallejo did not arrive in the pueblo alone. He was accompanied by the other members of the California diputacion. Nor did he come directly to Casa Carrillo. Word reached the family that he stopped at the Jamul Rancho to see their cousin,Governor Pio Pico.

It was Governor Pio Pico's continued insistence that the diputacion meet with him in San Diego that now brought all of them to the pueblo. Joaquin Carrillo received a written message from Vallejo upon his arrival in the pueblo. Josefa read it to him while Francisca listened.

"At last," he wrote, "I am in San Diego, and in five days I look forward to making Francisca my wife. It is with great anticipation that I also hope to visit with her each day before our wedding. Of course, you know that my duties as a member of the diputacion will use most of my day. Therefore, I plead with you to allow her to meet with me in the late afternoon at Senor Bandini's casa. The time is short, and I look forward to getting better acquainted with her."

Their papa looked at Josefa and frowned. "He wants Francisca to meet him at Bandini's casa?"

"They would not be alone," Josefa said.

"But...Bandini's casa? Bandini's casa?"

Francisca saw that her Papa was insulted, and she said, "Let us send him a message, Papa. We will write that he may meet me here in the sala at Casa Carrillo."

"His time is important," Josefa said. "The decisions of the diputacion affect all of California."

"It is only a short walk across the plaza from Bandini's casa," Francisca said. "If he is truly galante, as they say, he will not expect me to meet him at someone else's casa."

Josefa smiled. "Francisca is right, Papa."

Within the hour, Francisca and Josefa prepared a message for their Papa's approval. In it, they invited Mariano Vallejo to meet with the family for chocolate in the late afternoon of that very same day.

They did not receive a return message. Both her Papa and Josefa worried.

"Perhaps we have insulted him," her papa said.

"Please," Francisca said. "Dress for his arrival. He must know that the Carrillo family is proud."

Mariano Vallejo did appear in the late afternoon, and he was more handsome that Francisca remembered. Dark thick sideburns swept low on his brown cheeks. Heavy brows emphasized his dark eyes. In greeting, he grasped his future father-in-law warmly with both hands and then bowed straight from the waist to each of the women...Josefa, and finally, Francisca. Smiling broadly, he did not turn from Francisca until she raised her head to meet his eyes. "You have grown into an even more beautiful Senorita," he said.

Then, he glanced about the courtyard. "I have never seen so many flowers blooming in one place at this time of year."

Their papa invited him to walk along the portico and through the courtyard, calling his attention to Francisca's carefully groomed flower garden. Josefa poured chocolate from a blue willow designed pitcher into matching cups. The set was a recent gift brought to California from England by way of Valparaiso through Enrique Fitches new store. He had traded hides for this English import. In the sala, Mariano talked proudly, actually boastfully, about his participation in the diputacion.

"I think," he said, "that we must separate military and civil matters in California. We place too much dependence upon a governor's views. We need a governor and a diputacion with a commandante-general serving under both of them."

Francisca thought about something her teacher had said. She repeated it now. "Perhaps our governor should be a man who has lived in California. A true Californio who knows California."

Vallejo looked at his future wife in surprise. "I would like to hope so," he said.

One by one, family members left the sala until Francisca was alone with Mariano. For awhile, Mariano said nothing, only studying Francisca sitting across from him. Normally, her black hair hung in a braided pigtail down the center of her back. Tonight, it flowed freely. There was a collection of brightly colored beads around her sun-darkened neck.

"I think I have chosen well," he said.

Francisca rolled her eyes flirtatiously. "My papa has chosen well for me too," she said. They laughed together.

After a time, he said, "We have been honored in a very special way."

Francisca looked at Mariano expectantly.

"Juan Bandini wants us to come to his home for the festivities after the wedding," Vallejo said.

"Perhaps the second night," Francisca said forthrightly.

"But, you see…" Vallejo started.

"My family has known Juan Bandini since the first day he arrived in California," she said. "He will understand that plans have already been made for the fandango here at Casa Carrillo."

Vallejo appeared embarrassed when Francisca spoke so directly to him. He said, "Are you remembering that Juan Bandini is the substitute representative to the Mexican Congress?"

"Are you remembering that my cousin, Carlos Carrillo, is now in Mexico representing California in the Congress? Are you remembering that my papa is giving my hand in marriage, and he has made plans?"

Commandante Vallejo slumped back on the sofa. "Perhaps you had better tell me," he said, somewhat apologetically.

Francisca outlined the plans for the wedding and the celebration while he listened quietly.

"What shall I tell Bandini?" he asked.

"It would be a great honor if he would consent to a baile, a formal dance, at Casa Bandini on the second night of our celebration. We would invite the members of the diputacion, and ask Governor Pio Pico to make a speech. Perhaps Senor Bandini would lead us in a waltz. It is said that he introduced the waltz to Californians."

"I have the feeling," Mariano said, "that our marriage may influence the entire government of California!"

"Supper should be ready now," she said, changing the subject.

"I came only for chocolate. The diputacion will be meeting soon at Bandini's."

Then Francisca reached out and took Mariano's big hand.

"I will send my brother to tell Bandini that you are staying for dinner."

Vallejo stood to his full height, placing both of his large hands upon her cheeks. "You may plan the wedding," he said softly. "I will run the government. We will have a good marriage, Francisca. Goodnight."

39. Josefa in San Diego

When Enrique was offered an opportunity to serve as shipmaster for a California coastal trip by his old employer, Virmond, he took it. As part of the deal, he could find and load lumber for use in building a house.

Josefa found her bed cold and uninviting without Enrique beside her. In her wakefulness, she also found herself worrying about Francisca's wedding day. With her children, she began walking to the other side of the pueblo and along the trail until the bay came into view. Fate had continuously separated her from Enrique during times when she needed him most. Would it always be this way? When she had been at sea with him, she did not worry, but here with her family, waiting his return, she imagined so many disastrous things. He had been gone for months. He was overdue.

Finally, one early morning, far out on the horizon, she thought she could make out the shape of sails. They seemed to appear and disappear again and again, but they did not come closer. She studied the distant white spots for nearly an hour. When there was no change, she finally gave up and returned to the casa, trying to help with the preparation of food for the wedding festivities, but she could not do it. What she had seen bothered her.

She spoke to her papa about it, and they mounted horses, riding along the river toward Point Loma. For awhile, they saw nothing. They left the trail, urging their horses through high grass, ducking under low-limbed scrub oaks until they reached a clearing on the high bank overlooking the beach, the bay and beyond. Josefa fixed her eyes upon the horizon and studied its length minutely.

"There, Papa, see? It is still in the same place."

Suddenly, she realized that along this rise there was normally a breeze at anytime of year, but the air was dead still now. "It is a vessel," she said. "It is caught in a lull."

At last, in the late afternoon, a breeze came up, and they saw a barque with three square sails moving closer. It caught the wind and its sails finally billowed full.

"He made it…" Josefa said prayerfully. "It is the Leonor."

Joaquin rode back to the casa to tell the family. Josefa waited. Hours passed. Then she saw her whole family eagerly riding toward the beach. Her papa, her brothers, Francisca and even Mariano Vallejo. Others in the pueblo who saw them leave knew a ship was arriving and mounted horses to follow along the trail.

Josefa saw a surfboat go over the side of the Leonor and watched human figures climb down the ropes to it. Then she saw the surfboat rocking along slowly toward shore in the rising and falling waves.

She left the bluff and followed a trail to the beach, but it was still an exhaustingly long wait. In a very short time, the whole pueblo seemed to arrive…talking excitedly. Josefa moved far back on a slight rise where she could better watch the movement of the surfboat.

At last, the crew of the surfboat hurled paddles over the side to wash ashore. Almost at the same time, they jumped into the water, pushing the boat with its passengers until it touched the sand.

Then, for a moment, Josefa stiffened when she saw her husband lift a female passenger from the boat. Some of the men of the pueblo surged into the water to help pull the boat farther ashore. Josefa dropped the reins of her horse, hurrying to join the others.

She saw Enrique gently place the woman he carried on the dry sand, and then the crowd surrounding them. She heard Francisca calling to her. She saw that Francisca now held the woman in her arms. There was a breathless reaction from the crowd. Then, still not seeing or recognizing, only feeling, Josefa gasped.

"Gracias, Dios!" she exclaimed, crossing herself. She ran across the beach, breaking her way through the happy crowd, reaching out breathlessly. Enrique had brought Rosa home.

40. Francisca

The entire family at Casa Carrillo was up before dawn on Francisca's wedding day. So were the people of San Diego and the soldiers living in the barracks on presidio hill above the pueblo.

There had been a light rain during the night, and now a breeze spread the scent of wet earth and scattered leaves on the pueblo plaza. The breeze also carried the voices of people working in and around their casas: women tending the fires of outdoor ovens, men saddling family horses and children gleefully dressing in their most colorful clothes. It was a day for celebration.

Breezes blended the flavors of breakfasts in preparation...carne asada, meat barbecued on a spit, eggs, frijoles and tortillas along with the smoke of oak charcoal. There were also the scents that tantalized the children...corn and wheat pastries sprinkled with sugar and filled with dried fruits from the harvest of summer. Every woman in the pueblo prepared extra food to take to Casa Carrillo for the wedding festivities. It was one of those times when everyone became a child again.

All except Francisca. When Francisca did not see her papa in the courtyard, she peeked into his bedroom. There he sat on the side of the bed wearing a sombrero, but without pants or shoes. He was earnestly, quietly playing his violin.

"Papa," she exclaimed. "When will you saddle our horses?"

"Enrique is doing it," he said, without interrupting the long melodic sweep of his bow.

Francisca stood quietly for a moment and listened to her papa's music. It was a soft sweet sound—that only needed the rhythmic addition of castanets. "It is Indian," she said.

Joaquin's eyes closed. "Perhaps Mexican-Indian, something from Sonora. I have never heard it nor played it."

"Does it have a name?"

"Si," her papa said. "I have named it."

He stood and slowly walked to his daughter, playing all the while. "I call it 'Francisca's Song'."

She smiled, shrugged and left him playing, but for a moment, her papa's music swelled, and she imagined hearing a hundred violins as she swayed along the tiled portico. She would hear this melody over and over in her mind for the rest of her life. She looked out the back gate of the courtyard to the corral. Enrique and her younger brothers had horses lined up and tied to the corral posts, each getting a final brushing before cinching saddles. Mariano Vallejo's horse was ornamented with special saddle, stirrups and equipment he had brought from Monterey.

In the pantry, she found her mama, Josefa and two women of the pueblo preparing vegetables.

"When will you dress?" Francisca asked them.

"Do not worry, Francisca," Josefa said. "We will be ready when it is time."

The front gate opened, and Rosa entered the courtyard. "Where have you been?" Francisca asked.

Rosa smiled only faintly through the persistent gloom that enveloped her.

"I had to show little Romualdo the river." she said.

"Today?" Francisca asked incredulously.

"It is part of coming home," she said ever so softly. Young Romualdo joined his cousins in a corner of the courtyard.

Even in her black mourning dress, face masked against grief, Rosa looked beautiful, Francisca thought. "It means so much to have you here today," she said.

"I need all of you," Rosa said.

"I hope you are staying?"

"No. My home is in Santa Barbara now. I want my children to grow up there."

Rosa was several months into her pregnancy, and her child, Romualdo, was eighteen months old. She doted over Romualdo. She never failed to remind herself that the child was conceived in a guest room of Mission San Luis Rey, and in some way, all of the mysteries of the church were part of him, his life, his destiny. The family had talked together continuously since her arrival, but this was the first time she revealed her plans about returning to Santa Barbara.

Rosa took Francisca's arm. "How will you wear your hair today?" she asked.

"Just the way you wore it for your wedding."

"Let's get the combs. I'd like to fix it."

By midmorning, riders filled the trail between the pueblo and Mission San Diego de Alcala...men, women and children riding mules and horses. Mariano Vallejo and her papa rode at the head of the grand pageant while Francisca followed closely behind. Josefa and Rosa, along with their younger brothers, came next. Francisca looked back down the trail behind her. As far as she could see, people in festive dress followed. Beyond her family, she saw Juan Bandini and his large family and all the members of the Juan Estudillo family. Her cousins, the Picos, with all of their children, and a group of Indians attached to the pueblo as servants. As she studied the trail and the hundreds of people on it today, Along the way, Francisca kept catching her breath in disbelief. All of this was happening for her and Mariano.

Some people already sang, and she could hear guitars playing far in back of her. She reined her horse once when a quail scurried across their path and then gasped when several deer on the opposite bank of the river darted from their watering place. A mocking bird scolded hysterically at the endless threat of riders near her nesting place. The recent rains brought green grass, lighting the brown hills.

"This is your day, Francisca. Perhaps the best day in your life," Rosa told her. "Try not to worry. Everyone wants this day to be perfect for you."

41. Rosa and the Family

Rosa did not hurt inside just now. Rather, she felt numb. Only occasionally something occurred as they rode toward the mission that nudged her into awareness. There was the ever-present river below the trail where she and her sisters had played as children; where she and Romualdo had talked alone for the first time before they were married; where they dared lay out their lives together, speaking of his ambitions, dreaming of a rancho and a fine casa on a hill. How innocently they had planned. They had expected to live forever.

Now, Guerra took her into his family, taking responsibility for her care. For a time, she did not believe it happened. For two days and two nights she sat up in her bedroom waiting, expecting Romualdo to return. Sometimes she could feel him near her, comforting her, telling her that someone had made a mistake. He was with her during those nights and they talked again about their dreams for a lifetime together. But in the daytime, Guerra quietly reminded her that her very own papa had witnessed Romualdo's death. As was the custom in the military, he was buried as soon after rites as possible. Rosa could only grieve for his spirit and remain in a half-life state.

The Carrillo women of Santa Barbara clustered around her, cried with her, comforted her day after day. Their loving and caring somehow sustained her. Then Enrique Fitch appeared in the pueblo, asking her to come to Francisca's wedding. His presence partially awakened her to the reality of her family in San Diego.

In her cabin aboard Fitch's ship, she found a transition place away from other influences. She had never been without a plan, and it made her miserable to realize that her future was now so shattered. Only young Romualdo, playing and happily unaware, gave Rosa her sense of being. One evening while still aboard the vessel, she held him closely and whispered, "Through you, your Papa lives. His dreams become your destiny."

42. Josefa

Josefa turned and smiled at Enrique riding behind her with her brothers. How different this day was from their wedding day. For their love, she and Enrique had suffered all of the pain and isolation that governments and religious men could heap upon them. She recalled again her perilous ride to the beach intent upon holding the love she found with Enrique. It was followed by long weeks of seasickness on board the brig while enroute to Callao and Valparaiso and then their return to California to face the overpowering grips of condemnation and prison. It was still haunting.

She and Enrique had been the subject of rumors the length of California. She wondered whether, when the bells rang for a wedding at the church in the pueblo of Los Angeles, people thought of them and recalled that Enrique had purchased their bell as penance for his love of her.

Enrique was the most courageous man Josefa had ever known. "He can do anything," she often told her family and anyone else who would listen.

He was trustworthy and honest, she knew. When she had seen him lift Rosa from the surfboat, she had not known it was her sister. In that one moment, she had felt a terrible rush of blood. The thought of her husband touching another woman was more than she could bear. She regretted the feeling, but she knew she would kill before she would lose Enrique. She thought about the years ahead of them. In Enrique's warehouse, there was now a large load of lumber that had been floated ashore from the Maria Ester and stacked along the wall of Casa de Carrillo. One day soon, Enrique would build an American-style two-story casa for them. It would be just in time, she thought, feeling the new child inside her.

Enrique was the tallest man in the pueblo, and today, wearing a sombrero, he appeared a giant. Most men admired Enrique for both his size and his abilities. She knew it would not be long before he would be a very important person among them.

She tried not to think about Rosa's great loss today. The thought of her sister living unmarried for the rest of her life was crushing. She and Rosa and Francisca had looked forward to their marriages all of their lives. Rosa's loss was a loss for the entire family.

43. Enrique

Henry Fitch glanced across the canyon to a stretch of land where cattle grazed. Most of them belonged to Joaquin Carrillo. Then he looked over the heads of the young Carrillo children and the women riding in front of him. Today, for the first time in a long time, he saw Joaquin sitting high in his saddle. These people are now my family, Fitch thought. It surprised him how well he had finally adapted to this distant land...learning a new language, participating in another way of life, taking a new citizenship and accepting a new religion. He now realized the strength of commitment. He liked the way these people cared for their own. No person grew so old that he or she lost their place. In every family he saw an unbreakable bond.

He had talked to Mariano Vallejo for a short time during one of the young officer's visits at Casa Carrillo. Vallejo left Fitch with a fresh sense of his own destiny.

"When we explored to the north of San Francisco," Vallejo said, "I saw unbelievably fertile tracts of land for future ranchos. Keep this in mind. One day I will send you more information."

"Is it mission land?"

"Yes and no, but it does not matter. Things are changing in California! New laws will erase old laws."

44. Mariano

From time to time, Mariano caught Francisca's eye. She had a way of dipping her head and raising her sparkling dark eyes in the most insinuating way. Her glances, her smiles tugged at him. He hoped that her flirting was only for him. She came from a protective family, and she was an innocent child, of these things, he was certain. He wanted to take care of her. He wanted to commit to her.

He had not yet seen her as he saw her today. Her dark long hair was parted in the center and rolled in a tight bun at the back of her head with two large beaded combs holding it in place. Tight across each side of her head, the hair looped across her ears, accenting her deep ruby red earrings. With pride, he visualized her as hostess in his casa welcoming the members of the diputacion, the military officers of California, and yes, of course, the governor of California. He hoped, too, that they would make many babies together. She was irresistible.

He listened to Joaquin Carrillo boast about his herds of cattle and about his experiences as a soldier. Carrillo had the tough unflinching bearing of a good sergeant. Vallejo liked that.

"Too bad you have retired, Don Joaquin. I have never had a sergeant with your experience," he told the older man.

"I am available for occasional service," Joaquin said, "when it is not rodeo or mantanza time."

"I shall keep that in mind," Mariano answered.

As they neared the mission, a group of Indian boys appeared on the trail wearing robes and singing. Mariano stepped down He helped Francisca from her horse and turned the reins to the Carrillo boys. Joaquin Carrillo helped Ramona from her horse.

Both Mariano and Joaquin's horses were especially saddled for this occasion. Mariano's saddle was silver-mounted, its edges embroidered in both silver and gold. The bridle, too, was heavily decorated in silver. The reins were woven of select horse mane. At regular intervals in the rein, there was a link of silver connecting its parts.

In back of the Vallejo saddle, there was a piece of soft leather in the shape of a half moon, an anquera. It covered the hindquarters of the horse. It, too, was elaborately embossed and lined with sheepskin, the wool side next to the horse. The women sat on the saddles, the men on the anqueras.

The spurs Mariano wore today were special. They were inlaid with gold designs and the straps of the spurs were decorated with silver and gold thread.

Both Mariano and Joaquin wore tight fitting vests, sombreros, and handmade embroidered shirts decorated in lace down the front. Mariano's vest was white, made especially for the occasion.

Now, they followed the choir of Indian boys through the Indian rancheria that led in the direction of the church. The boys sang a plain chant in unison while one of them played a handmade five-stop bamboo flute.

All of the Indians of the rancheria, young and old, formed two lines, making a path through which the wedding procession passed. Padre Fernando Martin, wearing rich white satin vestments, stood at the side door of the church. He beckoned to Joaquin Carrillo and gave him instructions. Joaquin, Rosa and Josefa accompanied Francisca across the empty nave into the courtyard by way of a side door on the opposite side. Mariano remained behind.

45. Rosa

In a small room off the courtyard, Rosa carefully repaired the damage done to Francisca's hair during the ride from the pueblo. Josefa removed the rebozo and blanket that had protected her sister's dress from trail dust.

Rosa opened a small package and unfurled something that none of them had seen for a long time. "Will you wear it for the ceremony?" she asked.

Francisca reached out, smiling her pleasure. Rosa held the same delicate hand-embroidered white silk mantilla she had worn for her own wedding. Now, each of the women touched it...silk threads of crimson and yellow embroidered into a rich design of roses. The roses appeared embedded in green leaves.

"Do you remember it?" Rosa asked.

"I could never forget it," Francisca said. "I was standing on the portico when Captain John Wilson gave it to you."

"As a wedding gift," Rosa reminded her.

"Si," Francisca said. "As a wedding gift."

After each of the women had kissed Francisca, they entered the church, leaving their papa to escort her to the altar.

Having visited nearly all of the mission churches between San Diego and Santa Barbara, Rosa judged the interior of San Diego de Alcala the least adorned. Its walls were pale. Whatever designs might have once decorated the church had long since faded into only tinted hues. In every sense, it was simple.

Most of the crowd had been too far back along the trail to see Francisca and Mariano while riding. In the silence of the church, Rosa could hear the people of the pueblo stir with a kind of breathlessness as Francisca, followed by her papa, stepped in from the mission courtyard to take their place alongside Mariano. In that moment, she embodied all of the loving radiance of a virgin. Before the ceremony began, Padre Martin lifted his head, and the Indian boy's choir sang again, this time from the loft of the church at the very back of the nave.

They had learned to sing meaningful words in their own Diegan language because the priest had taught them in this way. As they imitated and learned from the priests, they also sang in Spanish. Church policy to the contrary, Padre Martin used secular language in his ceremonies. The priests found it necessary to present their messages in terms that fit the daily life and experience of their neophytes.

Now, they sang the "Alabado," a melody of praise familiar to everybody in attendance.

Rosa paid little heed to the words of the ceremony that followed. She saw Francisca and Mariano marking this new beginning in their lives, swearing to love and protect one another, to be faithful. With the two of them on their knees, she heard the soft murmur of their prayers together before Padre Martin. Then, Mariano placed a ring upon Francisca's finger, and finally, Rosa heard the blessings of the priest upon them and their future children.

At the end, Francisca and Mariano turned and faced those attending. They were now man and wife. The bells in the high-walled companaria in the mission courtyard began to ring, carrying the message of their union across the hills and canyons for a league in every direction. Vallejo looked very proud escorting Francisca down the aisle, pausing frequently to receive good wishes.

Their papa followed closely behind, and Josefa walked with Enrique. For the first time since Romualdo's death, Rosa found herself walking alone in public. Surrounded by people she had known all of her life, she felt almost unbearable loneliness.

Outside, a group of Indian musicians waited to join the celebration. It was a different music now. With a mix of guitars, violins, and carved bone flutes, they provided their version of Aragonese jotas, minuets and other European music.

The ceremony was not complete until Mariano and Joaquin's horses were brought to the front of the church for them. Francisca joined Mariano on his horse. As they rode slowly away, the musicians followed for a short distance and the crowd cheered. With the ceremonies ended, children climbed on their horses to race toward the pueblo. So did many of the men.

Padre Martin joined Rosa as she rode along the river canyon. Rosa felt content riding behind the long procession with the padre. This priest had arrived at the mission just the year before she was born. He had baptized her, presided at her confirmation and conducted her marriage ceremony. He reminded her of these events in her life while they rode. He had always been a fast-moving robust man who somehow seemed out of place in robes.

"Padre Martin would have made a good soldier," her papa once said.

Today, however, his face seemed sallow and gray. He spoke with spirit, but his movements did not reflect it. He appeared bent and dropped his head as they rode.

"Are you feeling well?" Rosa asked.

"Si," he answered. "I am merely growing old." Later, he said, "I want you to know that many of the California padres are deeply aware of the great sacrifice your husband made on behalf of the missions."

"Was it in vain, Padre?" she asked.

"Nothing done in the service of God is in vain, Child, but sometimes it is hard to read His purpose. We brought the message of God to this far place. It will be here long after our missions crumble. That is our consolation. I must say, though, that I was shaken when Padre Antonio Peyri left California. Undoubtedly, others will follow. Many feel they can do nothing more."

"Will you go?" Rosa asked.

"I have nowhere to go. Mission San Diego is my home. I want to die here." Then, he glanced at Rosa, looking very serious, and said, "When you reach the casa, you should change to fiesta clothes."

Rosa had almost forgotten that she still wore mourning clothes. They did seem so out of place today. "You are right, Padre. There is no more time for weeping."

In the distance they heard muskets firing a salute. The sound came from the presidio.

The courtyard gates of Casa de Carrillo were open wide when they arrived, and the music had started. People filled the courtyard, spilling out into the orchard and the pueblo plaza.

At every turn, men with guitars and violins combined to make music. There were long lines of people for food and there was plenty for all. Every household shared its most prized aguardiente and wine. Mariano and Francisca happily greeted guests, receiving congratulations and talking. How easily they do it, Rosa thought. As soon as she could break through the crowd, she hurried to her room and changed into more festive clothes. Julio's wife had remained behind today, caring for both her own children and the youngest of the Carrillo family babies. Young Romualdo could walk now, but Rosa carried him through the crowd to the pantry, fed him, and kept him close to her while talking to visitors.

When the dancing started, men swarmed around her. One of the older women took young Romualdo, insisting that Rosa enjoy herself.

170

Rosa suddenly felt her heart beat with the excitement of the music and the many couples dancing in the courtyard. There were so many varieties of contra danza, and the jota. Then there were new ones. Enrique introduced a happy movement he called a polka, and as he whistled the tune, he swung his big frame about the courtyard with Josefa. Joaquin soon found the melody on his violin, and other musicians picked up the rhythm. Other couples followed Enrique as he sang out in his big voice, "Put your little foot, put your little foot, put your little foot right there…"

When Enrique Fitch had finished, Juan Bandini could not resist introducing the dance for which he was so well known, the waltz. With his charming wife, Dolores Estudillo de Bandini, he tempted others to follow his lead. Bandini was a slim, small-boned man who looked especially suave when dancing. His rhythm was perfect. Soon, the courtyard was filled with waltzing Californios. Rosa enjoyed the gay freedom of the new dances. When one of the men asked her to waltz, he whirled her in wide circles until all stepped back to watch them. In those moments, she awakened to a new reality.

With nightfall, Rosa walked about the pueblo. It had been so long since she had seen it. Bonfires appeared in several places on the plaza, and each fire seemed to attract its own musicians. She watched Mariano and Francisca stroll from location to location where their wedding was celebrated. Some groups sang, others danced. The newlyweds joined whatever activities were underway at each spot, but long before the celebration of that day ended, Rosa saw her sister and Mariano enter the Bandini casa where they would be staying together while they remained in San Diego.

46. Francisca

The celebration at Casa Bandini on the second night was a far more formal affair. It was limited to those families receiving invitations. When Francisca requested, Juan Bandini again danced the waltz with his wife, Dolores, and showed all who were present how it was done. Governor Pio Pico made a most elegant speech, reminding those present that he had known Francisca since early childhood and that he had long recognized Mariano Vallejo's ability as a military man. Over the years, he said, Vallejo's talents had been rewarded with both promotions and increased responsibilities in California.

It pleased Francisca to know that the diputacion planned to continue meetings in San Diego for several more days. In the large guest room of Bandini's hacienda she was learning all the wondrous feelings of lying with a man, and yearned for Mariano's arms both during afternoon siestas and late in the night. Later, she faced disappointment when she heard that the diputacion planned to shift to Los Angeles. She must remain in San Diego until Mariano sends for her.

47. John Wilson at San Diego

Shipmaster John Wilson and his partner, Supercargo James Scott maintained a warehouse at San Diego. With the increase in the slaughter of cattle at the missions and the demand for cash rather than merchandise, these traders bought vigorously. They offered far less for the hides than usual. Because many hides were not properly cured or dried, they hired Indians from Missions San Luis Rey and San Diego to stretch and peg the hides on raked areas of the beach where they could thoroughly dry.

"There must be another 5000 hides for us between here and San Francisco," Scott said.

"Aye," Wilson said. "If we get there first and have the money. But every trader on the coast must be collecting them. Did you see Fitch's warehouse?

"No."

"It's filled to the eaves."

They had long ago grown accustomed to the putrid smells and insects attracted by the hides. The botas of tallow smelled equally bad.

"We haven't visited the Joaquin Carrillo casa." Wilson said.

"There is little need," Scott answered. "All of Carrillo's hides and the San Diego Mission hides are now handled by Fitch."

Nearly a year had passed since he and Scot last struck anchor in San Diego. They had stayed in Valparaiso for months cashing in the inventory of a brig brimming with hides intended for American and European markets. Reaching San Diego again, they discovered they were in the midst of a trading bonanza. The priests were ordering cattle slaughtered in wasteful lots, determined that if the mission lands were taken, the church would at least salvage some of its wealth.

As he worked, pegging hides in the sand, Wilson kept thinking about the Carrillos. His thoughts wandered back to the time when he and Scott had taken responsibility for escorting Josefa Fitch from Monterey to San Gabriel. Enroute, he recalled, they had anchored at Santa Barbara, bringing Josefa to shore to visit her sister, Rosa.

He still remembered with pleasure when Rosa had come to him on the beach to express her gratitude for his help. Then he reflected upon an even earlier time, Rosa's wedding day. He stood in a far corner that day watching her graceful movements while she danced. "What a fool I am," he murmured to himself. Unfortunately, those times remained etched in his brain. He simply could not be in this Senora's presence without feeling some loss in his life. Wilson had sailed these seas for years.

He and Scott had taken women as they found them in whatever port they landed…South America, Mexico, the Sandwich Islands and California. Yet, he would give his ship and all the hides in California for a woman the likes of this Senora.

"Did I tell you," Scott asked, "that we are invited to supper at Casa de Carrillo?"

Wilson felt a little jolt. "Damn you," he said. "You know you didn't."

Scott smiled. No doubt, he suspected his feelings. "Both Joaquin Carrillo and Henry Fitch, including Fitch's boys, came to the warehouse while you were out on the brig. They seemed to have something on their mind."

"I hope you accepted," Wilson said.

"Aye," Scott said.

"Keep in mind that the women are married," Wilson said. He knew his words sounded strained.

"It's odd that you should say that," Scott murmured.

Scott looked seriously at his partner. "Fitch told me that Rosa's husband was killed in one of those damned little revolts that happen so often in California."

John Wilson stopped where he worked, poised with a long peg and sledge hammer over one of the hides. Then Scott said, "They tell me she is very pregnant with her second child."

Wilson visualized Rosa's delicately sculptured brown face filled with grief. He could also imagine her belly swelled with child. It didn't effect his feelings in any way. Wilson was strong, he knew, but a woman like Rosa made him feel invincible.

48. John Wilson - Under Sail Three Days Later

Since daybreak, the Ayacucho had risen and fallen and rolled in the recurring northwesterly winds, conditions made worse by heavy clouds and threats of rain. She was a sturdy brig. Wilson stood on deck, constantly commanding the sails, keeping his Kanaka crew close to the rigging and hoping to reach the lee side of Santa Catalina Island and a calmer sea.

"Catalina ahead," a crew member called.

"Lean her starboard," Wilson commanded.

Between island and mainland, the winds remained strong, but they were steady and more predictable. Within a few hours, they would drop anchor to do business at San Pedro, Mission San Gabriel, and the Pueblo de Los Angeles.

Wilson saw the cook struggle out of the small galley with a tray headed toward the cabin under the poop deck. He called, "I'll take that." Then, "What is it?"

"It's tea and crackers, Captain. To settle their stomachs, you know."

Wilson balanced the tray on his fingers, raising it over one shoulder, whistling softly as he made his way to the cabin he normally occupied except when he had special guests on board.

The door opened almost before he could knock.

"Good morning, Lassies," he said. "I trust that you slept well last night."

Both Carrillo girls laughed. "I have never been so sick," Francisca said.

Wilson still had difficulty accepting the fact that this child was now married and would undoubtedly have a large family before she was twenty. She was both lovely and vivacious.

He placed the metal tray on the built-in chest of drawers. "And how are you, Senora?" he said, turning to Rosa.

"I don't think my baby likes it," she said. Captain Wilson glanced at young Romualdo playing on the bed.

"Not that baby," she said, smiling weakly. "This one."

She pointed to her belly.

"These crackers will help settle your stomach," Wilson advised, "and the weather is calming. You must come out on deck and breathe deeply. The breezes are filled with good health. At the stern, you can see Santa Catalina Island where some trading ships hide part of their inventory to avoid paying duty. At the bow, you'll sight Point Fermin and San Pedro Bay."

Young Romualdo crawled across the bed and reached to Captain Wilson. Wilson took the boy into his arms. "If you will trust me with your son," he said, "I'll give him a lesson in sailing this brig."

Rosa enjoyed his humor and the fact that he wanted to play with Romualdo, Jr. She wrapped Romualdo in a heavy wool shawl, and Wilson carried the boy out on deck. For a moment, the entire crew stopped work...the man tightening the rigging, those shifting the sails to catch the wind, the Kanaka in charge of the deck when Wilson wasn't available, and the Sandwich Islander in the crow's nest...all appeared unbelieving as they watched their captain.

"Damn it!" Wilson shouted. "Attend to your work before you run us aground."

Young Romualdo frowned, straightened his body and let out a shout in imitation of the captain. Wilson could scarcely believe his own exhilaration and the trembling affection he felt while holding this child. He could not remember ever feeling so tender. He roared with laughter.

He pointed to the billowing forecastle sail as he walked around the plank deck past the galley to the bow. "See how beautifully she cuts through the waves, Romualdo. Feel her rise and fall. It takes a good sailor to keep his feet."

Romualdo was a sturdy child—turning, babbling and squirming in Wilson's arms. Through the child, Wilson felt an indescribable energy. He continued talking, saying what could not be said if either the child or the wind had understood. "You see, Son, I am deeply in love with your mother. I loved her the moment I first saw her, but it was too late. Now, it is as if God and all of his angels have offered me a second chance. I can scarcely believe such a lovely creature would be found in this distant place. Tell me, Romualdo, how can I make both of you mine this time?"

The boy let out another shout, pointing, "Mama!"

Wilson whirled. Rosa stood only a few feet away, her head covered by the mantilla he had given her as a present when she married Romualdo, and she was smiling.

"You are right, Captain," she said. "The breezes do have healing qualities."

Both stared straight ahead from the rail into the sea. He dared not look into her liquid-brown eyes. "Why didn't you stay in San Diego to have your child?" he asked.

"It is only a feeling," she said. "I wanted the child born where he was conceived. Where I lived with his papa."

When she realized that she had again referred to the child she carried as a male, she glanced at Wilson to see whether he smiled, but he did not. It pleased her to know that he took her seriously.

"Where will you live in Santa Barbara?" he asked.

"Don Jose and Dona Maria Guerra have both asked me to be part of their family."

"Will you live there a year from now?" he asked.

"Perhaps…"

"Five years?"

The captain was not actually questioning her, she suddenly realized. He was telling her something, and it embarrassed her. Obviously, she should not, could not live with the Guerras all of her life. She said, "I cannot think so far into the future now. Perhaps after the baby is born, I can plan."

Almost without realizing, she found herself answering question after question, pouring out the events of her life…her childhood, learning to read and write, her Papa's admiration of Romualdo Pacheco, her Papa's reaction to her husband's death and then her own feelings at the time of hearing about it.

"My own life has ended," she said.

"I think not," he said. His piercing blue eyes and weathered face never left her. "As you care for your children, your old life continues. But there is also a way to another life."

Captain Wilson told her about his life…childhood in Dundee, Scotland; his strict upbringing and schooling until at seventeen, he rebelled by signing onto a trading ship headed for South America.

"Some days aboard that ship crossing the Atlantic, I lived in terror," he told her. "It was a month before we saw a port. At Rio de Janeiro, I plotted to jump ship. I planned it again at Buenos Aires. When we came around the Horn, I decided to stay aboard until we reached Lima. There, I deserted ship. I made some friends in Lima, and I felt more comfortable there than I had at home. I went to work for a man who had an interest in a fleet of trading ships."

"How did you get a ship of your own?"

"My employer told each of the captains I sailed with to teach me navigation. I felt a strange power far out on the ocean as I learned to estimate our place on a map in relationship to the rest of the world...learned to use a compass, an astrolabe, a quadrant. All the while, I learned to use sail and wind to make a vessel move through water. It came like second nature. Eventually, I was assigned a ship. My partner, James Scott, first worked as supercargo for William Goodwin Dana on board the *Waverly*."

"Scott sailed with my cousin, Margarita's husband?"

"Aye. Scott and I became partners when Dana took a wife and settled in Santa Barbara. Then Dr. Robertson retired. He asked us if we wanted to buy the *Ayacucho*."

When it was time for dinner, Wilson asked Rosa and Francisca to join him at a small table in the galley. It is not elegant," he warned, "but I would enjoy your company."

To Rosa's surprise, Francisca complained of a headache. She had never had a headache in her life! "But," she said, and her eyes danced mischievously, "Romualdo and I can have our supper together in the cabin where I can rest. You must go ahead without me. Provided, of course, you can fit your belly at that small table in the galley!" .

Rosa raised her nose slightly, now fully understanding her sister's intentions. "All right, then," she said. "You may take care of Romualdo."

When Rosa appeared on deck, she wore an elegant deep blue dress with a full cover of layered lace over it. Her dark hair was drawn tightly across her ears into a bun at the back of her head, and she wore several strands of beads along with brightly colored earrings. She had not dressed so completely for a long time, not even for the fiesta after Francisca's wedding.

As a final gesture, she draped her shoulders with the rich embroidered silk mantilla Captain Wilson had given her years ago. Before leaving the cabin, Francisca playfully touched Rosa's neck and arms with a rose blossom fragrance.

To Rosa's surprise, Captain Wilson also dressed for the occasion. He stood waiting in long coat, white shirt and tie. He appeared to draw a long deep breath when he saw her. Rosa could feel her soft olive-colored cheeks flush as she moved across the deck. He extended his arm, and they strolled.

"I do hope," he said, "that the calm keeping us at anchor holds for a while longer. This is the first date I've ever had on board a ship."

Now, a Kanaka crew member played a soft tune on his guitar, singing a song from the Islands. Scott lifted an open bottle of brandy in salute from where he stood on the deck. Rosa chose to ignore her sister standing by their cabin smiling.

"Will you tell me more about Dundee?" she asked when the cook, now also doubling as waiter, served them a portion of broiled red snapper he had caught in the bay that afternoon. He placed the fish in a bed of freshly cooked vegetables bought from a farmer at San Pedro. Rosa admired the plates, the sterling ware and the cut glass serving bowl.

"Is this the way you usually dine, Captain?" she asked.

"The ship is my home, Lassie."

"I must say I do feel at home, too. About Dundee...?"

Wilson's face visibly softened. "I love it still," he said, "but it was not good for me. I needed to stretch, and I wanted movement in my life."

"It is so far away," Rosa said. "I cannot imagine living so far from home. Is it close to the sea?"

"Aye, it is that," Wilson said. "It is a beautiful little seaport city on the Firth of Tay. It was dubbed a royal burgh long ago by William the Lion when he was King of Scotland."

"Are you Catholic?" Rosa suddenly asked, somehow feeling embarrassed by her question.

She felt his soft blue eyes fall across her face. "No, Lass," he said, "and it is difficult to believe that such a one as me should ever find so much that pleases him in this Catholic part of the world. In the great reformation, Dundee became a stronghold for Protestantism. No person who professed Catholicism remained in the city. The place was sacked and burned and thousands of people died. It is a city that depends largely upon the sea...fishing, whaling, shipbuilding. For the boy who cannot tolerate its discipline and restraint, there is the even harsher discipline of the sea."

Rosa felt an emptiness creep through her as he talked.

She tried not to show her disappointment, but she felt she was making a mistake. A terrible mistake. She allowed herself special feelings toward this man who was no part of the church.

She thought about leaving the deck, but something compelled her to remain. She tried not to look at him, but when he stopped talking, she glanced up to find him searching her face, waiting for her to respond.

"Is it that bad, Lassie?" he asked.

"Why aren't you catholic?" she suddenly, impulsively demanded.

"For the same reason that you are not a Protestant," he said. "I was born to a certain way of thinking and praying just as certainly as you were born to your ways."

The Kanaka cook placed a bowl in front of them. It was filled with ripe bananas and papaya from Mexico. He lighted candles in the niche of the galley walls behind Rosa and then the Captain. Wilson's head became a silhouette. It was a very manly head, she thought.

A breeze swept through the door of the galley when the cook stepped outside. A moment later, the brig began to rock in the water. A Kanaka crewman looked into the galley. "Shall we raise the anchor, Captain?"

Wilson looked long at Rosa without moving. "We can surely work out something," he said to her. Then, he stood and walked out to the deck.

In a moment, she heard him shouting orders in the wind. She heard chains scraping as men turned the windlass to bring the anchor to deck. She hurried to the cabin. Francisca was already in bed. Romualdo lay asleep in her arms. When the sails unfurled, she felt the brig jerk. It was as if God, himself, had taken hold. While she prayed, she felt His power in the sea and wind, but when she closed her eyes, she saw the shadowed face of Captain John Wilson as it had appeared in the candlelight of the galley. She dared not feel this way about one man while carrying the child of another! She kept repeating the thought to herself until sleep overtook her.

For nearly a week, Rosa had felt the movements of the child she carried growing stronger. Before reaching San Buenaventura Mission, she noticed the same tightness across her abdomen that she had experienced during the days before Romualdo was born.

At anchor offshore from San Buenaventura Mission, she remained aboard ship. To her surprise, so did Captain John Wilson. When she spoke to him, he only said, "Scott is the supercargo on this vessel. He does the trading. There is little need for me to go ashore during this short stop." Then, he asked, "How are you feeling?"

"Quite all right," she said. She was not accustomed to a man who asked pointed questions with such apparent feeling. Her beloved Romualdo had always remained reticent even when he seemed to wonder about her. As far as having a child was concerned, Romualdo had viewed that in the way of most Mexican men...having children was woman's business.

When James Scott left the *Ayacucho*, he took two large surfboats loaded with manufactured merchandise. When he returned, the merchandise was gone and the same boats were heaped high with hides and tallow. The crew came aboard exhausted, hungry and thirsty. During these times, Rosa noted, Captain Wilson seemed as attentive to the needs of his crew as to the ship itself. When their work was done, the cook prepared and served fresh cooked meat, vegetables and fruit brought from shore. They also brought aboard two live lambs and a young pig for the cook to slaughter and serve after the brig was under sail.

Rosa and Francisca watched everything from a distance. James Scott, after eating ravenously, came to them.

"Did you know Padre Francisco Suner?" he asked Rosa.

"Si," she said. "The blind priest."

"I'm sorry to tell you he died recently."

Then he added as an afterthought, "It won't be long until most of the priests are gone."

"Is Padre Uria alone now?" Rosa asked.

"Yes," Scott said. "But he has his cats and a number of Indians who are close to him."

Rosa felt restless during this stop. She looked forward to arriving in Santa Barbara and seeing Adriana, and enjoying the warmth of the Guerra casa and her cousins. She wanted to be part of the conversations, the parties and the daily excitement of that lively household. But in exchange for this joy, she would soon be leaving Francisca who would sail to her husband, Mariano Vallejo, in Sonoma.

Rosa also felt another emotional jolt. In a very short time, she would be separated from Capt. John Wilson. He had an immensity that compelled her, stimulated her. It seemed impossible in her present condition to consider him as a man who might love her, but sometimes, she allowed it. Sometimes, in idle thoughts, she rejoiced not only in the vitality of his mind, but in his bodily strength. I must not imagine him too close to me, she thought. But she did.

49. John Wilson - Santa Barbara Bay

"We are in the bay, Captain," the night watch said, shaking John Wilson awake. Wilson climbed out of the bunk he occupied below deck and made his way in the darkness to the deck ladder. At the top, the big Kanaka sailor said, "The youngest girl asked to see you."

"Francisca?" Wilson asked.

The youngest one," the Sandwich Islander repeated.

Wilson glanced in the direction of the cabin where Rosa and Francisca should be sleeping. He could see the flicker of candlelight through the window curtain.

To the starboard, he made out the outline of the hard dark mountains below which the Santa Barbara Mission, presidio and pueblo nested. The *Ayacucho* moved quietly, almost imperceptibly into the bay. Wilson called for a change of the great square sails so that the brig angled in the direction of the beach. "Prepare to drop anchor," he called.

He waited no longer. He hurried to the back of the deck and knocked on the cabin door. Francisca opened it, dark eyes wide with fear.

"We need hot water, Captain," she said.

Wilson looked across the girl's shoulder to where Rosa lay in bed. He turned and called to a member of the crew. "Wake up the cook," he said. "Have him heat a tub of water!"

He heard Rosa's soft moans and watched her painful writhing movements under the covers.

"Have you ever delivered a child, Francisca?" he asked.

"No," she said, "but I was in the room while the midwife delivered my youngest brother. Do you know how it is done?"

Wilson looked at Francisca incredulously and then, again, at Rosa. Her long dark hair fell loosely across the pillow, cradling her flushed face. Her son, Romualdo, lay near her. In the candlelight, her face glowed. No mother and child could be more beautiful, he thought. But another child was on the way.

"We best go to work, Lassie," he said to Francisca.

What he was about to do was unimaginable in California society, Wilson knew. A man without claim or relationship to a woman involving himself in such a personal matter as helping deliver a child could be the subject of talk along the California coast for years. The child would probably be remembered in the pueblo all of its life as the one delivered on board ship by Captain Wilson.

He quickly dismissed all such irrelevant thought, laying the covers back. Without hesitation, he ripped Rosa's gown open from neck to hem, exposing her whole body. Francisca prepared a small bed in the corner on the floor of the cabin and removed Romualdo to it. She also further separated Rosa's legs.

"The bag is broken," Francisca said. She moistened a towel in a pan of water taken from the kettle on the wood stove and wiped Rosa's legs.

"My God, that's not all," Wilson said. "The top of the infant's head is visible."

Wilson watched the muscles of Rosa's abdomen contract. She screamed in pain. "Push, Lassie," he heard himself saying as more of the infant's head appeared. "Push."

Rosa took a deep breath. Wilson hurriedly washed his hands. Soon, the cook set a large tub of hot water inside the door.

Wilson gently supported the newborn's head as it appeared face down. There was another contraction, and Rosa screamed and attempted to twist to her side, but both Wilson and Francisca held her in position. Rosa was crying brokenly. Wilson reached and found a small portion of the infant's back and chest. With Rosa's next contraction, he pulled gently so the shoulders and arms of the newborn child appeared. The visible portion of the child lay stretched along his hand and lower arm. Wilson could feel the miracle occurring. The contractions and pushing clearly consumed Rosa. She panted breathlessly. With each contraction, Wilson aided her until he gently raised a dripping living entity, still attached to the umbilical cord. The child cried. He laid the wet and slippery newborn gently over Rosa's breast.

Francisca wiped the infant's back and arms while Wilson watched the umbilical cord pulsate its nourishing blood. Rosa's labor contractions did not cease completely. As the infant lay in her arms, the last of the cord and the placenta were disgorged. When the cord ceased to pulsate, appearing empty, Francisca lifted the child upright while Wilson cut the cord and tied the finest knot in his seafaring career.

With the movement and handling, the newborn kicked and stretched into life. Now, Francisca lovingly cleansed the child. Again, she laid it along Rosa's breast, took a weary breath and left the cabin.

Wilson sat quietly beside the woman he loved. For a while, he dared touch her shoulder, and she half-opened her eyes and smiled at him. When she spoke, it was a whisper. "May I name my son Juan?" she asked.

He thought about this question for a time before answering. Finally, he said, "No." His answer was firm.

"Please," she whispered. "I want a child named for you."

Wilson leaned over the bed and touched her cheek with his hand. "I want you to name your next son after me," he said.

50. Rosa

Wilson insisted that Rosa remain in bed in her cabin even after the surfboats began making trips back and forth to the beach. In Scotland, he told her, it was not uncommon for a woman recovering from childbirth to remain in bed for ten days. However, Rosa, had different ideas. Her mother was a Mexican-Indian. If a woman felt like it, she might give birth one day and return to the fields with the infant upon her back the next day.

If she now delayed going ashore, it was partly John Wilson's influence and partly because she was so comfortable. The captain not only challenged her thinking in long conversations each day, but he also knew how to make her laugh. She liked both. Then, sometimes, she dared to think that through his forthright consuming blue eyes, he was making love to her.

He and James Scott soon arranged the deck as a general store with exciting goods for sale and trade…fabrics, farm tools, kitchenware, dishes, jewelry. The brig became a gently rocking place of music and fiesta, the movement of surfboats between shore and vessel a pageant, the pueblo and the mountains a backdrop for celebration. Each day, more Santa Barbara Carrillos and Guerras crowded aboard to celebrate the birth of a new child in their extended family, welcoming Rosa back home. Since none of them knew Francisca, they insisted upon taking her and baby Romualdo ashore, but when they did so, one of the other women remained behind as both company and companion for Rosa.

On the fourth day, in spite of protests from Wilson, Rosa awakened and called for water to wash her hair. Dona Margarita Dana had stayed with her on board the previous night.

Rosa felt so light when she walked about the cabin, even enjoying the rocking sensation of the brig. Margarita washed her long hair with special perfumed soap which Captain Wilson provided, then rinsed it in lemon juice. Afterward, she sat on deck in the sun while her cousin braided her hair into two long loose strands.

Rosa saw Captain Wilson nod in the direction of two of his crew. Soon, these Sandwich Islanders appeared strumming small guitars and singing in their high falsetto voices. Since they sang in their own language, Rosa did not understand the words, but their eyes were on the infant child asleep in her lap. Somehow, the song related to her new baby.

"It is one of their ancient mother and child songs," Wilson explained. "It involves a legend about a woman who wanted a child, but she could not have one. Just when she was on the verge of flinging herself from a high cliff into the sea, a bird appeared bearing a gift wrapped in sandalwood bark. When the woman opened the bundle, it was her child."

Both Rosa and Margarita laughed. "That would be a good way to have children," Margarita remarked.

Before the usual crowd appeared on the brig to trade that day, Margarita asked, "What have you named your new son?"

"I have named him for his new uncle," Rosa replied casually. "Mariano…"

"Does Francisca know…?"

"No," Rosa said. "I only finally decided last night."

No one discussed the conditions of her new son's birth, neither Francisca nor Rosa, and certainly not John Wilson. It would remain a secret among the three of them forever. In the late afternoon with hair washed, a bath and wearing her brightest colored beads and earrings, Rosa, with her second son, boarded a surfboat to go ashore.

Each day, for the next several days, Rosa made a point of spending long hours sitting on the wide-covered portico of the Guerra casa. Little Romualdo played near her on the tile floor while she held and fed infant Mariano. As she hoped, John Wilson found her there.

On the last day that he planned to remain in port, he said, "I'm not happy about leaving you, Lassie, but I know that some time must pass for you and me. After Scott and I take Francisca to Yerba Buena to meet her husband and finish trading there, we will sail directly south again. We'll pick up our hides and tallow stored at San Pedro and San Diego and sail for Valparaiso to trade for American and English goods. Then, we'll go out to the Sandwich Islands to trade for goods arriving there aboard other trading ships from Manila and Canton."

With each word, Rosa found the pain mounting. She could not restrain tears.

"How long?" she managed to ask.

"The round trip will take about nine months," he said quietly.

When he stood to leave, she also stood. Romualdo balanced uncertainly in a standing position, clinging to John Wilson's leg. Wilson picked him up, then reached out and drew Rosa and infant Mariano into his arms. He held them quietly.

"When I return, Dear Rosa, I intend to become a citizen of Mexico and a good catholic, and if you agree, we will become a family."

When Dona Maria Antonio appeared on the porch, Wilson withdrew his embrace, politely bidding adios to the older woman. Rosa's adopted Indian child, Adriana, appeared from nowhere, gathering the baby and Romualdo into her arms. For a moment, Rosa watched John Wilson adjust one of the stirrups on his rented horse. Then, she rushed from the portico and across the courtyard to where he stood.

Without hesitation, she came into his arms, and this time, he kissed her. In tears, she said, "I will wait for you, Juan Wilson! And if you wish, my next son will bear your name!"

51. Rosa at Santa Barbara

One morning several weeks later, Don Guerra asked his wife, children, grandchildren and household servants to remain at the breakfast table.

"We are going to have special guests in our home within a few days," he told them. We must clean everything thoroughly and prepare foods unlike any other we've enjoyed for awhile. Do you understand?"

A chorus of "Si's" bounced against the open ceiling of the big dining room and down the portico leading to bedrooms. Rosa found herself alone with the Guerra parents soon afterward. "Are you going to tell me who is coming?" her aunt asked.

"You can be proud of yourself, My Sweet. We are preparing for a visit from our new governor, Pio Pico. "We must plan a fandango on the plaza and invite everyone in the pueblo. His dispatch tells me he is planning a special announcement."

"Now, what could that be?"

"You know I petitioned long ago for the St. Julian grant."

By the time of the celebration, the entire pueblo knew about it. Women of every casa prepared food. Family blankets covered the square in front of the Guerra house, leaving space for the musicians and dancing. A rise in the soil was intended as the stage from which the governor would speak.

During the day of the celebration, Rosa oversaw the Chumash Indian servants as they baked bread and fruit pastries. In the early part of the day, before the fandango, Rosa assisted her aunt in serving the governor sherry and bites of fresh bread. Cousin Pio Pico was a family hero for his part in getting Enrique Fitch freed. In the evening, each of the Guerra sisters, as well as Rosa, took a turn dancing with the governor. "I knew Romualdo well, Rosa," he told her as they danced. "He was a brave soldier."

By the time the governor spoke that evening, Rosa was exhausted. She located Adriana among the playing children and started for the Guerra Casa as the Governor spoke. She paused at the iron gate and turned to face him.

"I am pleased that I can spend this special time with you in your beautiful pueblo," he said above the cheers. "I am also pleased this evening that I can acknowledge the many great services provided the California territory by one of your leading citizens, Don Jose Guerra de la Noriega. As a reward, it is my pleasure to grant his longstanding petition for the great St. Julian Rancho."

The governor waited while everyone cheered. "It is also my pleasure tonight to award the eldest daughter of the Guerra family, Margarita II, and her husband, William Goodwin Dana of Boston, the beautiful 38,000 acre Nipomo Rancho. He continued talking as he beckoned the couple forward to receive the handwritten statement of their grant.

Rosa knew that if Romualdo were alive this minute, he, too, would be receiving his grant. He dreamed of and petitioned for lands of a valley near Mission San Luis Obispo. She felt like crying as she opened the gate into the Guerra casa gardens. Then she heard the governor call, "Rosa Carrillo de Pacheco."

She also heard her aunt's voice, "Come back, Rosa. Now!"

Adriana took her hand and pulled her back into the crowd. "For your husband's years of service to the territory, I grant his petition in your name. It amounts to 48,000 acres in the region of Mission San Luis Obispo. We cannot bring Romualdo back to you, but we can honor him through you."

Rosa took the grant document, but her eyes were too blurred to read it. The Governor gallantly kissed her hand.

******

Months passed without ship's mail bringing Rosa a message from Juan Wilson. Then suddenly, three dispatches arrived. She left her children with Adriana and went to her special cove on the beach.

"My Dearest Rosa," the first began. "The weather in Peru is ever so light and sunny, keeping me constantly filled with thoughts of you. The ship's captain who will deliver this message actually awaits its completion before giving the order to sail. It may be four months before I see you in the flesh, but I do look forward to it. With Deepest Love, Juan Wilson."

She held it next to her heart. It pleased her to realize that he signed the message as "Juan." She quickly opened the next note: "I may be the luckiest Scotsman in the world to have met a woman such as you. I even appreciate the head start in family with boys like Romualdo and Mariano and a daughter like Adriana. I leave Valparaiso for the Sandwich Islands tonight."

The third message was written on two pages. "We have about completed our business on Oahu. It has been hard for me this trip because I so continuously think about you and my family-to-be. Make whatever arrangements you will for our marriage. I only want everything to be proper for the rest of our lives.

Here, on this island, I have met an interesting man who can help us solve an important problem...how to assure Romualdo and Mariano of the best possible education. It will require a great sacrifice for you, I fear, but if you are willing, we will place them in this Congregational Mission School under the tutorship of a Mr. Blackstone, the headmaster. Mr. Blackstone is a Scotsman and a missionary of some standing. More soon, My Love. I am sailing for California."

******

It seemed an eternity before Juan's ship, the Ayacucho, dropped anchor in the bay. Nine months had passed. It was early morning. Word spread rapidly throughout the pueblo and the presidio. Every trail to the beach filled with citizens, all going the same direction. When someone began singing the morning song, everyone joined. The entire village sang their traditional song. Rosa sang too, bursting with joy. She sang with heartfelt thanks, knowing Juan had arrived safely. In the trees, the sunshine and the sand, Rosa felt a new world opening to her. If a woman could possibly love two men at once, she knew she loved the vision of her first husband, Romualdo, and now, the reality of Juan.

Wilson's partner, Scott, along with Kanaka crew members arrived in the first three surf boats laden with merchandise which they displayed on the beach on old sail sheets. Items were priced in numbers of cowhides that Scott expected in exchange.

When Wilson arrived, unlike his usual stripped to the waist ship wear, he wore a suit with white collar shirt, bow tie and all of the attire of a Scots gentleman. At first, Rosa actually didn't recognize him, but then she burst out laughing, knowing he had dressed for her. Without words, he took her in his arms. They walked all day and talked of nothing but their love and their future together. They clung to each other in long stretches of caressing and breathless affection. They did not try to hide. Rosa knew they were two lonesome people desperately in need of love. At last, they sat down on back steps of the Guerra porch. When her aunt saw them, she insisted they eat.

"We are planning our marriage," Juan said.

Aunt Antonia looked surprised.

"You didn't tell your family?" Juan asked Rosa.

There was a moment of silence. Rosa was embarrassed.

Then her aunt said, "We knew from the continuous smile on her face. Now, come eat. The family has arranged for the wedding."

Deep in the night, Rosa slipped out of the room where Adriana, Romualdo and baby Mariano slept soundly. She ran through the dark to the beach where she knew Juan slept with his partner and crew. They slept there to safeguard the trade goods they displayed on the beach.

"I love you," she whispered in Juan's ear. He silently slipped out of his bed roll. She led him to her secret cove far down the beach, and without hesitation, removed her clothes. He didn't try to understand. He did the same. Their long day of affection, the constant touch of one another, their separation at nightfall left uncontrollable urges, love beyond measure. She felt his fierce search for her middle. Their bodies met in madness. And then a loving spiritual dance began.

Early the next morning, Rosa awakened Adriana. Adriana helped dress Romualdo and Mariano. They walked up the hill to the mission. They were alone, and in the moment, the sanctuary of the church felt cavernous, the cold adobe structure was filled with smells of burning candles.

Feeling wondrously blissful, Rosa found herself asking all kinds of prayerful thoughts. She had been granted the land Romualdo wanted so badly. She had been blessed with his sons, and God had given her an adopted Indian daughter. How could she best serve the intentions of God, make real the hopes Romualdo held for his family, and offer eternal love to Juan? For her, in this moment, the means became clear. The message was almost audible. Rosa dropped to her knees on the dirt floor of the church and the voice of her mama's ghost touched her.

"Use your gifts...use your womanhood...use your poetry, and all that you can create. Defy all who would limit you."

Rosa thought again of Juan Wilson. She wondered what Romualdo would say about her uncontrolled behavior. She prayed that she was not opposing God and everything he had given her. In the moment, she spoke directly to her dead husband. "Juan can help me fulfill your dreams too," she told him. "I want him for my husband."

Without opening her eyes, she felt the smile of young Romualdo. He must grow up to fill the place of his papa, Rosa decided, and Juan Wilson must serve as guide. She reached over and took her son. Then, she pulled Adriana, still holding baby Mariano, under one arm. This was her family. Now, she would have Juan Wilson.

Four joyous days later, she and Juan married in the mission church. Like every wedding in Santa Barbara, it was a pueblo-wide celebration. Rosa dressed simply for the occasion, but one part of her wear caught the eyes of all. She wore her deep-colored, floral designed mantilla, the one given her as a wedding gift by Wilson himself when she married Romualdo. It was on that day that she first met the eye of Juan Wilson and felt him reaching out to her.

Only one worrisome bit of news distracted the entire pueblo during the celebration By way of an overland traveler, they heard that three ships of the American Navy had dropped anchor at Monterey and Yerba Buena.

52. Rosa - 1846

Within days after her marriage to Captain John Wilson, Rosa, with her children, joined him aboard the Ayacucho destined for San Luis Obispo. After landing, they had a dawn-to-sundown walk across thousands of acres of land granted to her by the governor.

She sought a hill dividing the approach to two valleys. It was one Romualdo had described for her. It's top offered an ideal location with a nearly 360-degree view. While she carried Baby Marino in a soft sling across her shoulder, Wilson gave Romualdo Jr. a ride on his shoulders. Adriana walked, ran and occasionally twirled several meters ahead of them all day. With dusk, their goal achieved, they laid out a bed in the high grass.

"It is just as tranquil as you described, My Love," Wilson whispered in her ear.

In the early morning, they looked about them at the two green valleys. She found it easy to mention Romualdo to Wilson, and he encouraged her. "He was important in your life," Wilson said. "I have people who were once important to me, too, but I rarely think of them. They are thousands of miles away, and our lives will never touch again."

"We must build a small house immediately to lay claim to this grant," she said.

"Aye. I'll bring some of the members of my crew ashore, and we'll go to work. When the house is finished, I will return you to Santa Barbara, then fill my last orders to the north."

It took much longer than planned to make the adobe bricks and construct a starter house. It was the beginning of a home that would take years to develop into the hacienda Rosa dreamed it should become. While work continued, she and Adriana, taking turns carrying the baby, walked a trail that led them to Mission San Luis Obispo. Here, they met a young priest. He helped her find Indians living in the nearby Indian rancheria who had experience in making adobe bricks. She hired them and brought them to the ranch.

Wilson, stripped to the waist, worked alongside his Kanaka ship's crew. Although the crew worked fast and hard, they were not sure of what they were doing. The Indians gradually took over.

One night as they lay together, Wilson said, "I want to take you back to Santa Barbara now and finish my trading to the north. Then, we can return here and stay forever."

Rosa remained silent. The thought of leaving her land tore at her. For a time, she was distracted as his kisses covered her cheeks and breasts, but when he lay back with a contented sigh, she listened to the faint voice of her spirit mother reaching through stars and a half-moon. "Fulfill your dream, My Child," the familiar voice said. "Fulfill your dream."

She sat up abruptly. Her startled movement awakened Wilson. Why must she defy the man she loved, she asked herself. Then aloud, she said. "I can't leave this place you've built for me, Juan. I must see it through. I cannot deny destiny."

"But you can defy me."

"Please don't look at it that way."

"What do you expect me to do?"

"Do what you must do. Then return to our bed here in our home. I'll wait for you for as long as you wish."

A moment later, she kissed his bare strong shoulders and chest. She could almost feel her mama's strength as she defied John Wilson. At the same time, she sought to show him she defied with deepest love.

53. Francisca - 1846

Francisca loved her home at the presidio in Yerba Buena. The bustle of a small contingent of soldiers, occasional traders, and a group of colonials from Sonora originally recruited by Anza made this remote place exciting. The settlers had made their homes on sand dunes around Mission Dolores some distance back from the winds of San Francisco Bay. The presidio served as an outlook for all ships through the Golden Gate.

A small celebration took place when Vallejo received a dispatch from the governor appointing him commandante-general of all the lands of the California territory. Another social event occurred when Francisca told all who were present at a presidio gathering that she was pregnant. These events gave her much to think about, write about and reason to meet every ship entering the bay that might carry a dispatch for her.

Then the order came for Mariano to move to the Mission Sonoma territory to fight Indians, watch for any aggression from the Russians who had built Fort Ross along northern shores, and watch with concern the activities of a place called Fort Sutter established by a German. The Fort was a typical log enclosure that collected American mountain men and newly arriving Americans hoping to settle in California.

"I've ordered the construction of a new two-story adobe house near the mission.," Vallejo told her.

Francisca wanted to conceal her disappointment about leaving the presidio. She knew they faced isolation in his new assignment. Just thinking about it made her feel lonesome. "How can you oversee the military of all of the California territory located so far from its population?" she asked.

"It's strategic," he said. "I won't be near our military, but I will be near those who might make trouble for us. There are more American mountain men at Fort Sutter than men in our entire army."

"Could you stop them if they invaded?"

"Probably not, but its my job to try."

Francisca smiled faintly. "I had hoped for a long quiet time for planting a garden and growing babies. I think I'm about to have it."

******

Soon after they arrived and settled into their sparsely furnished new home near Sonoma Mission, a dispatch arrived by land carrier with word about three American ships landing in Monterey. Their commander announced they were occupying California.

"Pio Pico and General Castro are there. They don't have many soldiers, but they can make enough of a war to keep those Americans off shore," Vallejo told Francisca. But he didn't sound that sure.

A half-dozen men from the Presidio at Buena Vista appeared at Sonoma a few days later. "American ships have now dropped anchor in San Francisco Bay and raised an American flag," their leader reported. "We could not fight those big ships."

Vallejo assigned the soldiers places in the barracks.

******

Within the week, American occupation became a reality in Sonoma. Late one night both Mariano and Francisco awakened in the same moment. Both heard gun fire from near the barracks. It brought Vallejo to his feet. He pulled on his pants, boots and jacket.

"Don't light any candles," he whispered. "Don't make any noise. Please, Francisca, hide in the closet."

Instead, Francisca grabbed a musket she knew was loaded and sat down in a chair in the sala. Mariano's attention was diverted by a sudden banging on the door. When he hesitated to open it, there was a crash against it, and a half-dozen mountain men fell, shoulders first, into the room.

"We are declaring the California territory an independent nation," one man said. All of them had been drinking. "You are our prisoner," another yelled. "Put your hands high."

Mariano stepped over to where Francisca sat. He took the musket and laid it on the floor. "You must guarantee my wife protection."

Everyone among the rebels nodded in deference to Mariano and the recognition that they had just captured the top Mexican military man in California. They took him prisoner without tying his hands or otherwise handicapping him. The American leader then spoke directly to Francisca. "We are leaving guards outside your house to protect you."

An hour later, Francisca decided the house was a trap that might be entered by anyone of these drunken men. She did not want to be a victim. She did not like being here alone. She slipped out of the house past a sleeping guard. In the barn, she saddled a horse and walked him a half mile down a path that led to a main trail that connected with Sutter's Fort. Her musket was still loaded, and if necessary, she knew she would use it.

54. Francisca at Sutter's Fort

Three days later, Francisca watched from a hiding place in a grove of trees as the contingent of ragged looking American volunteers guided her husband through the gate at Sutter's Fort. She was weak with hunger as well as wet from a heavy rain during most of one night. An hour later, thinking about the child she carried, and overwhelmed with exhaustion, she finally decided she had no choice. She rode to the gate of the fort. Against one wall, closeby, she saw a family group. They appeared to be recently arrived settlers. When the guard appeared to block her way, she pointed to the family. In her best English, learned long ago from her soldier teacher, she said, "I am here to see that family."

"The Reed family?" he asked.

"Yes."

"Go ahead, Mam."

She rode to where the family had made camp.

She was pleasantly surprised when one of the women looked up at her and smiled.

When Francisca climbed down from her horse, she realized her pregnancy was conspicuous, and it was obvious to the man and woman and children who smiled at her that she was wet to the skin. "Oh, Dear Woman, you need dry clothes," the older woman said.

She and her daughter guided Francisca into a tiny log building and helped her undress. After drying her, they offered her a dress belonging to the daughter. It was much too large, but it felt warm. They sat her down and fed her from a stew-like mix of meat and wild vegetables. Without wanting to do so, Francisca fell asleep where she sat. She felt someone lay her back within the shelter. It was late in the day before she awakened. She felt strong again, and thanked everyone.

The man of the family said, "We arrived here only three days ago. Perhaps we can help you, and you can give us some guidance."

"You may be sure my husband and I can help you, and we will. You saved my life. First, I must find him and help him."

"What is your husband's name?"

"His name is Mariano Vallejo. He is commandante-generale of the California territory. You must have seen him brought in earlier today. I am Francisca Carrillo de Vallejo."

"Yes," Mr. Reed said. "They took him to the administration building in the center. I didn't realize he was such an important man."

Francisca explained that they had only been married for a short while. Mr. Reed said, "We are not too popular among the other settlers arriving from the Sierra Nevada Mountains."

"Why?" Francisca dared ask.

"We were trapped in the mountains during the worst of the winter months. People think we survived by eating others who died."

Francisca felt also sick for a moment. Finally, "You are good people. I know you are. Don't tell me more."

She walked across the open area of the Fort to the door of the log constructed administration building. She stepped inside. She was suddenly surrounded by mountain men.

"Well, Miss, what can I do for you?" one said.

"Better yet, you sweet little thing, what can you do for me?"

"Someone said I would find my husband here," she answered.

The room was silent for a moment. "What is your husband's name?" a third man asked. He sat at a table where a card game was under way. He reached out and pulled her to his lap.

"No!" she screamed. "Let me go."

The door to a nearby office opened. She heard a familiar voice. Then she saw the uniform. "I left my wife in Sonoma," he announced to the group. "I must be hearing things. Surely, that isn't you, Francisca. Sitting on another man's lap. No. I am a very jealous man. I would kill any man who would touch my wife."

The man released her and backed out the door She jumped up and ran into Mariano's arms. "Ah, I see I was wrong, My Francisca. You are not sitting on another man's lap. I am so glad. I would not want to fight the men whose commander has just freed me."

The man who stood behind Mariano Vallejo was an American military officer. "My Dearest," Vallejo continued, "Meet Captain John Fremont."

"Did you follow your husband all of the way from Sonoma?" Fremont asked.

She dropped her head and nodded.

"Thank you, Captain," Vallejo said. "We will ride back to Sonoma now."

Outside, Francisca said, "I want you to meet someone."

55. Josefa in San Diego

Rumors about American occupation spread the length of California quickly as coastline trading ships and trail riders did their business. Word about United States military movements reached San Diego days before navy vessels dropped anchor. Both members of the American volunteers and the U.S. Navy came ashore.

The day they arrived in San Diego, Enrique and Carrillo worked far out on the mission rancho rounding up cattle. Josefa heard cannon fire from the bay, and rushed across the pueblo square to find her son. With family safely inside Casa Carrillo, she closed the big doors to the courtyard, and brought out muskets that had not been used for years. She offered Oopah, the Indian servant, a weapon, but she shrunk from it, too frightened to speak. Josefa and her sons waited quietly until they heard the noises of frightened people in the pueblo, and men shouting in the orchard and outside their door. From the portico, she heard noises on their courtyard wall. As an American soldier showed himself at the top of the wall, Josefa knew he did not see her. As he dropped lightly to the ground, she touched the point of her musket to the soldier's temple. Startled, he jumped, falling backward to the ground.

"Please Mam," he said, startled and trembling. "I mean no harm. I only wanted to open your gate for my squad of men. We have been assigned to go through your town looking for danger."

"You may lay quietly where you are and live," Josefa said.

"I will, he said.

Shaking inside, Josefa sat down on a stool and held the weapon across her lap. Men outside the courtyard doors shouted, "Are you all right, Mo."

"I am being held at gunpoint," Josefa's prisoner shouted. "Don't break in. She may shoot me."

An hour passed. Oopah brought Josefa a cup of chocolate. "Give it to our prisoner." Josefa said. Oopah did so.

"Thank ya' Mam."

He took a long swallow. "You know, Mam, I'm an American. Real men don't hurt women. I guarantee it. None of my men will hurt you. You can be sure of that."

"Do real men climb over walls into a woman's house?" Josefa shouted. He said nothing. After a while, she said, "You can sit up with your back to the wall if you like."

At last, Josefa heard familiar voices outside the door. Her papa and husband were home. Unafraid, she opened the heavy door to see a swarm of men outside, all talking to her husband.

"Come in, Gentlemen," he said. "I want you to try my wife's chocolate and sweets, and my father-in-law's wine."

"Is that it?" Josefa asked Enrique.

"Yes, My Love. You are about to become an American."

"How is that?"

"We are in American territory."

56. John Wilson at Monterey, 1846

John Wilson searched the gradually rising morning mist to find the beach and the custom house. In Monterey. he planned to take on fresh water and check with American consul Thomas Larkin. Larkin also operated an import-export business. He dealt with every trader along the coast of California.

After entering the bay and moving closer to shore, Wilson called one of his crew. "Study the three white vessels ahead, and tell me what you see."

"I see an American flag at the top of the largest vessel," he said. He studied the three masts and the shape of the hull. "I'm sure the second and third ships also fly the stars and stripes. Sir, I've seen these ships anchored at Honolulu several times over the years."

"We're looking at most of the United States Pacific fleet," Wilson said.

Wilson was uncertain about what he should or could do. Then he realized that the naval sloop closest to his own Ayacucho was not anchored. It had shifted sail and now moved toward his ship.

"Slow down and hold course," Wilson called to his crew.

They drifted until the naval sloop neared them. An officer, using a bull horn, called, "What's your cargo?"

"Manufactured goods and some hides," Wilson shouted.

"We're sending inspectors aboard."

After a long wait, an American naval officer and four crew men climbed aboard from a surfboat. "Are you carrying weapons or ammunition?" the young officer asked.

"One musket. One pistol. For hunting and personal use. Tell me, Officer, is this a war?"

"Aye. Mexico attacked Texas."

"What can you tell me."

"Not much, I'm afraid. I hear there are already American troops in California."

"Do you intend to block trade?"

203

"No, on the contrary. We are only blocking weapons and watching for troop movements.

The officer and an aide inspected below deck while other navy crew stood guard on top. The men below soon reappeared holding their noses. The smell of hides in such close quarters was too much for them.

Later, Wilson went ashore. Wilson and his partner, Scott, owned two ships. Under the circumstances, it seemed lucky that Scott had taken their second brig to the Mexican coast. In Monterey, Wilson found both sailors and marines patrolling the streets. Probably 50-60 of them, he estimated. It was an easy takeover.

First, he visited the John Cooper adobe. Cooper had built a wall around a compound of several buildings. It appeared as more a personal fort than a home. Wilson wanted to meet this man who had married Mariano Vallejo's sister and whom he knew to be the half-brother of American Consul Thomas Larkin. He had heard the story of how Cooper had taken Josefa into his home while Enrique Fitch was a prisoner of the church and state.

"What are we to do?" Encarnacion asked. "Governor Pico and General Castro rushed off to Los Angeles the moment they saw American Navy ships come into the bay."

"Where is your husband?" Wilson asked.

"He sailed for Mexican ports two months ago. The government owns its own vessel, the California. He is its master."

"Have you heard anything from either Yerba Buena or Sonoma?"

"There is wild talk. We hear that the American Navy has taken Yerba Buena, and American soldiers and volunteers have moved into Sonoma. They say my brother, Mariano, has been taken prisoner, and a strange flag hangs in the square."

"Stars and stripes?"

"No, a bear."

Wilson tried to comfort Encarnacion. "Most Americans living at Sutter's Fort know of your family. They know, too, that Mariano Vallejo can be their best friend among the Californios."

Before leaving the Cooper home, Wilson promised to send Encarnacion a variety of foods and household supplies by way of one of his crew members.

Encarnacion insisted upon serving him lunch. After tamales and ensalada de fruita, Wilson found Thomas Larkin in his two-story adobe home, located amidst many others that made up the residential neighborhood of Monterey.

Larkin's wife, Rachel, greeted him at the door. Wilson had known this couple from the time of their arrival in California. She was an American and probably the only blue-eyed woman in California.

"These are busy days, John," Larkin said as they climbed the stairs to his second floor office. "But I wanted to see you. I have a dispatch that will concern you. It actually arrived on board the Savannah, one of the navy ships here in Monterey. Apparently Scott argued with the navy when he was commanded to let them come aboard to search his vessel. Now, they are holding him and your brig, Juanita. Scott sent a letter to me seeking help when he heard Commodore Sloat was coming to this port."

"My God," Wilson said.

"Well, Sloat did arrive here, and I vouched for Scott. Told him Scott was your partner, that you were not a gun runner. Sloat does not want any trouble he can avoid. Sloat sent word aboard the next navy vessel going south telling officials to free him."

"Thanks, my Friend. Scott has a temper, and it sometimes costs him."

"I had hoped to sail to Yerba Buena," Wilson said. "What do you think? I do big business there."

"Mariano Vallejo won't have trouble with the Americans. They like him and he likes them," Larkin said. "I don't think its a good place for us to go for a few months."

Late that day Wilson became convinced that he must sail back to San Luis Obispo as quickly as possible. His crew had finished unloading an order for Larkin at the Monterey custom house on the beach. Farther up the hill among the trees he saw the most motley group of men he'd ever seen in his lifetime. On horseback, weapons slung across shoulders, many dressed in deerskin coats, bearded, crude and noisy, someone said they had just arrived today.

Their leader dressed differently. He wore an American military uniform, and sat straight in his saddle. He appeared alert to every movement around him. He gave the order for his men to dismount and make camp.

When Wilson returned to the Larkin house to report filling the order, he told Thomas what he had seen. "Yes" Larkin said. "He left Sutter Fort several days ago. That is none other than Captain John Fremont and his mountain men volunteers. They are riding south, pueblo by pueblo, 'officially' occupying the California territory. He picks up a few more American recruits in every port city."

It looks like we are about to become Americans," Wilson said.

Larkin laughed. "I think you'll like it."

57. John Wilson - Off Central California's Coast

John Wilson knew he and his Kanaka crew faced a December storm like no other in their lives, but he wanted desperately to get back to San Luis Obispo to protect Rosa against the uncertain behavior of the band of American volunteers he saw in Monterey. He thought he had experienced the worst ever climate aboard the ship that brought him around Cape Horn in his earliest days, but the seas now seemed determined to devour him, his ship, his crew. When one of the men reported a leak in the hull that threatened to sink the Ayacucho, Wilson tried to pray to the only God he knew…this God of the Sea over whom he held so little control.

Their efforts to patch the wooden hull were useless. Their repairs tore away in seconds. The small bucket brigade out of the hull to the deck and over the rail proved useless. The crew did not give up until the main mast crashed across the deck, splintering everything in its path, breaking across Wilson's back.

"God spare me for a little while," Wilson shouted, hurting, and in half-consciousness, The storm was tearing the Ayacucho to shreds, and taking crew members with it, one by one. Wilson found himself helpless. His body was worn to exhaustion. "I don't want you to be alone, Rosa," he called into the wind. "I want you to be mine for at least a while. I want so much for your boys…"

Then he felt his helpless body whirl through space and crash into the churning water. He clung to something. A piece of the deck? A part of the mast? God, how he hurt. It's asking too much to hope I can hang over this floating piece in this water, he thought.

58. Rosa and Fremont in San Luis Obispo

The sudden appearance of Governor Pio Pico and General Juan Castro at her new home on the hill shocked Rosa. She didn't recognize Pio, her cousin, nor Castro, both childhood playmates in San Diego. "We escaped Monterey before the American ships landed. We barely left town before hearing that a battalion of volunteers came out of the north," Pio told her.

"Where are you headed," Rosa asked.

"Los Angeles," Castro said. He was breathless. "We hope we can organize soldiers and volunteers to stop this invasion."

"I am looking for your husband," Pio said.

"You didn't see him at Monterey?" Rosa asked.

"No..." Then, "Rosa, we're selling the missions to buy what equipment we can. We've already sold several."

Rosa could scarcely believe Pio. "You are actually selling church land and buildings?"

"Si."

"But the missions are churches of God."

"We are leaving the church buildings, rooms for the priests to live and a garden area. The rest is being confiscated by the state."

No woman in California had ever clamped her fists in such anger, Rosa knew, but she did so now. In her fury, she ran into the house. In the shadows of the bedroom she saw what she had not seen for sometime. It was the ghost of her mama. "Buy the mission, Rosa," her mama said. "Buy it now."

"How?"

"Use the pouch of gold Wilson left you for a crisis."

Rosa stared blankly at her mama's apparition. She followed it to the place where she knew Juan had hidden a metal box. She had not expected she would ever have cause to open it.

When she returned to the porch, Adriana followed with Mariano in her arms and young Romualdo beside her. "We will buy the mission," Rosa said.

"In addition to the church, I want both the garden and the vineyard across the arroyo left for the priest's use. Make the rest of the property in the name of my husband and his business partner."

******

The next day after Rosa purchased the mission, Padre Miguel Gomez visited her. "Thank you, Donna Rosa, for keeping the church from falling into uncertain hands."

"Thank you, Padre, for staying on with us." she said.

This young priest, Padre Gomez, had actually prepared for priesthood at the recently developed new college in Santa Barbara. He was the first graduate of Mexican descent. "With so much happening so fast," he said, "and the likelihood that the Americans will arrive any day, I wish that you would consider using some of the rooms of the mission as a place to live. It would be safer to live closer to others. There are a few other women whose husbands are away in military service or who spend their time far out on their rangelands. I am hoping they find their way to the mission."

A few days later a nearby rancho family escaped an Indian raid. Their horses were stolen and their houses ransacked. The possibility that one of her children might be injured or killed was more than Rosa was filling to risk. She and Adriana quickly packed mules and horses and headed for the mission. The rooms they occupied were large and farthest from the church sanctuary. One room included a small fireplace suited for cooking and warming.

"I'll breathe easier, Donna Rosa, knowing you are here." the Padre told her as he unpacked her mules.

It bothered Rosa to see the mission's interior walls crumbling and dust covering the tile floors. With help from some of the Indian women, she cleaned several rooms. Along with everyone else, she used the mission's large vegetable garden, and enjoyed meat from the dwindling mission herd. The buildings were furnished with very old, largely handmade furniture. She brought the best of it into the rooms she planned to occupy. Daily life from this time promised much. Juan Wilson would be arriving soon. For now, her lonesomeness was relieved by the activity of the Chumash Indians around the mission. But it was not all pleasant.

It rained all day, December 11, 1846. Water poured from the mission's tile roof and leaked in several places throughout the building. It grew dark early, and the arroyo overran its banks. It was after several days of conducting mass at Mission San Miguel and at the Assistencia on the Santa Margarita Rancho that Padre Gomez found his way back across the grade in mud too deep to walk a horse. Rosa was first aware of his return with the pounding on the door.

"I have terrible news," he blurted.

The children were asleep. She stepped out on the portico. Debris blocked the flow of water in the arroyo and flooded the plaza below.

"I saw three, maybe four hundred Americanos camped on the Santa Margarita Rancho," the priest said. His robe and his coat were soaked. "They are riding this direction now."

As they stood on the portico, the winds whipping at their clothes, Rosa saw the young padre's face in the candle light from the partially open door. It was filled with anguish. "Where is Jesus Pico?" he suddenly asked. "We must find him quickly." The man to whom he referred was the appointed local justice of the peace and majordomo of the community.

He hurried along the stairs with Rosa close behind. "They captured an Indian on the Santa Margarita Rancho," the priest said as they ran. "He carried a message written by Jesus Pico" The priest pulled his wide-brimmed hat over his eyes. The wind pressed his dark beard against his face. He was a powerful man, but now, in broken words, he said, "Yesterday, the Americans shot that Indian."

Rosa walked in the rain with only a light rebozo to protect her head and shoulders. She could tolerate the wet and cold, but with this news, she felt something inside her collapse.

They found Jesus Pico inside his small adobe casa at the back of the mission in the orchard. His wife, Dolores, and all of their children clustered inside. Smoke filled the dirt-floored casa, mixing with the stale smell of food cooked over a fire in a dilapidated fireplace.

Jesus listened quietly while Padre Gomez told him what he had heard. Jesus had been a soldier serving Mexican governmental causes the length of California. He was a cousin of both Governor Pio Pico and Rosa. Rosa realized that Jose's life was in serious danger.

Jesus shook his thick head in despair. "I should have known better," he said.

"What did your note say?" she asked.

"Estrada has a cache of ammunition buried on the rancho. It was left over after the revolt against Micheltorena. We hid it against another day. I asked him to send some of it to me."

"Before they shot the Indian," Padre Gomez said, "they herded all of the other Indians on the ranch to the assistencia to watch it. It was supposed to be a lesson to the others. It was a sickening moment for both the peaceful Chumash and Salinan people who worship there.

Pico's mind seemed to wander. "There are so few of us here," he said. "How can we protect our women and children?"

"Don't try," the Padre said. "No one else should suffer or die.:

"Go quickly to our rancho," Rosa said. "Hide there until this affair is behind us."

Jesus turned to his wife.

"Go," she said. "There is no time to waste. We will be safe here."

Looking hopeless, Jesus wrapped himself in his serape, pulled on his sombrero and headed for the mission stable for his horse.

******

Back in her mission rooms, she found Adriana comforting a crying Mariano. It was past his feeding time. Rosa lighted more candles and ringed the children around the fireplace for additional warmth. Earlier, she had prepared soup in a large black kettle and placed it in the coals of the fireplace. She brought baby Mariano to her lap and guided him to her nipple.

The room was heavy with the smell of wood smoke and damp adobe brick walls. She lay in the darkness on a cot between her children. She could almost feel the rock of Juan's ship sailing the dark sea, both wind and waves threatening the brig. Wilson will make strong men out of our boys, she thought. He had come to her offering unabashed love and made her life joyful again. In her belly, she could feel a third son, Juan's son, finding space for himself.

Perhaps because of the noise of rain and wind, Rosa did not sleep, and so she heard the loud clamp on the door. To her surprise, Adriana jumped up ahead of her, lighted a candle and opened the door. Several women from the mission settlement rushed into the room, guiding and holding more than a dozen children, all wrapped in blankets.

Rosa controlled her voice in spite of the trembling inside of her. So, now, she told herself, the Americans have arrived, and the priest is the only man in the settlement. She quietly urged the women to remove their wet clothing and dry both themselves and their children by the fire. Young Adriana worked at the fireplace. She was preparing hot chocolate.

Rosa leaned and kissed her adopted daughter. The child's presence reminded her over and over of the blessings in her own life…the conception of her first-born, Romualdo, in a Church of God, the insistence of all the world's sacredness upon her when Adriana sought her out, the birth of Mariano into the hands of the second man she would marry, the huge grant of land in her name and her own further certainty that she now carried a child sired by the man she loved more than any other.

******

At dawn, most of the Indian women and their children crept out of Rosa's quarters. One who remained took care of the children when Rosa, too, went out on the portico. From the high portico, she glanced around at the many thatched-roofed casas occupied by Chumash Indian women and a few older men. The young men spent their lives on the plains. For the most part they had deserted the mission way of life.

From behind a small building near the creek, she saw rain-soaked Americanos moving in and out of the church nave where they must have spent the night. As she watched the men in their strange mountain garb of deerskin pants, leather jackets, and leggings, one smiled and pointed toward her. None of them appeared threatening. She left the Indian casas and walked forthrightly through the large open area between the mission and the arroyo, now covered with mud from the creek's overflow. Huge amounts of debris, including tree limbs and brush, now covered the plaza.

She hurried up the steps toward the church, then hesitated. Several men stood near the door as guards. She frankly looked at each of the men, and they stared at her with obvious interest.

"Hey, now, where has a beauty like you been hiding?" one commented. She disregarded him.

The church's heavy hand-azed doors were open wide. She must win these men by defiance. She must remind them of the purpose of the church. She saw no danger in continuing. She found the nave in use as a barracks. But these men showed concern for the church as a sacred place, most especially the altar. After crossing herself with holy water, she walked past the bedrolls and weapons on the dirt floor. She felt all eyes upon her.

In the quietness, she felt assurance. She dropped to her knees at the roped off altar and remained until she was certain that God was aware of her and knew of the plight of the pueblo. Without men to take charge or negotiate with this enemy, she gradually decided the duty befell her. She recited the Rosary over and over.

Again, all eyes followed her as she left the church. Head covered with rebozo, she imagined the compelling chant of the Indian choir that once sang in the mission, and it lifted her. She wondered what these soldiers would think if they knew she owned most of the buildings and land round it.

When she heard a woman's call, she hurried down the steps to the plaza. She saw the Indian woman who cared for her children hurrying toward her. Rosa extended her arms and took baby Mariano in hand. Adriana clung to Romualdo.

"The son of Buchon," the Indian woman said brokenly, referring to an Indian boy who worked on a nearby rancho, "says the soldiers have captured Jesus Pico at your casa, and they are bringing him here."

In that moment, even as near as she felt to God after her prayers, Rosa resented the helplessness that overcame her. Why must all the men in family be gone at a time like this? Where could she turn? How could she help Jesus Pico?

She led her family slowly, uncertainly toward the casa where she would find Pico's wife. Along the way, several big rough Americanos tipped their hats. The Indian woman who walked with Rosa, kept whispering to the other women, telling of Pico's capture. They must let Rosa know if and when they saw Americanos returning with Jesus Pico. Rosa insisted that Pecho's wife and children stay with her in the mission. There, it was warm and dry. They continued feeding the fire.

In the late afternoon, the son of Buchon appeared at their door. He was not more than twelve. He was a handsome boy, tall and brown with a lean classical nose, perhaps partly Spanish. When the boy entered, Dolores stood motionless, her face stony.

"They have brought him in," the boy said. "They have taken him to the room of the commandante in the mission. Then his voice became a whisper. "They will shoot him, Senora."

"Why do you say that?" Rosa asked

"Some of the soldiers are Indians from the north. I asked them why they took Senor Pico prisoner. They said he is a traitor…that he must die."

As the young Chumash Indian prepared to leave, Rosa asked, "Will you watch for us and come back when you know more?"

"Si," he assured her, and disappeared.

Rosa sat quietly with her children. Dolores did the same. Both breast-fed their babies.

Time passed slowly in the unlighted room. Rosa considered going out again, hoping for more information. She could imagine the men pulling Jesus along on his horse, hands tied behind him. She could feel them taunting him, daring him, testing him.

When the son of Buchon appeared again, he looked grim and shaken. "They say that the commandante conducted a trial and Senor Jesus Pico is guilty of treason. The soldiers say he will be shot by a firing squad tomorrow and that all of us will be called to watch."

Who is this unmerciful man, Rosa asked herself. She felt the world crushing around her. Dolores began to sob. Even in the church, Rosa thought now, the soldiers must have mocked her, threatening the Christus and the Virgin Mary. What could she do? Jesus Pico, the strength of their isolated settlement, was a prison, accused of traitorous acts only because he wanted ammunition to defend the people of the San Luis Obispo district.

"It's enough!" Rosa found herself saying, startling the other women and even the children. "It's enough," she repeated. "If our justice of the peace must die…even if he must die…we must not cringe before this monster! I will not hide in dark corners."

Rosa drew a trembling breath. She called to the son of Buchon, still standing by the door. "Tell all of the women of the pueblo to come to my rooms. Have them bring their children." She whirled to where Dolores sat sobbing. "Save your tears. We must do what we can."

******

"El Capitan," Rosa said in her bravest voice.

The dark-haired Americano in his tight-fitting jacket stood abruptly behind the table when she entered his make-shift office. She had simply disregarded the guards beside the door. "Captain John Fremont at your service, Senora," he said. He eyed the gathering of women and children outside his door.

"My name is Rosa Carrillo de Pacheco de Wilson," she said. "Since neither the juez de paz nor my husband are present to greet you, I extend a welcome from the people of the San Luis Obispo territory."

"Well now," Fremont said. "That is very kind of you. I am pleased that you speak English. I'm afraid my Spanish is very clumsy."

213

He pulled a small straightback chair into position and invited her to sit down. She smiled, looking directly into the captain's eyes. Rosa had changed into her finest dress, and one of the women had brushed her hair tightly across the top of her head and ears, placing two combs to hold it in place. She had also draped a solid colored, deep blue mantilla partially over her head and across her shoulders.

Her mama had once told her that when she must defy, she should look her best. And, of course, even now, she must do it with love. She had seen the soldiers' eyes light up as she walked the length of the columned mission portico from her quarters to this room next to the church. But they appeared even further taken aback by the entourage of women and children who followed her. The women had gathered outside Fremont's quarters as Rosa entered.

She folded her hands in her lap, and looked up at Fremont. She said, "Many Californios have done business with Americanos and English-speaking people for years. Many of us speak English. I think too, that you may meet many Americanos and Englishmen, like my husband, who hold Mexican citizenship.

Rosa doubted that Fremont took her seriously. He smiled across at her.

"Many of the men in this battalion have already made Northern California their home," he said. "We march in peace, Senora. We do not mean harm."

"If you had arrived in sunshine," Rosa said quietly, "we could have given you a proper welcome, perhaps we could have had a fiesta."

"However, the weather will be even worse through San Marcos Pass to Santa Barbara," Rosa said. "Do you have a guide?"

"This may be a strange question to ask a woman," Fremont said, "but somehow I trust you, Senora. Give me the name of a man in the pueblo I can trust as a guide to Los Angeles."

"There is only one."

Fremont hesitated.

"If I may say so, Commandante, you need more than a guide. It would be helpful to you to be guided by one who knows the owners of every rancho and the majordomo of every pueblo."

"I see," he said. "I also see, Senora, that you are more than a beautiful woman. Are you ready to become an American citizen?"

"My husband says that every will be better."

"I agree. But where is your husband?"

"He is a shipmaster. I expect him to arrive any day.

Fremont leaned across the table and repeated his question. "Who do you recommend as a guide to the south?"

"One man you can trust?"

"Yes."

"My cousin, Jesus Pico. He is a trusted military officer, a cousin of both Governor Pio Pico and General Castro. He speaks English and has traveled the King's Highway many times."

"But..."

Her voice was firm. Her words flowed with certainty. "Let him help you," she said. Now, she knew the Captain as listening to more than her words. The women outside the door wept aloud and the children wailed.

"Senora, if you are misleading me."

"If you will trust me, Sir, I will trust you."

******

Rosa and the women of the settlement gathered on the portico again the next day as the long procession of Americanos mounted to ride out of San Luis Obispo. All waved as Jesus Pico kissed his wife and climbed his mount. Pico took his place to the right side of Fremont. Fremont tipped his hat to Rosa with utmost courtesy.

It would be months before she knew that her cousin, Jesus, served as translator between Fremont and General Andre Pico in the signing of the Treaty at Cahuenga Pass. This agreement stopped nearly all military aggression between the Californios and the Americanos. Rosa was soon lost in thought again. She waited with fear and anxiety for Juan Wilson to come home.

59. Rosa - At the Rancho

The American flag now hung in the plaza. Rosa watched little Romualdo salute it as the American volunteers had done before leaving town. She only wanted to return to the rancho. Things didn't change much for her. She found herself devoting more and more time to her journal and simply waiting. She knew with certainty Juan was right about sending the boys to the Sandwich Islands to a missionary school for their education. It would assure her that they spoke proper English and fit into the new world of the Californians. Most of all, she dared think, it would help Romualdo prepare for the greatness she and God wanted for him. She would talk to Juan Wilson about these things as soon as he returned.

Rosa's poetry and essays soon filled a book and next, a shelf in a closed cupboard. They served as a way for her to affirm thoughts, and plan for the future. One night, by candlelight, after the children were in bed, she wrote:

"Where have the winds
taken my brave man this night?
Where may I send my heart
to warm him?
How long can I wait for his return
to make me whole again?

"I fear for my Juan and his little ship," she wrote, "rolling in the dark gray waves. And I fear for my children and myself in this valley. I am desperately lonely."

Sometimes, rolled up tightly in bed, she thought about Juan, and then Romualdo, her first husband. In such moments she dared feel all of the world's loveliness drawn around her. She knew she would always loved both men. She could not think that she would never see either again.

60. Romualdo Pacheco Jr. - March, 1875

The river steamer Chrysopolis found her way down stream from Sacramento into San Francisco Bay during the night while we slept, and I awakened at six, my usual hour.

I washed and shaved carefully around the beard and mustache I had so carefully groomed over the years. A meticulously ironed white shirt and a fitted dark string tie almost completed my outfit. I was glad my face still showed the wrinkles of a person who had spent years working as a ranchero and some time aboard trader ships as a crewman with my stepfather's partner.

I also hoped my eyes reflected some of the brightness of an educated man; the education my mother and late stepfather arranged for my brother and me at the missionary school in the Sandwich Islands. We had no formal schools in California at the time. Even when we returned from Oahu, my mother arranged for tutors. I wanted to personify the men my mother loved and lost, Commandant Romualdo Pacheco, my father, and shipmaster John Wilson, my stepfather. Finally, I wanted to express the discernment and experience I had gained as justice of the peace, state senator, state treasurer and until a few days ago, Lieutenant Governor.

I felt somewhat envious when I glanced across the cabin at the scrubbed, high-cheeked face of my half-brother, John Wilson, Jr. His piercing blue eyes, youthful vigor and outgoing nature inspired people. He served as intern and assistant in my office.

Mary, my dearly beloved blue-eyed wife from Kentucky, was awake in the adjoining cabin. I thought she probably waited for our daughter, Maybella, to stir. I pulled on my dark suit coat as well as my overcoat. My brother, Mariano, was already at the rail when John and I stepped out of the cabin. Mariano was a member of my staff.

March winds swept across the deck, and the spray of salty bay waters stung my cheeks. I clasped the rail as we walked along the narrow outside passageway in front of the other cabins.

Outlines of San Francisco's wharves along with its wood and brick buildings formed a bluish blur of squares and rectangles, some dark, others so light that they faded in and out in the mist. The three of us walked briskly to the bow where the wind was strongest. For a moment, we experienced the sheer joy of the rise and fall of the vessel bucking the current. It was exhilarating.

My half-brother, young John, purposely sprang in the air as the bow tilted up. As he came down, he expressed the purest kind of pleasure. "You like this?" I asked him.

"I'll always be sorry I didn't get to sail with my papa," he said.

"I did, but I was much too young to remember,"

"I did too," Mariano laughed. "I was born on the Ayacucho."

Mariano and John, Jr. joined Mary and Maybella for breakfast in the dining room below.

"If I'm going to speak to the Young Republicans at a breakfast meeting," I told them, "I think I'll stay on deck and watch the docking." I also felt the need to avoid shaking a lot of hands. I took genuine comfort in my minutes alone these days.

I thought about Michel de Young again. He was publisher and editor of the San Francisco Chronicle. When I had visited him at his office, he had shown me an editorial he was holding for the right time, hoping for maximum effect. I never really thought he would use it.

Suddenly the gangplank was down, and there was no more time to think about the past. Everything must forward forcefully from this minute.

Enrique Fitch, Jr., my cousin and a reporter for the Chronicle, bounded aboard and gathered up the family. He had arranged a large covered carriage. Enroute to the hotel, our daughter Maybella delighted Mary and me by peeking through the closed flaps of the carriage. "Look Papa," she shrieked, "a street car." Then another peek, "We are going up a hill."

Fitch and Mariano had taken seats with the driver on the outside. I called to them. "Do you think there will be a large crowd so early in the morning?"

"It's a perfect time," Fitch called back. "This will be the best crowd of your career."

I really doubted that. Fitch didn't know about the warmth of the crowds I had experienced in San Luis Obispo and Santa Barbara over the years. But it didn't matter. I always enjoyed the overnight trip down the river from Sacramento.

We stepped down from the carriage in front of the Grand Hotel on Montgomery Street. It was a misty morning. There didn't seem to be anyone to greet us from the Young Republicans, but I had learned that protocol and grace were not always attributes of San Francisco's young men. It was a rough city.

All of us walked into the lobby, and I shook the mist from my high hat. Brother John Wilson hurried ahead, amazed by the ornateness of the lobby. Mary wiped the mist from Maybella's face, glanced about her, then gave Enrique Jr. a strange look. I, too, felt things were not going the way either of us expected. Then Mary took my arm and said, "Do you see what I see."

I smiled in disbelief. He was a big man with heavy black sideburns and a large mustache. My heart jumped when I recognized the woman beside him. I hurried across the red carpet and reached to my Aunt Francisca. Then, State Senator Mariano Vallejo clasped my shoulders, holding me for a long time. He had a wonderful laugh.

Several younger men and women appeared beside Uncle Mariano and Aunt Francisca. "Do you remember our children, Romualdo?" Aunt Francisca asked. She began pointing. "Platon, our physician son from the City of Vallejo and Luisa, Maria, Napoleon and Roselia..." The youngest lived in Benicia, the city given our Aunt's middle name.

"I do remember my Vallejo cousins," I said. I successfully introduced them to Mary and Maybella. This was an exciting moment for me.

It seemed to me that the Vallejos had fallen out of heaven. I was so eager to talk to Uncle Vallejo, a politician during both the Mexican period and the American time. I wondered if he had read the editorial "Michel de Young had written about me as a final blast that seemed to bring everything in Sacramento politics to a head. The words still rang in my head like a wonderful clarion bell.

"Come dine with us," Vallejo said, taking my arm.

"I wish I could, Uncle," Romualdo said. Can we talk later?"

"Wait just one minute," Aunt Francisca urged. "Your Aunt Josefa is with us."

As we walked down the wide hall toward the banquet room, Aunt Josefa appeared, more lovely with age, wearing a long full dress with lace covering, a mantilla draped over her head. I held her in my arms. Her husband Enrique, had died two years earlier. He had been a successful businessman in San Diego.

I could not express what happened inside of me at that moment. I remembered my Aunt Francisca and Aunt Josefa with such love. I glanced at my brothers, Mariano and John Jr. Surely, Enrique Fitch, Jr. had known his mother was in town. He worked here. He should be expressing more excitement.

I was even more surprised when we walked toward the banquet room. The Fitches and the Vallejos followed. Enrique Jr. said, "Come with me, Romualdo."

The room was elaborately decorated. When I looked around, my head reeled." This is the group you are talking to today," Enrique said, "Come with me, Romualdo. Time to relax and enjoy."

The place was filled with people. The sound of guitars, violins and castanets suggested a fiesta. Dancing broke out across the room. With Mary and Maybella at my side, we moved past cousins and aunts and uncles, and if any family member was missing, I had no way of knowing. I clasped shoulders with dozens of Guerras and Carrillos from Santa Barbara; Fitch cousins arrived from all over California…including San Diego, Santa Rosa, Petaluma, Sonoma, and Healdsburg. I had more relatives than I realized existed, all shaking my hand, embracing me, wishing me well.

Here were some of the children of children I knew while growing up. They scampered in and out around the legs of the adults. Many family members were dressed in traditional Mexican costumes. I kept looking around me expectantly. I could contain myself no longer.

While children surrounded me with their smiles and love, I took hands with both Mary and Maybella and walked deeper into the crowd, listening to the music, studying every face. Everybody seemed to part for us as we deliberately worked our way through the room. The rhythm of the castanets grew faster, and I felt my head throbbing with the excitement. "Mi Dios," I finally said, "Where is she?"

I still carried the week-old news item in my pocket that told of that day in the capitol building. I wanted desperately to share it with the person who had believed in me, considered it my destiny from the day she thought I was conceived at Mission San Luis Rey.

Bits of the news story raced through my mind while I looked excitedly around the banquet room. "Rumors have been rife in the city for the past twenty-four hours…" the story began. "Yesterday afternoon Lt. Governor Romualdo Pacheco was called for…it was known by only one or two state officers…this forenoon no little surprise was created in all circles by the word that Governor Newton Booth would resign to take his post in the United States Senate. At two o'clock in the afternoon, the Honorable Lewis Ramage,

Judge of the Sixth District Court, was sent for…The ceremony took place in the Governor's office with Pacheco, his wife and a select few witnesses.

I glanced around the room again at all of the family's smiling faces. I realized now that they had dressed this way for me…in the traditional clothes of old California. Then they opened a space for me, and she was waiting.

"Mama!" I said. There she stood, Rosa Carrillo de Pacheco de Wilson, draped in a beautiful embroidered silk mantilla with the most exquisite floral design in California. It was the same one given her by John Wilson before I was born. Her dark eyes sparkled. She looked as beautiful as the way I remembered her as a child when she told me over and over that I was born special, that I was truly conceived in a house of God. That I must do great things.

I lifted her up into my arms until her face was even with mine. "We made it Mama!"

"Si," she said. Her eyes appeared moist as she leaned toward me, whispering "Governor…Governor Romualdo Pacheco."

I realized in that moment that I had dreamed all of my life of hearing her say those simple words.

It was time to sing and dance!

Printed in the United States
71415LV00007B/59